THE THIRD MAN
& OTHER STORIES

GRAHAM GREENE

THE THIRD MAN
& OTHER STORIES

With an introduction by
PROFESSOR RICHARD GREENE

MACMILLAN COLLECTOR'S LIBRARY

This omnibus edition first published by Collector's Library 2011

Reissued by Macmillan Collector's Library 2017
an imprint of Pan Macmillan
The Smithson, 6 Briset Street, London ECIM 5NR
EU representative: Macmillan Publishers Ireland Ltd,
1st Floor, The Liffey Trust Centre, 117–126 Sheriff Street Upper,
Dublin 1, DOI YC43
Associated companies throughout the world
www.panmacmillan.com

ISBN 978-1-5098-2805-0

9 8

A CIP catalogue record for this book is available from the British Library.

Casing design and endpaper pattern by Andrew Davidson
Typeset by Antony Gray
Printed and bound in China by Imago

MIX
Paper | Supporting
responsible forestry
FSC® C116313

Visit www.panmacmillan.com to read more about all our books
and to buy them. You will also find features, author interviews and
news of any author events, and you can sign up for e-newsletters
so that you're always first to hear about our new releases.

Contents

INTRODUCTION

Harry Lime stands almost invisible in a black doorway. A cat sits between his well-polished shoes and licks its paws. The light from an upper window flashes on the hidden face. He looks up to the scolding Frau and then across at his approaching friend Martins. The eyebrow is raised under the brim of a tilted hat – a smile widens until the lips part, considering, calculating. Then the light is gone, and Harry too.

This is how most of us first encountered Harry Lime – as played by Orson Welles in Carol Reed's film of 1949. What we have of him is stolen from shadow, a phantasm on the great screen, a flickering of things known and unknown.

Harry Lime's creator, Graham Greene, was born in 1904; his father was a master and then headmaster of Berkhamsted School, which 'began just beyond my father's study, through a green baize door'. That door symbolised a divided life. By thirteen, he was a boarder at the school. Regarded as a Judas in the dormitory, he was bullied and betrayed by his close friends. His parents allowed him to live at home again, that is, on their side of the green baize door, but something in him was changed. He had learned that no one is precisely who he appears to be and that no loyalties are simple.

In his most admired novels, Greene played out those divisions of heart again and again. Pinkie, the razor-wielding thug of *Brighton Rock*, ponders the chances of mercy. The priest in *The Power and the Glory* mixes whisky and martyrdom in a single glass. In *The Heart of the Matter*, 'Scobie the Just' betrays his wife, his profession, and his God out of pity for a girl who is bored by his conscience. In the *The End of the Affair*, Bendrix and Sarah are caught in a passionate triangle with a God whose love is jealous and demands possession.

Where, then, did Harry Lime come from? Greene wrote to his mistress Catherine Walston on 30 September 1947:

> I believe I've got a book coming . . . The act of creation's awfully odd & inexplicable like falling in love . . . I walked all up Piccadilly & back, went in a gent's in Brick Street, & suddenly in the gent's, I saw the three characters, the beginning, the middle & the end, & in some ways all the ideas I had – the first sentence of the thriller about the dead Harry who wasn't dead, the risen-from-the-dead story, & the one the other day in the train – all seem to come together. I hope to God it lasts.

It did last – Greene went on to write a novella, and then the screenplay for the film. But what else was there to the story of Harry Lime than a moment of inspiration in the gent's? Some have seen in the story hints of Greene's friendship with Kim Philby, who belonged to the Cambridge spy-ring and defected to Russia in 1963. Greene had come to like Philby as a friend and drinking companion while working under him in the Iberian sub-section of MI6 in St Albans in 1943–4. Greene left the service because of Philby's attempts to gain control of counter-intelligence against the Soviets, but later claimed that he was put off merely by what he thought was an excess of ambition – a surprisingly slight reason for Greene to have left MI6 in the midst of a war. It is possible that Greene actually spotted Philby as a traitor or that Philby tried to recruit him. If so, then Greene would have been placed in a conflict of loyalties of just the sort that faces Rollo Martins in *The Third Man*.

The connection between Lime and Philby is decidedly speculative, and based on just scraps of evidence. Certainly, in postwar Vienna, Greene saw more than enough cruelty and deception to inspire a tale such as *The Third Man*. The chief of police told him of a racket whereby penicillin, available only in military hospitals, was being stolen by orderlies for sale on the black market. Often the pilfered drug was diluted with impure water with devastating consequences for the patients who received it. This was Harry Lime's racket.

As ever, Greene doubts things too easily known, and his story divides into nearly irreconcilable perspectives, just as the city is divided into zones under the control of the Great Powers. The novella is oddly obsessed with how difficult it is to capture the truth in writing. The story is told by the policeman Calloway, a man who prides himself on the exactness of his files; he is something of a realist, even a positivist, but somehow he misses the fact that a car accident is a murder and has to admit he is made 'a fool'. The American Rollo Martins is a writer of cowboy novels and a sentimentalist, 'a buffoon'. Hero-worshipping his old friend, he dismisses Calloway's account of Harry's racketeering and tries to prove that he was murdered. The two men are trapped by their ways of telling a story, and Martins is comically mistaken for a highbrow novelist willing to discuss Virginia Woolf and the stream-of-consciousness.

Having known Lime only as a generous lover, his girlfriend Anna Schmidt scolds Martins: ' "For God's sake stop making people in *your* image. Harry was real. He wasn't just your hero and my lover. He was Harry." ' She sees a great difference between facts and reality: ' "I told you – a man doesn't alter because you find out more about him. He's still the same man." ' Is that Greene's point in this novel, that there is something unchanging about Harry, who is both a Catholic and a reprobate? That even Harry possesses a soul and that the Christ depicted in Dr Winkler's exclusive Jansenist crucifix actually died for him? Harry would be rather like Pinkie in *Brighton Rock*, whose evil is beyond dispute yet whose fate is mysterious; a priest remarks at the end of that novel: ' "You can't conceive, my child, nor can I or anyone the . . . appalling . . . strangeness of the mercy of God." '

If these things are so, then in *The Third Man*, Graham Greene is telling us why he cannot write the sort of novels that had been fashionable in the 1920s. For him, the self does not simply bob along in the waters of consciousness, but is mysterious and abiding. Although Greene often insisted he was not a 'Catholic novelist' but a novelist who happened to be Catholic, in *The Third Man* he seems to say something entirely different: a Catholic writer's technique is distinctive – his characters will have a soul and their fate lies beyond the last page.

In Greene's short fiction, all hearts are divided. An early story, 'The Basement Room', provided the basis for another of Carol Reed's great films *The*

Fallen Idol (1948), in which Ralph Richardson played the lead. The short story (published in this volume under the latter title) is far grimmer than the screen-play that succeeded it. Here, Greene depicts the seven-year-old Philip who passes through green baize doors into a world of unbearable experience. The boy has much in common with Henry James's Maisie, and must try to comprehend adult hatreds. He is devoted to the butler Baines, a man locked in a hellish marriage to the housekeeper who tries to wheedle information on Baines's hidden life out of the boy. Indeed, the house itself seems to stand for the horrors of consciousness, a protected nursery at the top, the main part empty while his parents are travelling – and something fearful in the servants' quarters: 'This was life: a strange passion he couldn't understand moving in the basement room.' When he dashes from the house, 'it was life he was in the middle of'. Burdened with secrets, the boy believes himself responsible for the catastrophe that follows.

At the age of seven, the free part of Philip's life is over: 'He never opened his Meccano set again, never built anything, never created anything, died, the old dilettante, sixty years later . . . ' The word dilettante catches the reader's eye. Psychoanalysed in youth, Greene is considering how the injuries of childhood can quietly defeat a writer's ambitions and corrupt him: 'Letters could lie all right, but they made the lie permanent; they lay as evidence against you; they made you meaner than the spoken word.' In this story, the written word does not, of itself, promise liberty or healing.

Between these two famous tales, *The Third Man* and *The Fallen Idol*, this volume inserts a sequence of stories of a very different tone and texture. Indeed, they connect those earlier works to each other with a swinging bridge of ironies.

'Looking over my short stories now, which stretch in time from 1929 to the eve of the 1970s,' Greene wrote in *Ways of Escape* (1980), 'I am struck by an odd fact – humour enters very late and very unexpectedly.' He was speaking of *May We Borrow Your Husband?*, a collection of stories published in 1967 and included here in its entirety. Written 'in a single mood of sad hilarity', these short stories emerge from a great change in his life. As part of a settlement with the Inland Revenue, Greene became a tax exile in France from the beginning of 1966, a move which also enabled him to begin something like a settled life with the mistress of his later years Yvonne Cloetta. Some of the tales arose from overheard, even misunderstood, conversations at a favourite restaurant in Antibes.

The shortest stories are plainly the product of dark whimsy. In 'Beauty', Greene sends up the aestheticism and sexuality of the 1920s as an older woman in a period toque allows her life to be ruled by a Pekinese called 'Beauty' – she pampers him, regards him as delicate and precious, but at night he rummages in the bins, emerging with a length of some animal's intestine for a trophy. In 'Chagrin in Three Parts', two women soon to become lovers exchange stories in a restaurant about their disappointments with the bodies of men: ' "Perhaps smoked like an eel one might enjoy it." ' In 'A Shocking Accident', a man is haunted all his life by his father's having been killed by a pig that fell from a balcony five storeys up. He cannot marry happily until he knows his fiancée's reaction to this strange secret. In 'The Overnight Bag', a man flying BOAC claims that he is carrying the corpse of his wife's baby (not by him) in his cabin baggage. In 'Mortmain', a man's all-too-matey former mate inhabits his present marriage; she plants friendly letters like bombs throughout the flat, even in the bed – and they are timed to go off at the worst possible moments. In 'The Invisible Japanese Gentlemen', a young novelist boasts to her fiancée of the career her publisher foresees for her owing to her great 'powers of observation'; yet she fails entirely to notice the curious and ceremonial behaviour of some Japanese at a table nearby.

Greene's sense of what might constitute a comedy can come as a surprise to some readers. 'May We Borrow Your Husband', the story that gives its title to the collection, depicts a couple on their honeymoon at a hotel in Antibes. The narrator, an 'unheroic' older man writing, as Greene did, a biography of the Restoration poet and rake, the Earl of Rochester, sees that a homosexual couple is trying to seduce the young husband. The writer is placed in the awkward position of entertaining the girl while the three men go off on their escapades. There follows a Jamesian collision: 'she belonged to the age of trust just as I belonged to the age of cynicism'. Although he insists on his own 'scruples' and is outraged by the seduction, the narrator too has something of the hunter in him. The girl's 'hateful' name is Poopy, and she never exists for him even though, pitiably, she confides in him about her supposed failures in sex. The narrator's attraction to her is at best a yearning for his own past, and he does not reveal these thoughts: ' . . . if I didn't bother to convey them to her, why should I bother to convey them to you, *hypocrite lecteur*?' This thoroughly unreliable narrator cannot decide what to make of events, leaving the reader to judge: 'It was a little like a novel which hesitates on the verge between comedy and tragedy.'

'Cheap in August' is equally disturbing, as Greene takes the exact measure of a passing kindness. After some years of marriage to a New England professor, Mary Watson feels restless: 'Next year, she thought, when I am forty, I must feel grateful that I have preserved the love of a good man.' However, for now, she slips away, during one of his absences, to Jamaica where she discovers 'with disappointment the essential morality of a holiday resort in the cheap season; there were no opportunities for infidelity, only for writing postcards . . . ' She holds aloof from most of the other tourists but falls into the company of Hickslaughter, an old man with an 'elephantine back-side'. He is that rare thing in Greene's fiction, an unsuccessful American, and he fears death. Mary Watson's quest for sex in August is changed, though only slightly. Hickslaughter wins her pity and her affection: 'she wept a little, but not seriously, at the temporary nature of this meeting'.

There is no easy sentiment in this sequence of stories. Even some characters who cling to fidelity are fools of a sort. In 'Two Gentle People', a pair of strangers, both unhappy in marriage, meet in a park in Paris, where the man puts an injured pigeon out of its misery by wringing its neck. The woman is just bold enough to compliment him on his fine umbrella. They go to dinner and enact a whole love affair, marriage and death between the courses. Then, a pair of sensitive cowards, they part without even exchanging addresses. When it is all over, the greatest protest the man can make against his own continuing misery is to say in bed to his horrible wife: 'I was thinking that things might have been different.'

Graham Greene recalled that during the war he wrote humorous short stories in times of danger as an escape from fear:

> So perhaps the stories which make up the collection *May We Borrow Your Husband?*, all written during what should have been the last decade of my life, are an escape in humour from the thought of death – this time of certain death. Writing is a form of therapy: sometimes I wonder how all those who do not write, compose or paint can manage to escape the madness, the melancholia, the panic fear which is inherent in the human condition.

BIOGRAPHY

Born in 1904 in Berkhamsted, Graham Greene was educated at a school where his father was headmaster. He read history at Balliol College, Oxford, from 1922–5. He converted to Roman Catholicism in 1926, and married in 1927. While employed as a sub-editor at *The Times*, he produced his first novel, *The Man Within* (1929). He went on to write some of the outstanding novels of the twentieth century, among them *Brighton Rock* (1938), *The Power and the Glory* (1940), *The Heart of the Matter* (1948) and *The End of the Affair* (1951). He was a prolific journalist, reviewer, scriptwriter and dramatist and was a perennial candidate for the Nobel Prize. A restless traveller, he wrote about many of the world's most dangerous places, including Liberia, Mexico, Vietnam, the Congo, Haiti, Para–guay and Central America. From the mid-1960s, he lived chiefly in France. Graham Greene died of leukaemia in Switzerland in 1991.

FURTHER READING

Biographies

Richard Greene, *Graham Greene: A Life in Letters*, Little, Brown & Co., London, 2007

Anthony Mockler, *Graham Greene: Three Lives*, Hunter McKay, Arbroath, 1994

Michael Shelden, *Graham Greene: The Man Within*, William Heinemann, London, 1994

Norman Sherry, *The Life of Graham Greene*, 3 volumes, Jonathan Cape, London, 1989–2004

Criticism

Bernard Bergonzi, *A Study in Greene: Graham Greene and the Art of the Novel*, Oxford University Press, Oxford, 2006

Richard Kelly, *Graham Greene: A Study of the Short Fiction*, Twayne, New York, 1992

David Lodge, *Graham Greene*, Columbia University Press, New York, 1966

THE THIRD MAN

Preface

The Third Man was never written to be read but only to be seen. Like many love affairs it started at a dinner table and continued with many headaches in many places: Vienna, Venice, Ravello, London, Santa Monica.

Most novelists, I suppose, carry round in their heads or in their notebooks the first ideas for stories that have never come to be written. Sometimes one turns them over after many years and thinks regretfully that they would have been good once, in a time now dead. So years back, on the flap of an envelope, I had written an opening paragraph: 'I had paid my last farewell to Harry a week ago, when his coffin was lowered into the frozen February ground, so that it was with incredulity that I saw him pass by, without a sign of recognition, among the host of strangers in the Strand.' I, no more than my hero, had pursued Harry, so when Sir Alexander Korda asked me to write a film for Carol Reed – to follow our *Fallen Idol* – I had nothing more to offer than this paragraph. Though Korda wanted a film about the four-power occupation of Vienna, he was prepared to let me pursue the tracks of Harry Lime.

To me it is almost impossible to write a film play without first writing a story. Even a film depends on more than plot, on a certain measure of characterisation, on mood and atmosphere; and these seem to me almost impossible to capture for the first time in the dull shorthand of a script. One can reproduce an effect caught in another medium, but one cannot make the first act of creation in script form. One must have the sense of more material than one needs to draw on. *The Third Man*, therefore, though never intended for publication, had to start as a story before those apparently interminable transformations from one treatment to another.

On these treatments Carol Reed and I worked closely together, covering so many feet of carpet a day, acting scenes at each other. No third ever joined our conferences; so much value lies in the clear cut-and-thrust of argument between two people. To the novelist, of course, his novel is the best he can do with a particular subject; he cannot help resenting many of the changes necessary for turning it into a film or a play; but *The Third Man* was never intended to be more than the raw material for a picture. The reader will notice many differences between the story and the film, and he should not imagine these changes were forced on an unwilling author: as likely as not they were suggested by the author. The film in fact, is better than the story because it is in this case the finished state of the story.

Some of these changes have obvious superficial reasons. The choice of an American instead of an English star involved a number of alterations. For example, Mr Joseph Cotten quite reasonably objected to the name Rollo. The name had to be an absurd one, and the name Holley occurred to me when I remembered that figure of fun, the American poet Thomas Holley Chivers. An American, too, could hardly have been mistaken for the great English writer Dexter, whose literary character bore certain echoes of the gentle genius of Mr E. M. Forster. The confusion of identities would have been impossible, even if Carol Reed had not rightly objected to a rather far-fetched situation involving a great deal of explanation that increased the length of a film already far too long. Another minor point: in deference to American opinion a Rumanian was substituted for Cooler, since Mr Orson Welles' engagement had already supplied us with one American villain. (Incidentally, the popular line of dialogue concerning Swiss cuckoo clocks was written into the script by Mr Welles himself.)

One of the very few major disputes between Carol Reed and myself concerned the ending, and he has been proved triumphantly right. I held the view that an entertainment of this kind was too light an affair to carry the weight of an unhappy ending. Reed on his side felt that my ending – indeterminate though it was, with no words spoken – would strike the audience, who had just seen Harry die, as unpleasantly cynical. I admit I was only half convinced; I was afraid few people would wait in their seats during the girl's long walk from the graveside and that they would leave the cinema under the impression that the ending was as conventional as mine and more drawn-out. I had not given enough consideration to the mastery of Reed's direction, and at that stage, of course, we neither of us could have anticipated Reed's brilliant discovery of Mr Karas, the zither player.

The episode of the Russians kidnapping Anna (a perfectly possible incident in Vienna) was eliminated at a fairly late stage. It was not satisfactorily tied into the story, and it threatened to turn the film into a propagandist picture. We had no desire to move people's political emotions; we wanted to entertain them, to frighten them a little, to make them laugh.

Reality, in fact, was only a background to a fairy tale; none the less the story of the penicillin racket is based on a truth all the more grim because so many of the agents were more innocent than Joseph Harbin. The other day in London a surgeon took two friends to see the film. He was surprised to find them subdued and depressed by a picture he had enjoyed. They then told him that at the end of the war when they were with the Royal Air Force they had themselves sold penicillin in Vienna. The possible consequences of their act had never before occurred to them.

One never knows when the blow may fall. When I saw Rollo Martins first I made this note on him for my security police files: 'In normal circumstances a cheerful fool. Drinks too much and may cause a little trouble. Whenever a woman passes raises his eyes and makes some comment, but I get the impression that really he'd rather not be bothered. Has never really grown up and perhaps that accounts for the way he worshipped Lime.' I wrote there that phrase 'in normal circumstances' because I met him first at Harry Lime's funeral. It was February, and the grave-diggers had been forced to use electric drills to open the frozen ground in Vienna's Central Cemetery. It was as if even nature were doing its best to reject Lime, but we got him in at last and laid the earth back on him like bricks. He was vaulted in, and Rollo Martins walked quickly away as though his long gangly legs wanted to break into a run and the tears of a boy ran down his thirty-five-year-old face. Rollo Martins believed in friendship, and that was why what happened later was a worse shock to him than it would have been to you or me (you because you would have put it down to an illusion and me because at once a rational explanation – however wrongly – would have come to my mind). If only he had come to tell me then, what a lot of trouble would have been saved.

If you are to understand this strange, rather sad story you must have an impression at least of the background – the smashed dreary city of Vienna divided up in zones among the Four Powers: the Russian, the British, the American, the French zones, regions marked only by noticeboards, and in the centre of the city, surrounded by the Ring with its heavy public buildings and its prancing statuary, the Innere Stadt under the control of all Four Powers. In this once fashionable Inner City each power in turn, for a month at a time, takes, as we call it, 'the chair', and becomes responsible for security; at night, if you were fool enough to waste your Austrian schillings on a nightclub, you would be fairly certain to see the International Power at work – four military police, one from each power, communicating with each other, if they communicated at all, in the common language of their enemy. I never knew Vienna between the wars, and I am too young to remember the old Vienna with its Strauss music and its bogus easy charm; to me it is simply a city of undignified ruins which turned that February into great glaciers of snow and ice. The Danube was a grey flat muddy river a long way off across the Second Bezirk, the Russian zone where the Prater lay smashed and desolate and full of weeds, only the Great Wheel revolving slowly over the foundations of merry-go-rounds like abandoned millstones, the rusting iron of smashed tanks which nobody had cleared away, the frost-nipped weeds where the snow was thin. I haven't enough imagination to picture it as it had once been, any more than I can picture Sacher's Hotel as other than a transit hotel for English officers or see the Kärntnerstrasse as a fashionable shopping street instead of a street which exists, most of it, only at eye level, repaired up to the first storey. A Russian soldier in a fur cap goes by with a rifle over his shoulder, a few tarts cluster round the American Information Office, and men in overcoats sip ersatz coffee in the windows of the Old Vienna. At night it is just as well to stick to the Inner City or the zones of three of the Powers, though even there the kidnappings occur – such senseless kidnappings they sometimes seemed to us – a Ukrainian girl without a passport, an old man beyond the age of usefulness, sometimes, of course, the technician or the traitor. This was roughly the Vienna to which Rollo Martins came on 7 February last year. I have reconstructed the affair as best I can from my own files and from what Martins told me. It is as accurate as I can make it – I have tried not to invent a line of dialogue, though I can't vouch for Martins' memory; an ugly story if you leave out the girl: grim and sad and unrelieved, if it were not for that absurd episode of the British Council lecturer.

2

A British subject can still travel if he is content to take with him only five English pounds which he is forbidden to spend abroad, but if Rollo Martins had not received an invitation from Lime of the International Refugee Office he would not have been allowed to enter Austria, which counts still as occupied territory. Lime had suggested that Martins might write up the business of looking after the international refugees, and although it wasn't Martins' usual line, he had consented. It would give him a holiday, and he badly needed a holiday after the incident in Dublin and the other incident in Amsterdam; he always tried to dismiss women as 'incidents', things that simply happened to him without any will of his own, acts of God in the eyes of insurance agents. He had a haggard look when he arrived in Vienna and a habit of looking over his shoulder that for a time made me suspicious of him until I realised that he went in fear that one of, say, six people might turn up unexpectedly. He told me vaguely that he had been mixing his drinks – that was another way of putting it.

Rollo Martins' usual line was the writing of cheap paper-covered Westerns under the name of Buck Dexter. His public was large but unremunerative. He couldn't have afforded Vienna if Lime had not offered to pay his expenses when he got there out of some vaguely described propaganda fund. Lime could also, he said, keep him supplied with paper *Bafs* – the only currency in use from a penny upwards in British hotels and clubs. So it was with exactly five unusable pound notes that Martins arrived in Vienna.

An odd incident had occurred at Frankfurt, where the plane from London grounded for an hour. Martins was eating a hamburger in the American canteen (a kindly airline supplied the passengers with a voucher for sixty-five cents' worth of food) when a man he could recognise from twenty feet away as a journalist approached his table.

'You Mr Dexter?' he asked.

'Yes,' Martins said, taken off his guard.

'You look younger than your photographs,' the man said. 'Like to make a statement? I represent the local forces paper here. We'd like to know what you think of Frankfurt.'

'I only touched down ten minutes ago.'

'Fair enough,' the man said. 'What about views on the American novel?'

'I don't read them,' Martins said.

'The well-known acid humour,' the journalist said. He pointed at a small grey-haired man with protruding teeth, nibbling a bit of bread. 'Happen to know if that's Carey?'

'No. What Carey?'

'J. G. Carey of course.'

'I've never heard of him.'

'You novelists live out of the world. He's my real assignment,' and Martins watched him make across the room for the great Carey, who greeted him with a false headline smile, laying down his crust. Dexter wasn't the man's assignment, but Martins couldn't help feeling a certain pride – nobody had ever before referred to him as a novelist; and that sense of pride and importance carried him over the disappointment when Lime was not there to meet him at the airport. We never get accustomed to being less important to other people than they are to us – Martins felt the little jab of dispensability, standing by the bus door, watching the snow come sifting down, so thinly and softly that the great drifts among the ruined buildings had an air of permanence, as though they were not the result of this meagre fall, but lay, for ever, above the line of perpetual snow.

There was no Lime to meet him at the Hotel Astoria, the terminus where the bus landed him, and no message – only a cryptic one for Mr Dexter from someone he had never heard of called Crabbin. 'We expected you on tomorrow's plane. Please stay where you are. On the way round. Hotel room booked.' But Rollo Martins wasn't the kind of man who stayed around. If you stayed around in a hotel lounge, sooner or later incidents occurred; one mixed one's drinks. I

29

can hear Rollo Martins saying to me, 'I've done with incidents. No more incidents,' before he plunged head first into the most serious incident of all. There was always a conflict in Rollo Martins – between the absurd Christian name and the sturdy Dutch (four generations back) surname. Rollo looked at every woman that passed, and Martins renounced them for ever. I don't know which one of them wrote the Westerns.

Martins had been given Lime's address and he felt no curiosity about the man called Crabbin; it was too obvious that a mistake had been made, though he didn't yet connect it with the conversation at Frankfurt. Lime had written that he could put Martins up in his own flat, a large apartment on the edge of Vienna that had been requisitioned from a Nazi owner. Lime could pay for the taxi when he arrived, so Martins drove straight away to the building lying in the third (British) zone. He kept the taxi waiting while he mounted to the third floor.

How quickly one becomes aware of silence even in so silent a city as Vienna with the snow steadily settling. Martins hadn't reached the second floor before he was convinced that he would not find Lime there, but the silence was deeper than just absence – it was as if he would not find Lime anywhere in Vienna, or, as he reached the third floor and saw the big black bow over the door handle, anywhere in the world at all. Of course it might have been a cook who had died, a housekeeper, anybody but Harry Lime, but he knew – he felt he had known twenty stairs down – that Lime, the Lime he had hero-worshipped now for twenty years, since the first meeting in a grim school corridor with a cracked bell ringing for prayers, was gone. Martin's wasn't wrong, not entirely wrong. After he had rung the bell half a dozen times a small man with a sullen expression put his head out from another flat and told him in a tone of vexation, 'It's no use. There's nobody there. He's dead.'

'Herr Lime?'

'Herr Lime, of course.'

Martins said to me later, 'At first it didn't mean a thing. It was just a bit of information, like those paragraphs in *The Times* they call "News in Brief". I said to him, "When did it happen? How?"'

'He was run over by a car,' the man said. 'Last Thursday.' He added sullenly, as if really this were none of his business, 'They're burying him this afternoon. You've only just missed them.'

'Them?'

'Oh, a couple of friends and the coffin.'

'Wasn't he in hospital?'

'There was no sense in taking him to hospital. He was killed here on his own doorstep – instantaneously. The right-hand mudguard struck him on his shoulder and bowled him over like a rabbit.'

It was only then, Martins told me, when the man used the word 'rabbit', that the dead Harry Lime came alive, became the boy with the gun which he had shown Martins the means of 'borrowing'; a boy starting up among the long sandy burrows of Brickworth Common saying, 'Shoot, you fool, shoot! There,' and the rabbit limped to cover, wounded by Martins' shot.

'Where are they burying him?' he asked the stranger on the landing.

'In the Central Cemetery. They'll have a hard time of it in this frost.'

He had no idea how to pay for his taxi, or indeed where in Vienna he could find a room in which he could live for five English pounds, but that problem had to be postponed until he had seen the last of Harry Lime. He drove straight out of town into the suburb (British zone) where the Central Cemetery lay. One passed through the Russian zone to reach it, and took a short cut through the American zone, which you couldn't mistake because of the ice-cream parlours in every street. The trams ran along the high wall of the Central Cemetery, and for a mile on the other side of the rails stretched the monumental masons and the market gardeners – an apparently endless chain of gravestones waiting for owners and wreaths waiting for mourners.

Martins had not realised the size of this huge snow-bound park where he was making his last rendezvous with Lime. It was as if Harry had left a message for him, 'Meet me in Hyde Park', without specifying a spot between the Achilles statue and Lancaster Gate; the avenues of graves, each avenue numbered and lettered, stretched out like the spokes of an enormous wheel; they drove for a half-mile towards the west, and then turned and drove a half-mile north, turned south. . . . The snow gave the great pompous family headstones an air of grotesque comedy: a toupée of snow slipped sideways over an angelic face, a saint wore a heavy white moustache, and a shako of snow tipped at a drunken angle over the bust of a superior civil servant called Wolfgang Gottmann. Even this cemetery was zoned between the Powers: the Russian zone was marked by huge tasteless statues of armed men, the French by rows of anonymous wooden crosses and a torn tired tricolour flag. Then Martins remembered that Lime was a Catholic and was unlikely to be buried in the British zone for which they had been vainly searching. So back they drove through the heart of a forest where the graves lay like wolves under the trees, winking white eyes under the gloom of the evergreens. Once from under the trees emerged a group of three men in strange eighteenth-century black and silver uniforms, with three-cornered hats, pushing a kind of barrow: they crossed a ride in the forest of graves and disappeared again.

It was just chance that they found the funeral in time – one patch in the enormous park where the snow had been shovelled aside and a tiny group was gathered, apparently bent on some very private business. A priest had finished speaking, his words coming secretively through the thin patient snow, and a coffin was on the point of being lowered into the ground. Two men in lounge suits stood at the grave-side; one carried a wreath that he obviously had for-gotten to drop on to the coffin, for his companion nudged his elbow so that he came to with a start and dropped the flowers. A girl stood a little way away with her hands over her face, and I stood twenty yards away by another grave, watching with relief the last of Lime and noticing carefully who was there – just a man in a mackintosh I was to Martins. He came up to me and said, 'Could you tell me who they are burying?'

'A fellow called Lime,' I said, and was astonished to see the tears start to this stranger's eyes: he didn't look like a man who wept, nor was Lime the kind of man whom I thought likely to have mourners – genuine mourners with genuine tears. There was the girl of course, but one excepts women from all such generalisations.

Martins stood there, till the end, close beside me. He said to me later that as an old friend he didn't want to intrude on these newer ones – Lime's death belonged to them, let them have it. He was under the sentimental illusion that Lime's life – twenty years of it anyway – belonged to him. As soon as the affair was over – I am not a religious man and always feel a little impatient with the fuss that surrounds death – Martins strode away on his long legs, which always seemed likely to get entangled together, back to his taxi. He made no attempt to speak to anyone, and the tears now were really running, at any rate the few meagre drops that any of us can squeeze out at our age.

One's file, you know, is never quite complete; a case is never really closed, even after a century, when all the participants are dead. So I followed Martins: I knew the other three: I wanted to know the stranger. I caught him up by his taxi and said, 'I haven't any transport. Would you give me a lift into town?'

'Of course,' he said. I knew the driver of my jeep would spot me as we came out and follow us unobtrusively. As we drove away I noticed Martins never looked behind – it's nearly always the fake mourners and the fake lovers who take that last look, who wait waving on platforms, instead of clearing quickly out, not looking back. Is it perhaps that they love themselves so much and want to keep themselves in the sight of others, even of the dead?

I said, 'My name's Calloway.'

'Martins,' he said.

'You were a friend of Lime?'

'Yes.' Most people in the last week would have hesitated before they admitted quite so much.

'Been here long?'

'I only came this afternoon from England. Harry had asked me to stay with him. I hadn't heard.'

'Bit of a shock?'

'Look here,' he said, 'I badly want a drink, but I haven't any cash – except five pounds sterling. I'd be awfully grateful if you'd stand me one.'

It was my turn to say 'Of course'. I thought for a moment and told the driver the name of a small bar in the Kärntnerstrasse. I didn't think he'd want to be seen for a while in a busy British bar full of transit officers and their wives. This bar – perhaps because it was exorbitant in its prices – seldom had more than one self-occupied couple in it at a time. The trouble was too that it really only had one drink – a sweet chocolate liqueur that the waiter improved at a price with cognac – but I got the impression that Martins had no objection to any drink so long as it cast a veil over the present and the past. On the door was the usual notice saying the bar opened from six till ten, but one just pushed the door and walked through the front rooms. We had a whole small room to ourselves; the only couple were next door, and the waiter, who knew me, left us alone with some caviare sandwiches. It was lucky that we both knew I had an expense account.

Martins said over his second quick drink, 'I'm sorry, but he was the best friend I ever had.'

I couldn't resist saying, knowing what I knew, and because I was anxious to vex him – one learns a lot that way – 'That sounds like a cheap novelette.'

He said quickly, 'I write cheap novelettes.'

I had learned something anyway. Until he had had a third drink I was under the impression that he wasn't an easy talker, but I felt fairly certain he was one of those who turn unpleasant after their fourth glass.

I said, 'Tell me about yourself – and Lime.'

'Look here,' he said, 'I badly need another drink, but I can't keep on scrounging from a stranger. Could you change me a pound or two into Austrian money?'

'Don't bother about that,' I said and called the waiter. 'You can treat me when I come to London on leave. You were going to tell me how you met Lime?'

The glass of chocolate liqueur might have been a crystal, the way he looked at it and turned it this way and that. He said, 'It was a long time ago. I don't suppose anyone knows Harry the way I do,' and I thought of the thick file of agents' reports in my office, each claiming the same thing. I believe in my agents; I've sifted them all very thoroughly.

'How long?'

'Twenty years – or a bit more. I met him my first term at school. I can see the place. I can see the noticeboard and what was on it. I can hear the bell ringing. He was a year older and knew the ropes. He put me wise to a lot of things.' He took a quick dab at his drink and then turned the crystal again as if to see more clearly what there was to see. He said, 'It's funny. I can't remember meeting any woman quite as well.'

'Was he clever at school?'

'Not the way they wanted him to be. But what things he did think up! He was a wonderful planner. I was far better at subjects like History and English than Harry, but I was a hopeless mug when it came to carrying out his plans.' He laughed: he was already beginning, with the help of drink and talk, to throw off the shock of the death. He said, 'I was always the one who got caught.'

'That was convenient for Lime.'

'What the hell do you mean?' he asked. Alcoholic irritation was setting in.

'Well, wasn't it?'

'That was my fault, not his. He could have found someone cleverer if he'd chosen, but he liked me.' Certainly, I thought, the child is father to the man, for I too had found Lime patient.

'When did you see him last?'

'Oh, he was over in London six months ago for a medical congress. You know, he qualified as a doctor, though he never practised. That was typical of Harry. He just wanted to see if he could do a thing and then he lost interest. But he used to say that it often came in handy.' And that too was true. It was odd how like the Lime he knew was to the Lime I knew: it was only that he looked at Lime's image from a different angle or in a different light. He said, 'One of the things I liked about Harry was his humour.' He gave a grin which took five years off his age. 'I'm a buffoon. I like playing the silly fool, but Harry had real wit. You know, he could have been a first-class light composer if he had worked at it.'

He whistled a tune – it was oddly familiar to me. 'I always remember that. I saw Harry write it. Just in a couple of minutes on the back of an envelope. That was what he always whistled when he had something on his mind. It was his signature tune.' He whistled the tune a second time, and I knew then who had written it – of course it wasn't Harry. I nearly told him so, but what was the point? The tune wavered and went out. He stared down into his glass, drained what was left, and said, 'It's a damned shame to think of him dying the way he did.'

'It was the best thing that ever happened to him,' I said.

He didn't take in my meaning at once: he was a little hazy with his drinks. 'The best thing?'

'Yes.'

'You mean there wasn't any pain?'

'He was lucky in that way, too.'

It was my tone of voice and not my words that caught Martins' attention. He asked gently and dangerously – I could see his right hand tighten – 'Are you hinting at something?'

There is no point at all in showing physical courage in all situations: I eased my chair far enough back to be out of reach of his fist. I said, 'I mean that I had his case completed at police headquarters. He would have served a long spell – a very long spell – if it hadn't been for the accident.'

'What for?'

'He was about the worst racketeer who ever made a dirty living in this city.'

I could see him measuring the distance between us and deciding that he couldn't reach me from where he sat. Rollo wanted to hit out, but Martins was steady, careful. Martins, I began to realise, was dangerous. I wondered whether after all I had made a complete mistake: I couldn't see Martins being quite the mug that Rollo had made out. 'You're a policeman?' he asked.

'Yes.'

'I've always hated policemen. They are always either crooked or stupid.'

'Is that the kind of book you write?'

I could see him edging his chair round to block my way out. I caught the waiter's eye and he knew what I meant – there's an advantage in always using the same bar for interviews.

Martins brought out a surface smile and said gently, 'I have to call them sheriffs.'

'Been in America?' It was a silly conversation.

'No. Is this an interrogation?'

'Just interest.'

'Because if Harry was that kind of racketeer, I must be one too. We always worked together.'

'I dare say he meant to cut you in – somewhere in the organisation. I wouldn't be surprised if he had meant to give you the baby to hold. That was his method at school – you told me, didn't you? And, you see, the headmaster was getting to know a thing or two.'

'You are running true to form, aren't you? I suppose there was some petty racket going on with petrol and you couldn't pin it on anyone, so you've picked a dead man. That's just like a policeman. You're a real policeman, I suppose?'

'Yes, Scotland Yard, but they've put me into a colonel's uniform when I'm on duty.'

He was between me and the door now. I couldn't get away from the table without coming into range. I'm no fighter, and he had six inches of advantage anyway. I said, 'It wasn't petrol.'

'Tyres, saccharin – why don't you policemen catch a few murderers for a change?'

'Well, you could say that murder was part of his racket.'

He pushed the table over with one hand and made a dive at me with the other; the drink confused his calculations. Before he could try again my driver had his arms round him. I said, 'Don't treat him rough. He's only a writer with too much drink in him.'

'Be quiet, can't you, sir,' my driver said. He had an exaggerated sense of officer-class. He would probably have called Lime 'sir'.

'Listen, Callaghan, or whatever your bloody name is . . . '

'Calloway. I'm English, not Irish.'

'I'm going to make you look the biggest bloody fool in Vienna. There's one dead man you aren't going to pin your unsolved crimes on.'

'I see. You're going to find me the real criminal? It sounds like one of your stories.'

'You can let me go, Callaghan. I'd rather make you look the fool you are than black your bloody eye. You'd only have to go to bed for a few days with a black eye. But when I've finished with you, you'll leave Vienna.'

I took out a couple of pounds' worth of bafs and stuck them in his breast pocket. 'These will see you through tonight,' I said, 'and I'll make sure they keep a seat for you on tomorrow's London plane.'

'You can't turn me out. My papers are in order.'

'Yes, but this is like other cities: you need money here. If you change sterling on the black market I'll catch up with you inside twenty-four hours. Let him go.'

Rollo Martins dusted himself down. He said, 'Thanks for the drinks.'

'That's all right.'

'I'm glad I don't have to feel grateful. I suppose they were on expenses?'

'Yes.'

'I'll be seeing you again in a week or two when I've got the dope.' I knew he was angry. I didn't believe then that he was serious. I thought he was putting over an act to cheer up his self-esteem.

'I might come and see you off tomorrow.'

'I shouldn't waste your time. I won't be there.'

'Paine here will show you the way to Sacher's. You can get a bed and dinner there. I'll see to that.'

He stepped to one side as though to make way for the waiter and slashed out at me. I just avoided him, but stumbled against the table. Before he could try again Paine had landed him one on the mouth. He went bang over in the alleyway between the tables and came up bleeding from a cut lip. I said, 'I thought you promised not to fight.'

He wiped some of the blood away with his sleeve and said, 'Oh, no, I said I'd rather make you a bloody fool. I didn't say I wouldn't give you a black eye as well.'

I had had a long day and I was tired of Rollo Martins. I said to Paine, 'See him safely into Sacher's. Don't hit him again if he behaves,' and turning away from both of them towards the inner bar (I deserved one more drink), I heard Paine say respectfully to the man he had just knocked down, 'This way, sir. It's only just around the corner.'

3

What happened next I didn't hear from Paine but from Martins a long time afterwards, as I reconstructed the chain of events which did indeed – though not quite in the way he had expected – prove me to be a fool. Paine simply saw him to the head porter's desk and explained there, 'This gentleman came in on the plane from London. Colonel Calloway says he's to have a room.' Having made that clear, he said, 'Good-evening, sir,' and left. He was probably a bit embarrassed by Martins' bleeding lip.

'Had you already got a reservation, sir?' the porter asked.

'No. No, I don't think so,' Martins said in a muffled voice, holding his handkerchief to his mouth.

'I thought perhaps you might be Mr Dexter. We had a room reserved for a week for Mr Dexter.'

Martins said, 'Oh, I am Mr Dexter.' He told me later that it occurred to him that Lime might have engaged a room for him in that name because perhaps it was Buck Dexter and not Rollo Martins who was to be used for propaganda purposes. A voice said at his elbow, 'I'm so sorry you were not met at the plane, Mr Dexter. My name's Crabbin.'

The speaker was a stout middle-aged young man with a natural tonsure and one of the thickest pairs of horn-rimmed glasses that Martins had ever seen. He went apologetically on, 'One of our chaps happened to ring up Frankfurt and heard you were on the plane. HQ made one of their usual foolish mistakes and wired you were not coming. Something about Sweden, but the cable was badly mutilated. Directly I heard from Frankfurt I tried to meet the plane, but I just missed you. You got my note?'

Martins held his handkerchief to his mouth and said obscurely, 'Yes. Yes?'

'May I say at once, Mr Dexter, how excited I am to meet you?'

'Good of you.'

'Ever since I was a boy, I've thought you the greatest novelist of our century.'

Martins winced. It was painful opening his mouth to protest. He took an angry look instead at Mr Crabbin, but it was impossible to suspect that young man of a practical joke.

'You have a big Austrian public, Mr Dexter, both for your originals and your translations. Especially for *The Curved Prow*, that's my own favourite.'

Martins was thinking hard. 'Did you say – room for a week?'

'Yes.'

'Very kind of you.'

'Mr Schmidt here will give you tickets every day, to cover all meals. But I expect you'll need a little pocket money. We'll fix that. Tomorrow we thought you'd like a quiet day – to look about.'

'Yes.'

'Of course any of us are at your service if you need a guide. Then the day after tomorrow in the evening there's a little quiet discussion at the Institute – on the contemporary novel. We thought perhaps you'd say a few words just to set the ball rolling, and then answer questions.'

Martins at that moment was prepared to agree to anything to get rid of Mr Crabbin and also to secure a week's free board and lodging; and Rollo, of course, as I was to discover later, had always been prepared to accept any suggestion – for a drink, for a girl, for a joke, for a new excitement. He said now, 'Of course, of course,' into his handkerchief.

'Excuse me, Mr Dexter, have you got toothache? I know a very good dentist.'

'No. Somebody hit me, that's all.'

'Good God! Were they trying to rob you?'

'No, it was a soldier. I was trying to punch his bloody colonel in the eye.' He removed the handkerchief and gave Crabbin a view of his cut mouth. He told me that Crabbin was at a complete loss for words. Martins couldn't understand why because he had never read the work of his great contemporary, Benjamin Dexter: he hadn't even heard of him. I am a great admirer of Dexter, so that I could understand Crabbin's bewilderment. Dexter has been ranked as a stylist with Henry James, but he has a wider feminine streak than his master – indeed his enemies have sometimes described his subtle, complex, wavering style as old-maidish. For a man still just on the right side of fifty his passionate interest in embroidery and his habit of calming a not very tumultuous mind with tatting – a trait beloved by his disciples – certainly to others seems a little affected.

'Have you ever read a book called *The Lone Rider of Santa Fé*?'

'No, I don't think so.'

Martins said, 'This lone rider had his best friend shot by the sheriff of a town called Lost Claim Gulch. The story is how he hunted that sheriff down – quite legally – until his revenge was completed.'

'I never imagined you reading Westerns, Mr Dexter,' Crabbin said, and it needed all Martins' resolution to stop Rollo saying, 'But I write them.'

'Well, I'm gunning just the same way for Colonel Callaghan.'

'Never heard of him.'

'Heard of Harry Lime?'

'Yes,' Crabbin said cautiously, 'but I didn't really know him.'

44

'I did. He was my best friend.'

'I shouldn't have thought he was a very – literary character.'

'None of my friends are.'

Crabbin blinked nervously behind the horn-rims. He said with an air of appeasement, 'He was interested in the theatre though. A friend of his – an actress, you know – is learning English at the Institute. He called once or twice to fetch her.'

'Young or old?'

'Oh, young, very young. Not a good actress in my opinion.'

Martins remembered the girl by the grave with her hands over her face. He said, 'I'd like to meet any friend of Harry's.'

'She'll probably be at your lecture.'

'Austrian?'

'She claims to be Austrian, but I suspect she's Hungarian. She works at the Josefstadt.'

'Why claims to be Austrian?'

'The Russians sometimes get interested in the Hungarians. I wouldn't be surprised if Lime had helped her with her papers. She calls herself Schmidt. Anna Schmidt. You can't imagine a young English actress calling herself Smith, can you? And a pretty one, too. It always struck me as a bit too anonymous to be true.'

Martins felt he had got all he could from Crabbin, so he pleaded tiredness, a long day, promised to ring up in the morning, accepted ten pounds' worth of *Bafs* for immediate expenses, and went to his room. It seemed to him that he was earning money rapidly – twelve pounds in less than an hour.

He *was* tired: he realised that when he stretched

himself out on his bed in his boots. Within a minute he had left Vienna far behind him and was walking through a dense wood, ankle-deep in snow. An owl hooted, and he felt suddenly lonely and scared. He had an appointment to meet Harry under a particular tree, but in a wood so dense how could he recognise any one tree from the rest? Then he saw a figure and ran towards it: it whistled a familiar tune and his heart lifted with the relief and joy at not after all being alone. The figure turned and it was not Harry at all – just a stranger who grinned at him in a little circle of wet slushy melted snow, while the owl hooted again and again. He woke suddenly to hear the telephone ringing by his bed.

A voice with a trace of foreign accent – only a trace – said, 'Is that Mr Rollo Martins?'

'Yes.' It was a change to be himself and not Dexter.

'You wouldn't know me,' the voice said unnecessarily, 'but I was a friend of Harry Lime.'

It was a change too to hear anyone claim to be a friend of Harry's. Martins' heart warmed towards the stranger. He said, 'I'd be glad to meet you.'

'I'm just round the corner at the Old Vienna.'

'Couldn't you make it tomorrow? I've had a pretty awful day with one thing and another.'

'Harry asked me to see that you were all right. I was with him when he died.'

'I thought – ' Rollo Martins said and stopped. He had been going to say, 'I thought he died instantaneously,' but something suggested caution. He said instead, 'You haven't told me your name.'

'Kurtz,' the voice said. 'I'd offer to come round to you, only, you know, Austrians aren't allowed in Sacher's.'

'Perhaps we could meet at the Old Vienna in the morning.'

'Certainly,' the voice said, 'if you are *quite* sure that you are all right till then?'

'How do you mean?'

'Harry had it on his mind that you'd be penniless.' Rollo Martins lay back on his bed with the receiver to his ear and thought: Come to Vienna to make money. This was the third stranger to stake him in less than five hours. He said cautiously, 'Oh, I can carry on till I see you.' There seemed no point in turning down a good offer till he knew what the offer was.

'Shall we say eleven, then, at the Old Vienna in the Kärntnerstrasse? I'll be in a brown suit and I'll carry one of your books.'

'That's fine. How did you get hold of one?'

'Harry gave it to me.' The voice had enormous charm and reasonableness, but when Martins had said good-night and rung off, he couldn't help wondering how it was that if Harry had been so conscious before he died he had not had a cable sent to stop him. Hadn't Callaghan too said that Lime died instantaneously – or without pain, was it? – or had he put the words into Callaghan's mouth? It was then the idea first lodged firmly in Martins' mind that there was something wrong about Lime's death, something the police had been too stupid to discover. He tried to discover it himself with the help of two cigarettes, but he fell asleep without his dinner and with the mystery still unsolved. It had been a long day, but not quite long enough for that.

4

'What I disliked about him at first sight,' Martins told me, 'was his toupée. It was one of those obvious toupées – flat and yellow, with the hair cut straight at the back and not fitting close. There *must* be something phoney about a man who won't accept baldness gracefully. He had one of those faces too where the lines have been put in carefully, like a make-up, in the right places – to express charm, whimsicality, lines at the corners of the eyes. He was made up to appeal to romantic schoolgirls.'

This conversation took place some days later – he brought out his whole story when the trail was nearly cold. We were sitting in the Old Vienna at the table he had occupied that first morning with Kurtz, and when he made that remark about the romantic schoolgirls I saw his rather hunted eyes focus suddenly. It was a girl – just like any other girl, I thought, hurrying by outside in the driving snow.

'Something pretty?'

He brought his gaze back and said, 'I'm off that for ever. You know, Calloway, a time comes in a man's life when he gives up all that sort of thing . . . '

'I see. I thought you were looking at a girl.'

'I was. But only because she reminded me for a moment of Anna – Anna Schmidt.'

'Who's she? Isn't she a girl?'

'Oh, yes, in a way.'

'What do you mean, in a way?'

'She was Harry's girl.'

'Are you taking her over?'

'She's not that kind, Calloway. Didn't you see her

at his funeral? I'm not mixing my drinks any more. I've got a hangover to last me a lifetime.'

'You were telling me about Kurtz,' I said.

It appeared that Kurtz was sitting there, making a great show of reading *The Lone Rider of Santa Fé*. When Martins sat down at his table he said with indescribably false enthusiasm, 'It's wonderful how you keep the tension.'

'Tension?'

'Suspense. You're a master at it. At the end of every chapter one's left guessing . . . '

'So you were a friend of Harry's,' Martins said.

'I think his best,' but Kurtz added with the smallest pause, in which his brain must have registered the error, 'except you, of course.'

'Tell me how he died.'

'I was with him. We came out together from the door of his flat and Harry saw a friend he knew across the road – an American called Cooler. He waved to Cooler and started across the road to him when a jeep came tearing round the corner and bowled him over. It was Harry's fault really – not the driver's.'

'Somebody told me he died instantaneously.'

'I wish he had. He died before the ambulance could reach us though.'

'He could speak, then?'

'Yes. Even in his pain he worried about you.'

'What did he say?'

'I can't remember the exact words, Rollo – I may call you Rollo, mayn't I? he always called you that to us. He was anxious that I should look after you when you arrived. See that you were looked after. Get your return ticket for you.' In telling me, Martins said, 'You see I was collecting return tickets as well as cash.'

'But why didn't you cable to stop me?'

'We did, but the cable must have missed you. What with censorship and the zones, cables can take anything up to five days.'

'There was an inquest?'

'Of course.'

'Did you know that the police have a crazy notion that Harry was mixed up in some racket?'

'No. But everyone in Vienna is. We all sell cigarettes and exchange schillings for *Bafs* and that kind of thing. You won't find a single member of the Control Commission who hasn't broken the rules.'

'The police meant something worse than that.'

'They get rather absurd ideas sometimes,' the man with the toupée said cautiously.

'I'm going to stay here till I prove them wrong.'

Kurtz turned his head sharply and the toupée shifted very very slightly. He said, 'What's the good? Nothing can bring Harry back.'

'I'm going to have that police officer run out of Vienna.'

'I don't see what you can do.'

'I'm going to start working back from his death. You were there and this man Cooler and the chauffeur. You can give me their addresses.'

'I don't know the chauffeur's.'

'I can get it from the coroner's records. And then there's Harry's girl . . . '

Kurtz said, 'It will be painful for her.'

'I'm not concerned about her. I'm concerned about Harry.'

'Do you know what it is that the police suspect?'

'No. I lost my temper too soon.'

'Has it occurred to you,' Kurtz said gently, 'that

you might dig up something – well, discreditable to Harry?'

'I'll risk that.'

'It will take a bit of time – and money.'

'I've got time and you were going to lend me some money, weren't you?'

'I'm not a rich man,' Kurtz said. 'I promised Harry to see you were all right and that you got your plane back . . . '

'You needn't worry about the money – or the plane,' Martins said. 'But I'll make a bet with you – in pounds sterling – five pounds against two hundred schillings – that there's something queer about Harry's death.'

It was a shot in the dark, but already he had this firm instinctive sense that there was something wrong, though he hadn't yet attached the word 'murder' to the instinct. Kurtz had a cup of coffee halfway to his lips and Martins watched him. The shot apparently went wide; an unaffected hand held the cup to the mouth and Kurtz drank, a little noisily, in long sips. Then he put down the cup and said, 'How do you mean – queer?'

'It was convenient for the police to have a corpse, but wouldn't it have been equally convenient, perhaps, for the real racketeers?' When he had spoken he realised that after all Kurtz might not have been unaffected by his wild statement: hadn't he perhaps been frozen into caution and calm? The hands of the guilty don't necessarily tremble; only in stories does a dropped glass betray agitation. Tension is more often shown in the studied action. Kurtz had drunk his coffee as though nothing had been said.

'Well – ' he took another sip – 'of course I wish you

luck, though I don't believe there's anything to find. Just ask me for any help you want.'

'I want Cooler's address.'

'Certainly. I'll write it down for you. Here it is. In the American zone.'

'And yours?'

'I've already put it – underneath. I'm unlucky enough to be in the Russian zone – so don't visit me very late. Things sometimes happen round our way.' He was giving one of his studied Viennese smiles, the charm carefully painted in with a fine brush in the little lines about the mouth and eyes. 'Keep in touch,' he said, 'and if you need any help . . . but I still think you are very unwise.' He touched *The Lone Rider*. 'I'm so proud to have met you. A master of suspense,' and one hand smoothed the toupée, while another, passing softly over the mouth, brushed out the smile as though it had never been.

5

Martins sat on a hard chair just inside the stage door of the Josefstadt Theatre. He had sent up his card to Anna Schmidt after the matinée, marking it 'a friend of Harry's'. An arcade of little windows, with lace curtains and the lights going out one after another, showed where the artists were packing up for home, for the cup of coffee without sugar, the roll without butter to sustain them for the evening performance. It was like a little street built indoors for a film set, but even indoors it was cold, even cold to a man in a heavy overcoat, so that Martins rose and walked up and down underneath the little windows. He felt, he said, rather like a Romeo who wasn't sure of Juliet's balcony.

He had had time to think: he was calm now, Martins not Rollo was in the ascendant. When a light went out in one of the windows and an actress descended into the passage where he walked, he didn't even turn to take a look. He was done with all that. He thought, Kurtz is right. They are all right. I'm behaving like a romantic fool. I'll just have a word with Anna Schmidt, a word of commiseration, and then I'll pack and go. He had quite forgotten, he told me, the complication of Mr Crabbin.

A voice over his head called, 'Mr Martins,' and he looked up at the face that watched him from between the curtains a few feet above his head. It wasn't a beautiful face, he firmly explained to me, when I accused him of once again mixing his drinks. Just an honest face: dark hair and eyes which in that light looked brown; a wide forehead, a large mouth which didn't try to charm. No danger anywhere, it seemed to Rollo Martins, of that sudden reckless moment when the scent of hair or a hand against the side alters life. She said, 'Will you come up, please? The second door on the right.'

There are some people, he explained to me carefully, whom one recognises instantaneously as friends. You can be at ease with them because you know that never, never will you be in danger. 'That was Anna,' he said, and I wasn't sure whether the past tense was deliberate or not.

Unlike most actresses' rooms this one was almost bare; no wardrobe packed with clothes, no clutter of cosmetics and grease-paints; a dressing-gown on the door, one sweater he recognised from Act II on the only easy chair, a tin of half-used paints and grease. A kettle hummed softly on a gas ring. She said, 'Would you like a cup of tea? Someone sent me a packet last week – sometimes the Americans do, instead of flowers, you know, on the first night.'

'I'd like a cup,' he said, but if there was one thing he hated it was tea. He watched her while she made it, made it, of course, all wrong: the water not on the boil, the teapot unheated, too few leaves. She said, 'I never quite understand why English people like tea.'

He drank his cupful quickly like a medicine and watched her gingerly and delicately sip at hers. He said, 'I wanted very much to see you. About Harry.'

It was the dreadful moment; he could see her mouth stiffen to meet it.

'Yes?'

'I had known him twenty years. I was his friend. We were at school together, you know, and after that – there weren't many months running when we didn't meet . . . '

She said, 'When I got your card, I couldn't say no. But there's nothing really for us to talk about, is there? – nothing.'

'I wanted to hear –'

'He's dead. That's the end. Everything's over, finished. What's the good of talking?'

'We both loved him.'

'I don't know. You can't know a thing like that – afterwards. I don't know anything any more except –'

'Except?'

'That I want to be dead too.'

Martins told me, 'Then I nearly went away. What was the good of tormenting her because of this wild idea of mine? But instead I asked her one question. "Do you know a man called Cooler?" '

'An American?' she asked. 'I think that was the man who brought me some money when Harry died. I didn't want to take it, but he said Harry had been anxious – at the last moment.'

'So he didn't die instantaneously?'

'Oh, no.'

Martins said to me, 'I began to wonder why I had got that idea so firmly into my head, and then I thought it was only the man in the flat who told me so – no one else. I said to her, "He must have been very clear in his head at the end – because he remembered about me too. That seems to show that there wasn't really any pain." '

'That's what I tell myself all the time.'

'Did you see the doctor?'

'Once. Harry sent me to him. He was Harry's own doctor. He lived near by, you see.'

Martins suddenly saw in that odd chamber of the mind that constructs such pictures, instantaneously, irrationally, a desert place, a body on the ground, a group of birds gathered. Perhaps it was a scene from one of his own books, not yet written, forming at the gate of consciousness. It faded, and he thought how odd that they were all there, just at that moment, all Harry's friends – Kurtz, the doctor, this man Cooler; only the two people who loved him seemed to have been missing. He said, 'And the driver? Did you hear his evidence?'

'He was upset, scared. But Cooler's evidence exonerated him. No, it wasn't his fault, poor man. I've often heard Harry say what a careful driver he was.'

'He knew Harry too?' Another bird flapped down

and joined the others round the silent figure on the sand who lay face down. Now he could tell that it was Harry, by the clothes, by the attitude like that of a boy asleep in the grass at a playing-field's edge, on a hot summer afternoon.

Somebody called outside the window, 'Fräulein Schmidt.'

She said, 'They don't like one to stay too long. It uses up *their* electricity.'

He had given up the idea of sparing her anything. He told her, 'The police say they were going to arrest Harry. They'd pinned some racket on him.'

She took the news in much the same way as Kurtz. 'Everybody's in a racket.'

'I don't believe he was in anything serious.'

'No.'

'But he may have been framed. Do you know a man named Kurtz?'

'I don't think so.'

'He wears a toupée.'

'Oh.' He could tell that that struck home. He said, 'Don't you think that it was odd they were all there – at the death? Everybody knew Harry. Even the driver, the doctor . . . '

She said with hopeless calm, 'I've wondered that too, though I didn't know about Kurtz. I wondered whether they'd murdered him, but what's the use of wondering?'

'I'm going to get those bastards,' Rollo Martins said.

'It won't do any good. Perhaps the police are right. Perhaps poor Harry got mixed up – '

'Fräulein Schmidt,' the voice called again.

'I must go.'

'I'll walk with you a bit of the way.'

The dark was almost down; the snow had ceased for a while to fall, and the great statues of the Ring, the prancing horses, the chariots and eagles, were gun-shot grey with the end of evening. 'It's better to give up and forget,' Anna said. The moonlit snow lay ankle-deep on the unswept pavements.

'Will you give me the doctor's address?'

They stood in the shelter of a wall while she wrote it down for him.

'And yours too?'

'Why do you want that?'

'I might have news for you.'

'There isn't any news that would do any good now.' He watched her from a distance board her tram, bowing her head against the wind, a dark question mark on the snow.

6

An amateur detective has this advantage over the professional, that he doesn't work set hours. Rollo Martins was not confined to the eight-hour day: his investigations didn't have to pause for meals. In his one day he covered as much ground as one of my men would have covered in two, and he had this initial advantage over us, that he was Harry's friend. He was, as it were, working from inside, while we pecked at the perimeter.

Dr Winkler was at home. Perhaps he would not have been at home to a police officer. Again Martins had marked his card with the open-sesame phrase: 'A friend of Harry Lime's.'

Dr Winkler's waiting-room reminded Martins of an antique shop – an antique shop that specialises in religious *objects d'art*. There were more crucifixes than he could count, none of later date probably than the seventeenth century. There were statues in wood and ivory. There were a number of reliquaries: little bits of bone marked with saints' names and set in oval frames on a background of tinfoil. If they were genuine, what an odd fate it was, Martins thought, for a portion of St Susanna's knuckle to come to rest in Dr Winkler's waiting-room. Even the high-backed hideous chairs looked as if they had once been sat in by cardinals. The room was stuffy, and one expected the smell of incense. In a small gold casket was a splinter of the True Cross. A sneeze disturbed him.

Dr Winkler was the cleanest doctor Martins had ever seen. He was very small and neat, in a black tail-coat and a high stiff collar; his little black moustache was like an evening tie. He sneezed again: perhaps he was cold because he was so clean. He said, 'Mr Martins?'

An irresistible desire to sully Dr Winkler assailed Rollo Martins. He said, 'Dr Winkle?'

'Dr Winkler.'

'You've got an interesting collection here.'

'Yes.'

'These saints' bones . . . '

'The bones of chickens and rabbits.' Dr Winkler took a large white handkerchief out of his sleeve rather as though he were a conjurer producing his country's flag, and blew his nose neatly and thoroughly twice, closing each nostril in turn. You expected him to throw away the handkerchief after one use. 'Would you mind, Mr Martins, telling me the purpose of your visit? I have a patient waiting.'

'We were both friends of Harry Lime.'

'I was his medical adviser,' Dr Winkler corrected him and waited obstinately between the crucifixes.

'I arrived too late for the inquest. Harry had invited me out here to help him in something. I don't quite know what. I didn't hear of his death till I arrived.'

'Very sad,' Dr Winkler said.

'Naturally, under the circumstances, I want to hear all I can.'

'There is nothing I can tell you that you don't know. He was knocked over by a car. He was dead when I arrived.'

'Would he have been conscious at all?'

'I understand he was for a short time, while they carried him into the house.'

'In great pain?'

'Not necessarily.'

'You are quite certain that it was an accident?'

Dr Winkler put out a hand and straightened a crucifix. 'I was not there. My opinion is limited to the cause of death. Have you any reason to be dissatisfied?'

The amateur has another advantage over the professional: he can be reckless. He can tell unnecessary truths and propound wild theories. Martins said, 'The police have implicated Harry in a very serious racket. It seems to me that he might have been murdered – or even killed himself.'

'I am not competent to pass an opinion,' Dr Winkler said.

'Do you know a man called Cooler?'

'I don't think so.'

'He was there when Harry was killed.'

'Then of course I have met him. He wears a toupée.'

'That was Kurtz.'

Dr Winkler was not only the cleanest, he was also the most cautious doctor that Martins had ever met. His statements were so limited that you could not for a moment doubt their veracity. He said, 'There was a second man there.' If he had to diagnose a case of scarlet fever he would, you felt, have confined himself to a statement that a rash was visible, that the temperature was so and so. He would never find himself in error at an inquest.

'Had you been Harry's doctor for long?' He seemed an odd man for Harry to choose – Harry who liked men with a certain recklessness, men capable of making mistakes.

'For about a year.'

'Well, it's good of you to have seen me.' Dr Winkler bowed. When he bowed there was a very slight creak as though his shirt were made of celluloid. 'I mustn't keep you from your patients any longer.' Turning away from Dr Winkler, he confronted yet another crucifix, the figure hanging with arms above the head: a face of elongated El Greco agony. 'That's a strange crucifix,' he said.

'Jansenist,' Dr Winkler commented and closed his mouth sharply as though he had been guilty of giving away too much information.

'Never heard the word. Why are the arms above the head?'

Dr Winkler said reluctantly, 'Because He died, in their view, only for the elect.'

7

As I see it, turning over my files, the notes of conversations, the statements of various characters, it would have been still possible, at this moment, for Rollo Martins to have left Vienna safely. He had shown an unhealthy curiosity, but the disease had been checked at every point. Nobody had given anything away. The smooth wall of deception had as yet shown no real crack to his roaming fingers. When Rollo Martins left Dr Winkler's he was in no danger. He could have gone home to bed at Sacher's and slept with a quiet mind. He could even have visited Cooler at this stage without trouble. No one was seriously disturbed. Unfortunately for him – and there would always be periods of his life when he bitterly regretted it – he chose to go back to Harry's flat. He wanted to talk to the little vexed man who said he had seen the accident – or had he really not said so much? There was a moment in the dark frozen street when he was inclined to go straight to Cooler, to complete his picture of those sinister birds who sat around Harry's body, but Rollo, being Rollo, decided to toss a coin and the coin fell for the other action, and the deaths of two men.

Perhaps the little man – who bore the name of Koch – had drunk a glass too much of wine, perhaps he had simply spent a good day at the office, but this time, when Rollo Martins rang his bell, he was friendly and quite ready to talk. He had just finished dinner and had crumbs on his moustache. 'Ah, I remember you. You are Herr Lime's friend.'

He welcomed Martins in with great cordiality and

introduced him to a mountainous wife whom he obviously kept under very strict control. 'Ah, in the old days, I would have offered you a cup of coffee, but now – '

Martins passed round his cigarette case and the atmosphere of cordiality deepened. 'When you came yesterday I was a little abrupt,' Herr Koch said, 'but I had a touch of migraine and my wife was out, so I had to answer the door myself.'

'Did you tell me that you had actually seen the accident?'

Herr Koch exchanged glances with his wife. 'The inquest is over, Ilse. There is no harm. You can trust my judgement. The gentleman is a friend. Yes, I saw the accident, but you are the only one who knows. When I say that I saw it, perhaps I should say that I heard it. I heard the brakes put on and the sound of the skid, and I got to the window in time to see them carry the body to the house.'

'But didn't you give evidence?'

'It is better not to be mixed up in such things. My office cannot spare me. We are short of staff, and of course I did not actually *see* – '

'But you told me yesterday how it happened.'

'That was how they described it in the papers.'

'Was he in great pain?'

'He was dead. I looked right down from my window here and I saw his face. I know when a man is dead. You see, it is, in a way, my business. I am the head clerk at the mortuary.'

'But the others say that he did not die at once.'

'Perhaps they don't know death as well as I do.'

'He was dead, of course, when the doctor arrived. He told me that.'

'He was dead at once. You can take the word of a man who knows.'

'I think, Herr Koch, that you should have given evidence.'

'One must look after oneself, Herr Martins. I was not the only one who should have been there.'

'How do you mean?'

'There were three people who helped to carry your friend to the house.'

'I know – two men and the driver.'

'The driver stayed where he was. He was very much shaken, poor man.'

'Three men . . . ' It was as though suddenly, fingering that bare wall, his fingers had encountered, not so much a crack perhaps, but at least a roughness that had not been smoothed away by the careful builders.

'Can you describe the men?'

But Herr Koch was not trained to observe the living; only the man with the toupée had attracted his eyes – the other two were just men, neither tall nor short, thick nor thin. He had seen them from far above, foreshortened, bent over their burden; they had not looked up, and he had quickly looked away and closed the window, realising at once the wisdom of not being seen himself.

'There was no evidence I could really give, Herr Martins.'

No evidence, Martins thought, no evidence! He no longer doubted that murder had been done. Why else had they lied about the moment of death? They wanted to quieten with their gifts of money and their plane ticket the only two friends Harry had in Vienna. And the third man? Who was he?

He said, 'Did you see Herr Lime go out?'

'No.'

'Did you hear a scream?'

'Only the brakes, Herr Martins.'

It occurred to Martins that there was nothing – except the word of Kurtz and Cooler and the driver – to prove that in fact Harry had been killed at that precise moment. There was the medical evidence, but that could not prove more than that he had died, say, within a half-hour, and in any case the medical evidence was only as strong as Dr Winkler's word: that clean controlled man creaking among his crucifixes.

'Herr Martins, it just occurs to me – you are staying in Vienna?'

'Yes.'

'If you need accommodation and spoke to the authorities quickly, you might secure Herr Lime's flat. It is a requisitioned property.'

'Who has the keys?'

'I have them.'

'Could I see the flat?'

'Ilse, the keys.'

Herr Koch led the way into the flat that had been Harry's. In the little dark hall there was still the smell of cigarette smoke – the Turkish cigarettes that Harry always smoked. It seemed odd that a man's smell should cling in the folds of a curtain so long after the man himself had become dead matter, a gas, a decay. One light, in a heavily beaded shade, left them in semi-darkness, fumbling for door handles.

The living-room was completely bare – it seemed to Martins too bare. The chairs had been pushed up against the walls; the desk at which Harry must have written was free from dust or any papers. The parquet reflected the light like a mirror. Herr Koch opened a door and showed the bedroom: the bed neatly made with clean sheets. In the bathroom not even a used razor blade indicated that a few days ago a living man had occupied it. Only the dark hall and the cigarette smell gave a sense of occupation.

'You see,' Herr Koch said, 'it is quite ready for a newcomer. Ilse has cleaned up.'

That she certainly had done. After a death there should have been more litter left than this. A man can't go suddenly and unexpectedly on his longest journey without forgetting this or that, without leaving a bill unpaid, an official form unanswered, the photograph of a girl. 'Were there no papers, Herr Koch?'

'Herr Lime was always a very tidy man. His wastepaper basket was full and his briefcase, but his friend fetched that away.'

'His friend?'

'The gentleman with the toupée.'

It was possible, of course, that Lime had not taken the journey so unexpectedly, and it occurred to Martins that Lime had perhaps hoped he would arrive in time to help. He said to Herr Koch, 'I believe my friend was murdered.'

'Murdered?' Herr Koch's cordiality was snuffed out by the word. He said, 'I would not have asked you in here if I had thought you would talk such nonsense.'

'Why should it be nonsense?'

'We do not have murders in this zone.'

'All the same, your evidence may be very valuable.'

'I have no evidence. I saw nothing. I am not concerned. You must leave here at once, please. You have been very inconsiderate.' He hustled Martins back through the hall; already the smell of the smoke was fading a little more. Herr Koch's last word before he slammed his own door was, 'It's no concern of mine.'

Poor Herr Koch! We do not choose our concerns. Later, when I was questioning Martins closely, I said to him, 'Did you see anybody at all on the stairs, or in the street outside?'

'Nobody.' He had everything to gain by remembering some chance passer-by, and I believed him. He said, 'I noticed myself how quiet and dead the whole street looked. Part of it had been bombed, you know, and the moon was shining on the snow slopes. It was so very silent. I could hear my own feet creaking in the snow.'

'Of course, it proves nothing. There is a basement where anybody who had followed you could have hidden.'

'Yes.'

'Or your whole story may be phoney.'

'Yes.'

'The trouble is I can see no motive for you to have done it. It's true you are already guilty of getting money on false pretences. You came out here to join Lime, perhaps to help him . . .'

Martins said to me, 'What was this precious racket you keep on hinting at?'

'I'd have told you all the facts when I first saw you if you hadn't lost your temper so damned quickly. Now I don't think I shall be acting wisely to tell you. It would be disclosing official information, and your contacts, you know, don't inspire confidence. A girl with phoney papers supplied by Lime, this man Kurtz . . .'

'Dr Winkler . . .'

'I've got nothing against Dr Winkler. No, if you are phoney, you don't need the information, but it might help you to learn exactly what we know. You see, our facts are not complete.'

'I bet they aren't. I could invent a better detective than you in my bath.'

'Your literary style does not do your name-sake justice.' Whenever he was reminded of Mr Crabbin, that poor harassed representative of the British Council, Rollo Martins turned pink, with annoyance, embarrassment, shame. That too inclined me to trust him.

He had certainly given Crabbin some uncomfortable hours. On returning to Sacher's Hotel after his interview with Herr Koch he had found a desperate note waiting for him from the representative.

I have been trying to locate you all day [Crabbin wrote]. It is essential that we should get together and work out a proper programme for you. This morning by telephone I have arranged lectures at Innsbruck and Salzburg for next week, but I must have your consent to the subjects, so that proper programmes can be printed. I would suggest two lectures: 'The Crisis of Faith in the Western World' (you are very respected here as a Christian writer, but this lecture should be quite unpolitical and no references should be made to Russia or Communism) and 'The Technique of the Contemporary Novel'. The same lectures would be given in Vienna. Apart from this, there are a great many people here who would like to meet you, and I want to arrange a cocktail party for early next week. But for all this I must have a few words with you.

[The letter ended on a note of acute anxiety.] You
will be at the discussion tomorrow night, won't you?
We all expect you at 8.30 and, needless to say, look
forward to your coming. I will send transport to the
hotel at 8.15 sharp.

Rollo Martins read the letter and, without bothering
any further about Mr Crabbin, went to bed.

8

After two drinks Rollo Martins' mind would always
turn towards women – in a vague, sentimental,
romantic way, as a sex, in general. After three drinks,
like a pilot who dives to find direction, he would begin
to focus on one available girl. If he had not been
offered a third drink by Cooler, he would probably
not have gone quite so soon to Anna Schmidt's house,
and if – but there are too many 'ifs' in my style of
writing, for it is my profession to balance possibilities,
human possibilities, and the drive of destiny can never
find a place in my files.

Martins had spent his lunchtime reading up the
reports of the inquest, thus again demonstrating the
superiority of the amateur over the professional, and
making him more vulnerable to Cooler's liquor (which
the professional in duty bound would have refused). It
was nearly five o'clock when he reached Cooler's flat,
which was over an ice-cream parlour in the American
zone: the bar below was full of GIs with their girls, and
the clatter of the long spoons and the curious free
unformed laughter followed him up the stairs.

The Englishman who objects to Americans in

general usually carries in his mind's eye just such an exception as Cooler: a man with tousled grey hair and a worried kindly face and long-sighted eyes, the kind of humanitarian who turns up in a typhus epidemic or a world war or a Chinese famine long before his countrymen have discovered the place in an atlas. Again the card marked 'Harry's friend' was like an entrance ticket. Cooler was in officer's uniform, with mysterious letters on his flash, and no badges of rank, although his maid referred to him as Colonel Cooler. His warm frank handclasp was the most friendly act that Martins had encountered in Vienna.

'Any friend of Harry is all right with me,' Cooler said. 'I've heard of you, of course.'

'From Harry?'

'I'm a great reader of Westerns,' Cooler said, and Martins believed him as he did not believe Kurtz.

'I wondered – you were there, weren't you? – if you'd tell me about Harry's death.'

'It was a terrible thing,' Cooler said. 'I was just crossing the road to go to Harry. He and Mr Kurtz were on the sidewalk. Maybe if I hadn't started across the road, he'd have stayed where he was. But he saw me and stepped straight off to meet me and this jeep – it was terrible, terrible. The driver braked, but he didn't stand a chance. Have a Scotch, Mr Martins. It's silly of me, but I get shaken up when I think of it.' He said as he splashed in the soda, 'In spite of this uniform, I'd never seen a man killed before.'

'Was the other man in the car?'

Cooler took a long pull and then measured what was left with his tired kindly eyes. 'What man would you be referring to, Mr Martins?'

'I was told there was another man there.'

'I don't know how you got that idea. You'll find all about it in the inquest reports.' He poured out two more generous drinks. 'There were just the three of us – me and Mr Kurtz and the driver. The doctor, of course. I expect you were thinking of the doctor.'

'This man I was talking to happened to look out of a window – he has the next flat to Harry's – and he said he saw three men and the driver. That's before the doctor arrived.'

'He didn't say that in court.'

'He didn't want to get involved.'

'You'll never teach these Europeans to be good citizens. It was his duty.' Cooler brooded sadly over his glass. 'It's an odd thing, Mr Martins, with accidents. You'll never get two reports that coincide. Why, even Mr Kurtz and I disagreed about details. The thing happens so suddenly, you aren't concerned to notice things, until bang crash, and then you have to reconstruct, remember. I expect he got too tangled up trying to sort out what happened before and what after, to distinguish the four of us.'

'The four?'

'I was counting Harry. What else did he see, Mr Martins?'

'Nothing of interest – except he says Harry was dead when he was carried to the house.'

'Well, he was dying – not much difference there. Have another drink, Mr Martins?'

'No, I don't think I will.'

'Well, I'd like another spot. I was very fond of your friend, Mr Martins, and I don't like talking about it.'

'Perhaps one more – to keep you company. Do you know Anna Schmidt?' Martins asked, while the whisky tingled on his tongue.

'Harry's girl? I met her once, that's all. As a matter
of fact, I helped Harry fix her papers. Not the sort of
thing I should confess to a stranger, I suppose, but
you have to break the rules sometimes. Humanity's a
duty too.'

'What was wrong?'

'She was Hungarian and her father had been a
Nazi, so they said. She was scared the Russians would
pick her up.'

'Why should they want to?'

'We can't always figure out why they do these
things. Perhaps just to show that it's not healthy being
friends with an Englishman.'

'But she lives in the British zone.'

'That wouldn't stop them. It's only five minutes'
ride in a jeep from the Commandatura. The streets
aren't well lighted, and you haven't many police
around.'

'You took her some money from Harry, didn't
you?'

'Yes, but I wouldn't have mentioned that. Did she
tell you?'

The telephone rang, and Cooler drained his glass.
'Hello,' he said. 'Why, yes. This is Colonel Cooler.'
Then he sat with the receiver at his ear and an
expression of sad patience, while some voice a long
way off drained into the room. 'Yes,' he said once.
'Yes.' His eyes dwelt on Martins' face, but they
seemed to be looking a long way beyond him: flat
and tired and kind, they might have been gazing out
across the sea. He said, 'You did quite right,' in a
tone of commendation, and then, with a touch of
asperity, 'Of course they will be delivered. I gave my
word. Goodbye.'

He put the receiver down and passed a hand across his forehead wearily. It was as though he were trying to remember something he had to do. Martins said, 'Had you heard anything of this racket the police talk about?'

'I'm sorry. What's that?'

'They say Harry was mixed up in some racket.'

'Oh, no,' Cooler said. 'No. That's quite impossible. He had a great sense of duty.'

'Kurtz seemed to think it was possible.'

'Kurtz doesn't understand how an Anglo-Saxon feels,' Cooler replied.

9

It was nearly dark when Martins made his way along the banks of the canal: across the water lay the half-destroyed Diana Baths and in the distance the great black circle of the Prater Wheel, stationary above the ruined houses. Over there across the grey water was the Second Bezirk, in Russian ownership. St Stephans-kirche shot its enormous wounded spire into the sky above the Inner City, and, coming up the Kärntner-strasse, Martins passed the lit door of the Military Police Station. The four men of the International Patrol were climbing into their jeep; the Russian MP sat beside the driver (for the Russians had that day taken over the chair for the next four weeks) and the Englishman, the Frenchman and the American mounted behind. The third stiff whisky fumed into Martins' brain, and he remembered the girl in Amsterdam, the girl in Paris; loneliness moved along the crowded pavement at his side. He passed the corner of the street where Sacher's lay and went on. Rollo was in control and moved towards the only girl he knew in Vienna.

I asked him how he knew where she lived. Oh, he said, he'd looked up the address she had given him the night before, in bed, studying a map. He wanted to know his way about, and he was good with maps. He could memorise turnings and street names easily because he always went one way on foot.

'One way?'

'I mean when I'm calling on a girl – or someone.'

He hadn't, of course, known that she would be in, that her play was not on that night in the Josefstadt, or perhaps he had memorised that too from the posters. In at any rate she was, if you could really call it being in, sitting alone in an unheated room, with the bed disguised as a divan, and a typewritten script lying open at the first page on the inadequate too-fancy topply table – because her thoughts were so far from being 'in'. He said awkwardly (and nobody could have said, not even Rollo, how much his awkwardness was part of his technique), 'I thought I'd just look in and look you up. You see, I was passing . . . '

'Passing? Where to?' It had been a good half an hour's walk from the Inner City to the rim of the English zone, but he always had a reply. 'I had too much whisky with Colonel Cooler. I needed a walk and I just happened to find myself this way.'

'I can't give you a drink here. Except tea. There's some of that packet left.'

'No, no thank you.' He said, 'You are busy,' looking at the script.

'I didn't get beyond the first line.'

He picked it up and read: '*Enter Louise*. LOUISE: I heard a child crying.'

'Can I stay a little?' he asked with a gentleness that was more Martins than Rollo.

'I wish you would.'

He slumped down on the divan, and he told me a long time later (for lovers reconstruct the smallest details if they can find a listener) that then it was he took his second real look at her. She stood there, as awkward as himself, in a pair of old flannel trousers which had been patched badly in the seat; she stood with her legs firmly straddled as though she were opposing someone and was determined to hold her ground – a small rather stocky figure with any grace she had folded and put away for use professionally.

'One of those bad days?' he asked.

'It's always bad about this time.' She explained, 'He used to look in, and when I heard you ring, just for a moment, I thought . . .' She sat down on a hard chair opposite him and said, 'Please talk. You knew him. Just tell me anything.'

And so he talked. The sky blackened outside the window while he talked. He noticed after a while that their hands had met. He said to me, 'I never meant to fall in love, not with Harry's girl.'

'When did it happen?' I asked him.

'It was very cold and I got up to close the window curtains. I only noticed my hand was on hers when I took it away. As I stood up I looked down at her face and she was looking up. It wasn't a beautiful face – that was the trouble. It was a face to live with, day in, day out. A face for wear. I felt as though I'd come into a new country where I couldn't speak the language. I had always thought it was beauty one loved in a woman. I stood there at the curtains, waiting to pull them, looking out. I couldn't see anything but my own face, looking back into the room, looking for her. She said, "And what did Harry do that time?" and I wanted to say, "Damn Harry. He's dead. We both loved him, but he's dead. The dead are made to be forgotten." Instead, of course, all I said was, "What do you think? He just whistled his old tune as if nothing was the matter," and I whistled it to her as well as I could. I heard her catch her breath, and I looked round and before I could think: Is this the right way, the right card, the right gambit? – I'd already said, "He's dead. You can't go on remembering him for ever." '

She said, 'I know, but perhaps something will happen first.'

'What do you mean – something happen?'

'Oh, I mean perhaps there'll be another war, or I'll die, or the Russians will take me.'

'You'll forget him in time. You'll fall in love again.'

'I know, but I don't want to. Don't you see I don't want to?'

So Rollo Martins came back from the window and sat down on the divan again. When he had risen half a minute before he had been the friend of Harry, comforting Harry's girl; now he was a man in love with Anna Schmidt who had been in love with a man they had both once known called Harry Lime. He didn't speak again that evening about the past. Instead he began to tell her of the people he had seen. 'I can believe anything of Winkler,' he told her, 'but Cooler – I liked Cooler. He was the only one of his friends who stood up for Harry. The trouble is, if Cooler's right, then Koch is wrong, and I really thought I had something there.'

'Who's Koch?'

He explained how he had returned to Harry's flat and he described his interview with Koch, the story of the third man.

'If it's true,' she said, 'it's very important.'

'It doesn't prove anything. After all, Koch backed out of the inquest; so might this stranger.'

'That's not the point,' she said. 'It means that *they* lied: Kurtz and Cooler.'

'They might have lied so as not to inconvenience this fellow – if he was a friend.'

'Yet another friend – on the spot. And where's your Cooler's honesty then?'

'What do we do? Koch clamped down like an oyster and turned me out of his flat.'

'He won't turn me out,' she said, 'or his Ilse won't.'

They walked up the long road to the flat together; the snow clogged on their shoes and made them move slowly like convicts weighed down by irons. Anna Schmidt said, 'Is it far?'

'Not very far now. Do you see that knot of people up the road? It's somewhere about there.' The group was like a splash of ink on the whiteness, a splash that flowed, changed shape, spread out. When they came a little nearer Martins said, 'I think that's his block. What do you suppose this is, a political demonstration?'

Anna Schmidt stopped. She said, 'Who else have you told about Koch?'

'Only you and Colonel Cooler. Why?'

'I'm frightened. It reminds me . . . ' She had her eyes fixed on the crowd and he never knew what memory out of her confused past had risen to warn her. 'Let's go away,' she implored him.

'You're crazy. We're on to something here, something big . . . '

'I'll wait for you.'

'But you're going to talk to him.'

'Find out first what all those people . . . ' She said, strangely for one who worked behind the footlights, 'I hate crowds.'

He walked slowly on alone, the snow caking on his heels. It wasn't a political meeting, for no one was making a speech. He had the impression of heads turning to watch him come, as though he were somebody who was expected. When he reached the fringe of the little crowd, he knew for certain that it was the house. A man looked hard at him and said, 'Are you another of them?'

'What do you mean?'

'The police.'

'No. What are they doing?'

'They've been in and out all day.'

'What's everybody waiting for?'

'They want to see him brought out.'

'Who?'

'Herr Koch.'

It occurred to Martins that somebody besides himself had discovered Herr Koch's failure to give evidence, though that was hardly a police matter. He said, 'What's he done?'

'Nobody knows that yet. They can't make their minds up in there – it might be suicide, you see, and it might be murder.'

'Herr Koch?'

'Of course.'

A small child came up to his informant and pulled at his hand. 'Papa, papa.' He wore a wool cap on his head, like a gnome; his face was pinched and blue with cold.

'Yes, my dear, what is it?'

'I heard them talking through the grating, papa.'

'Oh, you cunning little one. Tell us what you heard, Hansel.'

'I heard Frau Koch crying, papa.'

'Was that all, Hansel?'

'No. I heard the big man talking, papa.'

'Ah, you cunning little Hansel. Tell papa what he said.'

'He said, "Can you tell me, Frau Koch, what the foreigner looked like?" '

'Ha, ha, you see, they think it's murder. And who's to say they are wrong? Why should Herr Koch cut his own throat in the basement?'

'Papa, papa.'

'Yes, little Hansel?'

'When I looked through the grating, I could see some blood on the coke.'

'What a child you are. How could you tell it was blood? The snow leaks everywhere.' The man turned to Martins and said, 'The child has such an imagination. Maybe he will be a writer when he grows up.'

The pinched face stared solemnly up at Martins. The child said, 'Papa.'

'Yes, Hansel?'

'He's a foreigner too.'

The man gave a big laugh that caused a dozen heads to turn. 'Listen to him, sir, listen,' he said proudly. 'He thinks you did it just because you are a foreigner. As though there weren't more foreigners here these days than Viennese.'

'Papa, papa.'

'Yes, Hansel?'

'They are coming out.'

A knot of police surrounded the covered stretcher which they lowered carefully down the steps for fear of sliding on the trodden snow. The man said, 'They can't get an ambulance into this street because of the ruins. They have to carry it round the corner.' Frau Koch came out at the tail of the procession; she had a shawl over her head and an old sackcloth coat. Her thick shape looked like a snowman as she sank in a drift at the pavement's edge. Someone gave her a hand and she looked round with a lost hopeless gaze at this crowd of strangers. If there were friends there she did not recognise them, looking from face to face. Martins bent as she passed, fumbling at his shoelace, but looking up from the ground he saw at his own eyes' level the scrutinising cold-blooded gnome-gaze of little Hansel.

Walking back down the street towards Anna, he looked back once. The child was pulling at his father's hand and he could see the lips forming round those syllables like the refrain of a grim ballad, 'Papa, papa.'

He said to Anna, 'Koch has been murdered. Come away from here.' He walked as rapidly as the snow would let him, turning this corner and that. The child's suspicion and alertness seemed to spread like a cloud over the city – they could not walk fast enough to evade its shadow. He paid no attention when Anna said to him. 'Then what Koch said was true. There *was* a third man,' nor a little later when she said, 'It must have been murder. You don't kill a man to hide anything less.'

The tramcars flashed like icicles at the end of the street: they were back at the Ring. Martins said, 'You had better go home alone. I'll keep away from you awhile till things have sorted out.'

'But nobody can suspect you.'

'They are asking about the foreigner who called on Koch yesterday. There may be some unpleasantness for a while.'

'Why don't you go to the police?'

'They are so stupid. I don't trust them. See what they've pinned on Harry. And then I tried to hit this man Callaghan. They'll have it in for me. The least they'll do is send me away from Vienna. But if I stay quiet – there's only one person who can give me away. Cooler.'

'And he won't want to.'

'Not if he's guilty. But then I can't believe he's guilty.'

Before she left him, she said, 'Be careful. Koch knew so very little and they murdered him. You know as much as Koch.'

The warning stayed in his brain all the way to Sacher's: after nine o'clock the streets are very empty, and he would turn his head at every padding step coming up the street behind him, as though that third man whom they had protected so ruthlessly were following him like an executioner. The Russian sentry outside the Grand Hotel looked rigid with the cold, but he was human, he had a face, an honest peasant face with Mongol eyes. The third man had no face: only the top of a head seen from a window.

At Sacher's Mr Schmidt said, 'Colonel Calloway has been in, asking for you, sir. I think you'll find him in the bar.'

'Back in a moment,' Martins said and walked straight out of the hotel again: he wanted time to think. But immediately he stepped outside a man came forward, touched his cap, and said firmly.

'Please, sir.' He flung open the door of a khaki-painted truck with a Union Jack on the windscreen and firmly urged Martins within. He surrendered without protest; sooner or later, he felt sure, enquiries would be made; he had only pretended optimism to Anna Schmidt.

The driver drove too fast for safety on the frozen road, and Martins protested. All he got in reply was a sullen grunt and a muttered sentence containing the word 'orders'. 'Have you orders to kill me?' Martins asked facetiously and got no reply at all. He caught sight of the Titans on the Hofburg, balancing great globes of snow above their heads, and then they plunged into ill-lit streets beyond, where he lost all sense of direction.

'Is it far?' But the driver paid no attention at all. At least, Martins thought, I am not under arrest: they have not sent a guard; I am being invited – wasn't that the word they used? – to visit the station to make a statement.

The car drew up and the driver led the way up two flights of stairs; he rang the bell of a great double door, and Martins was aware of many voices beyond it. He turned sharply to the driver and said, 'Where the hell . . . ?' but the driver was already halfway down the stairs, and already the door was opening. His eyes were dazzled from the darkness by the lights inside; he heard, but he could hardly see, the advance of Crabbin. 'Oh, Mr Dexter, we have been so anxious, but better late than never. Let me introduce you to Miss Wilbraham and the Gräfin von Meyersdorf.'

A buffet laden with coffee cups; an urn steaming; a woman's face shiny with exertion; two young men with the happy intelligent faces of sixth-formers; and, huddled in the background, like faces in a family album, a multitude of the old-fashioned, the dingy, the earnest and cheery features of constant readers. Martins looked behind him, but the door had closed.

He said desperately to Mr Crabbin, 'I'm sorry, but – '

'Don't think any more about it,' Mr Crabbin said. 'One cup of coffee and then let's go on to the discussion. We have a very good gathering tonight. They'll put you on your mettle, Mr Dexter.' One of the young men placed a cup in his hand, the other shovelled in sugar before he could say he preferred his coffee unsweetened. The younger man breathed into his ear, 'Afterwards would you mind signing one of your books, Mr Dexter?' A large woman in black silk bore down upon him and said, 'I don't mind if the Gräfin does hear me, Mr Dexter, but I don't like your books, I don't approve of them. I think a novel should tell a good story.'

'So do I,' Martins said hopelessly.

'Now, Mrs Bannock, wait for question time.'

'I know I'm downright, but I'm sure Mr Dexter values *honest* criticism.'

An old lady, who he supposed was the Gräfin, said, 'I do not read many English books, Mr Dexter, but I am told that yours . . . '

'Do you mind drinking up?' Crabbin said and hustled him through into an inner room where a number of elderly people were sitting on a semicircle of chairs with an air of sad patience.

Martins was not able to tell me very much about the meeting; his mind was still dazed with the death; when he looked up he expected to see at any moment the child Hansel and hear that persistent pedantic refrain, 'Papa, papa.' Apparently Crabbin opened the proceedings, and, knowing Crabbin, I am sure that it was a very lucid, very fair and unbiased picture of the contemporary English novel. I have heard him give that talk so often, varied only by the emphasis given to the work of the particular English visitor. He would have touched lightly on various problems of technique – the point of view, the passage of time – and then he would have declared the meeting open for questions and discussion.

Martins missed the first question altogether, but luckily Crabbin filled the gap and answered it satisfactorily. A woman wearing a brown hat and a piece of fur round her throat said with passionate interest, 'May I ask Mr Dexter if he is engaged on a new work?'

'Oh, yes – yes.'

'May I ask the title?'

' "The Third Man",' Martins said and gained a spurious confidence as the result of taking that hurdle.

'Mr Dexter, could you tell us what author has chiefly influenced you?'

Martins, without thinking, said, 'Grey.' He meant of course the author of *Riders of the Purple Sage*, and he was pleased to find his reply gave general satisfaction – to all save an elderly Austrian who asked, 'Grey. What Grey? I do not know the name.'

Martins felt he was safe now and said, 'Zane Grey – I don't know any other,' and was mystified at the low subservient laughter from the English colony.

Crabbin interposed quickly for the sake of the Austrians, 'That is a little joke of Mr Dexter's. He meant the poet Gray – a gentle, mild, subtle genius – one can see the affinity.'

'And he is called Zane Grey?'

83

'That was Mr Dexter's joke. Zane Grey wrote what we call Westerns – cheap popular novelettes about bandits and cowboys.'

'He is not a great writer?'

'No, no. Far from it,' Mr Crabbin said. 'In the strict sense I would not call him a writer at all.' Martins told me that he felt the first stirrings of revolt at that statement. He had never regarded himself before as a writer, but Crabbin's self-confidence irritated him – even the way the light flashed back from Crabbin's spectacles seemed an added cause of vexation. Crabbin said, 'He was just a popular entertainer.'

'Why the hell not?' Martins said fiercely.

'Oh, well, I merely meant – '

'What was Shakespeare?'

Somebody with great daring said, 'A poet.'

'Have you ever read Zane Grey?'

'No. I can't say – '

'Then you don't know what you are talking about.'

One of the young men tried to come to Crabbin's rescue. 'And James Joyce, where would you put James Joyce, Mr Dexter?'

'What do you mean put? I don't want to put anybody anywhere,' Martins said. It had been a very full day: he had drunk too much with Colonel Cooler; he had fallen in love; a man had been murdered – and now he had the quite unjust feeling that he was being got at. Zane Grey was one of his heroes: he was damned if he was going to stand any nonsense.

'I mean would you put him among the really great?'

'If you want to know, I've never heard of him. What did he write?'

He didn't realise it, but he was making an enormous impression. Only a great writer could have taken so arrogant, so original a line. Several people wrote Zane Grey's name on the backs of envelopes and the Gräfin whispered hoarsely to Crabbin, 'How do you spell Zane?'

'To tell you the truth, I'm not quite sure.'

A number of names were simultaneously flung at Martins – little sharp pointed names like Stein, round pebbles like Woolf. A young Austrian with an intellectual black forelock called out, 'Daphne du Maurier,' and Mr Crabbin winced and looked sideways at Martins. He said in an undertone, 'Be gentle with them.'

A kind-faced woman in a hand-knitted jumper said wistfully, 'Don't you agree, Mr Dexter, that no one, no one has written about *feelings* so poetically as Virginia Woolf? In prose, I mean.'

Crabbin whispered, 'You might say something about the stream of consciousness.'

'Stream of what?'

A note of despair came into Crabbin's voice. 'Please, Mr Dexter, these people are your genuine admirers. They want to hear your views. If you knew how they have *besieged* the Institute.'

An elderly Austrian said, 'Is there any writer in England today of the stature of the late John Galsworthy?'

There was an outburst of angry twittering in which the names of du Maurier, Priestley and somebody called Layman were flung to and fro. Martins sat gloomily back and saw again the snow, the stretcher, the desperate face of Frau Koch. He thought: if I had never returned, if I had never asked questions, would that little man still be alive? How had he benefited Harry by supplying another victim – a victim to assuage the fear of whom? – Herr Kurtz, Colonel Cooler (he could not believe that), Dr Winkler? Not one of them seemed adequate to the drab gruesome crime in the basement; he could hear the child saying, 'I saw blood on the coke,' and somebody turned towards him a blank face without features, a grey plasticine egg, the third man.

Martins could not have said how he got through the rest of the discussion. Perhaps Crabbin took the brunt; perhaps he was helped by some of the audience who got into an animated discussion about the film version of a popular American novel. He remembered very little more before Crabbin was making a final speech in his honour. Then one of the young men led him to a table stacked with books and asked him to sign them. 'We have only allowed each member one book.'

'What have I got to do?'

'Just a signature. That's all they expect. This is my copy of *The Curved Prow*. I would be so grateful if you'd just write a little something . . .'

Martins took his pen and wrote: 'From B. Dexter, author of *The Lone Rider of Santa Fé*,' and the young man read the sentence and blotted it with a puzzled expression. As Martins sat down and started signing Benjamin Dexter's title pages, he could see in a mirror the young man showing the inscription to Crabbin. Crabbin smiled weakly and stroked his chin, up and down, up and down. 'B. Dexter, B. Dexter, B. Dexter,' Martins wrote rapidly – it was not, after all, a lie. One by one the books were collected by their owners; little half-sentences of delight and compliment were dropped like curtsies – was this what it was to be a writer? Martins began to feel distinct irritation towards Benjamin Dexter. The complacent, tiring, pompous ass, he thought, signing the twenty-seventh copy of *The Curved Prow*. Every time he looked up and took another book he saw Crabbin's worried speculative gaze. The members of the Institute were beginning to go home with their spoils: the room was emptying. Suddenly in the mirror Martins saw a military policeman. He seemed to be having an argument with one of Crabbin's young henchmen. Martins thought he caught the sound of his own name. It was then he lost his nerve and with it any relic of common sense. There was only one book left to sign; he dashed off a last 'B. Dexter' and made for the door. The young man, Crabbin and the policeman stood together at the entrance.

'And this gentleman?' the policeman asked.

'It's Mr Benjamin Dexter,' the young man said.

'Lavatory. Is there a lavatory?' Martins said.

'I understood a Mr Rollo Martins came here in one of your cars.'

'A mistake. An obvious mistake.'

'Second door on the left,' the young man said.

Martins grabbed his coat from the cloakroom as he went and made down the stairs. On the first-floor landing he heard someone mounting the stairs and, looking over, saw Paine, whom I had sent to identify him. He opened a door at random and shut it behind him. He could hear Paine going by. The room where he stood was in darkness; a curious moaning sound made him turn and face whatever room it was.

He could see nothing and the sound had stopped. He made a tiny movement and once more it started, like an impeded breath. He remained still and the sound died away. Outside somebody called, 'Mr Dexter, Mr Dexter.' Then a new sound started. It was like somebody whispering – a long continuous monologue in the darkness. Martins said, 'Is anybody there?' and the sound stopped again. He could stand no more of it. He took out his lighter. Footsteps went by and down the stairs. He scraped and scraped at the little wheel and no light came. Somebody shifted in the dark, and something rattled in mid-air like a chain. He asked once more with the anger of fear, 'Is anybody there?' and only the click-click of metal answered him.

Martins felt desperately for a light switch, first to his right hand and then to his left. He did not dare go farther because he could no longer locate his fellow occupant; the whisper, the moaning, the click had all stopped. Then he was afraid that he had lost the door and felt wildly for the knob. He was far less afraid of the police than he was of the darkness, and he had no idea of the noise he was making.

Paine heard it from the bottom of the stairs and came back. He switched on the landing light, and the glow under the door gave Martins his direction. He opened the door and, smiling weakly at Paine, turned back to take a second look at the room. The eyes of a parrot chained to a perch stared beadily back at him. Paine said respectfully, 'We were looking for you, sir. Colonel Calloway wants a word with you.'

'I lost my way,' Martins said.

'Yes, sir. We thought that was what had happened.'

10

I had kept a very careful record of Martins' movements from the moment I knew that he had not caught the plane home. He had been seen with Kurtz, and at the Josefstadt Theatre; I knew about his visit to Dr Winkler and to Colonel Cooler, his first return to the block where Harry had lived. For some reason my man lost him between Cooler's and Anna Schmidt's flats; he reported that Martins had wandered widely, and the impression we both got was that he had deliberately thrown off his shadower. I tried to pick him up at the hotel and just missed him.

Events had taken a disquieting turn, and it seemed to me that the time had come for another interview. He had a lot to explain.

I put a good wide desk between us and gave him a cigarette. I found him sullen but ready to talk, within strict limits. I asked him about Kurtz and he seemed to me to answer satisfactorily. I then asked him about Anna Schmidt and I gathered from his reply that he must have been with her after visiting Colonel Cooler; that filled in one of the missing points. I tried him with Dr Winkler, and he answered readily enough. 'You've been getting around,' I said, 'quite a bit. And have you found out anything about your friend?'

'Oh, yes,' he said. 'It was under your nose but you didn't see it.'

'What?'

'That he was murdered.' That took me by surprise: I had at one time played with the idea of suicide, but I had ruled even that out.

'Go on,' I said. He tried to eliminate from his story all mention of Koch, talking about an informant who had seen the accident. This made his story rather confusing, and I couldn't grasp at first why he attached so much importance to the third man.

'He didn't turn up at the inquest, and the others lied to keep him out.'

'Nor did your man turn up – I don't see much importance in that. If it was a genuine accident, all the evidence needed was there. Why get the other chap in trouble? Perhaps his wife thought he was out of town; perhaps he was an official absent without leave – people sometimes take unauthorised trips to Vienna from places like Klagenfurt. The delights of the great city, for what they are worth.'

'There was more to it than that. The little chap who told me about it – they've murdered him. You see, they obviously didn't know what else he had seen.'

'Now we have it,' I said. 'You mean Koch.'

'Yes.'

'As far as we know, you were the last person to see him alive.' I questioned him then, as I've written, to find out if he had been followed to Koch's by somebody who was sharper than my man and had kept out of sight. I said, 'The Austrian police are anxious to pin this on you. Frau Koch told them how disturbed her husband was by your visit. Who else knew about it?'

'I told Cooler.' He said excitedly, 'Suppose immediately I left he telephoned the story to someone – to the third man. They had to stop Koch's mouth.'

'When you told Colonel Cooler about Koch, the man was already dead. That night he got out of bed, hearing someone, and went downstairs – '

'Well, that rules me out. I was in Sacher's.'

'But he went to bed very early. Your visit brought back the migraine. It was soon after nine when he got up. You returned to Sacher's at nine-thirty. Where were you before that?'

He said gloomily, 'Wandering round and trying to sort things out.'

'Any evidence of your movements?'

'No.'

I wanted to frighten him, so there was no point in telling him that he had been followed all the time. I knew that he hadn't cut Koch's throat, but I wasn't sure that he was quite so innocent as he made out. The man who owns the knife is not always the real murderer.

'Can I have another cigarette?'

'Yes.'

He said, 'How did you know that I went to Koch's? That was why you pulled me in here, wasn't it?'

'The Austrian police –'

'They hadn't identified me.'

'Immediately you left Colonel Cooler's, he telephoned to me.'

'Then that lets him out. If he had been concerned, he wouldn't have wanted me to tell you my story – to tell Koch's story, I mean.'

'He might assume that you were a sensible man and would come to me with your story as soon as you learned of Koch's death. By the way, how did you learn of it?'

He told me promptly and I believed him. It was then I began to believe him altogether. He said, 'I still can't believe Cooler's concerned. I'd stake anything on his honesty. He's one of those Americans with a real sense of duty.'

'Yes,' I said, 'he told me about that when he phoned. He apologised for it. He said it was the worst of having been brought up to believe in citizenship. He said it made him feel a prig. To tell you the truth, Cooler irritates me. Of course, he doesn't know that I know about his tyre deals.'

'Is he in a racket, too, then?'

'Not a very serious one. I dare say he's salted away twenty-five thousand dollars. But I'm not a good citizen. Let the Americans look after their own people.'

'I'm damned.' He said thoughtfully, 'Is that the kind of thing Harry was up to?'

'No. It was not so harmless.'

He said, 'You know, this business – Koch's death – has shaken me. Perhaps Harry did get mixed up in something bad. Perhaps he was trying to clear out again, and that's why they murdered him.'

'Or perhaps,' I said, 'they wanted a bigger cut of the spoils. Thieves fall out.'

He took it this time without any anger at all. He said, 'We won't agree about motives, but I think you check your facts pretty well. I'm sorry about the other day.'

'That's all right.' There are times when one has to make a flash decision – this was one of them. I owed him something in return for the information he had given me. I said, 'I'll show you enough of the facts in Lime's case for you to understand. But don't fly off the handle. It's going to be a shock.'

It couldn't help being a shock. The war and the peace (if you can call it peace) let loose a great number of rackets, but none more vile than this one. The black marketeers in food did at least supply food, and the same applied to all the other racketeers who provided articles in short supply at extravagant prices. But the penicillin racket was a different affair altogether. Penicillin in Austria was supplied only to the military hospitals; no civilian doctor, not even a civilian hospital, could obtain it by legal means. As the racket started, it was relatively harmless. Penicillin would be stolen by military orderlies and sold to Austrian doctors for very high sums – a phial would fetch anything up to seventy pounds. You might say that this was a form of distribution – unfair distribution because it benefited only the rich patient, but the original distribution could hardly have a claim to greater fairness.

This racket went on quite happily for a while. Occasionally an orderly was caught and punished, but the danger simply raised the price of penicillin. Then the racket began to get organised: the big men saw big money in it, and while the original thief got less for his spoils, he received instead a certain security. If anything happened to him he would be looked after. Human nature too has curious twisted reasons that the heart certainly knows nothing of. It eased the conscience of many small men to feel that they were working for an employer: they were almost as respectable soon in their own eyes as wage-earners; they were one of a group, and if there was guilt, the leaders bore the guilt. A racket works very like a totalitarian party.

This I have sometimes called stage two. Stage three was when the organisers decided that the profits were not large enough. Penicillin would not always be impossible to obtain legitimately; they wanted more money and quicker money while the going was good.

They began to dilute the penicillin with coloured water, and, in the case of penicillin dust, with sand. I keep a small museum in one drawer in my desk, and I showed Martins examples. He wasn't enjoying the talk, but he hadn't yet grasped the point. He said, 'I suppose that makes the stuff useless.'

I said, 'We wouldn't worry so much if that was all, but just consider. You can be immunised from the effects of penicillin. At the best you can say that the use of this stuff makes a penicillin treatment for the particular patient ineffective in the future. That isn't so funny, of course, if you are suffering from VD. Then the use of sand on a wound that requires penicillin – well, it's not healthy. Men have lost their legs and arms that way – and their lives. But perhaps what horrified me most was visiting the children's hospital here. They had bought some of this penicillin for use against meningitis. A number of children simply died, and a number went off their heads. You can see them now in the mental ward.'

He sat on the other side of the desk, scowling into his hands. I said, 'It doesn't bear thinking about very closely, does it?'

'You haven't shown me any evidence yet that Harry – '

'We are coming to that now,' I said. 'Just sit still and listen.' I opened Lime's file and began to read. At the beginning the evidence was purely circumstantial, and Martins fidgeted. So much consisted of coincidence – reports from agents that Lime had been at a certain place at a certain time; the accumulation of opportunities; his acquaintance with certain people. He protested once, 'But the same evidence would apply against me – now.'

'Just wait,' I said. For some reason Harry Lime had grown careless: he may have realised that we suspected him and got rattled. He held a quite distinguished position in the Relief Organisation, and a man like that is the more easily rattled. We put one of our agents as an orderly in the British Military Hospital: we knew by this time the name of our go-between, but we had never succeeded in getting the line right back to the source. Anyway, I am not going to bother the reader now, as I bothered Martins then, with all the stages – the long tussle to win the confidence of the go-between, a man called Harbin. At last we had the screws on Harbin, and we twisted them until he squealed. This kind of police work is very similar to secret-service work: you look for a double agent whom you can really control, and Harbin was the man for us. But even he only led us as far as Kurtz.

'Kurtz!' Martins exclaimed. 'But why haven't you pulled him in?'

'Zero hour is almost here,' I said.

Kurtz was a great step forward, for Kurtz was in direct communication with Lime – he had a small outside job in connection with international relief. With Kurtz, Lime sometimes put things on paper – if he was pressed. I showed Martins the photostat of a note. 'Can you identify that?'

'It's Harry's hand.' He read it through. 'I don't see anything wrong.'

'No, but now read this note from Harbin to Kurtz – which we dictated. Look at the date. This is the result.'

He read them both through twice.

'You see what I mean?' If one watched a world come to an end, a plane dive from its course, I don't suppose one would chatter, and a world for Martins had certainly come to an end, a world of easy friendship, hero-worship, confidence that had begun twenty years before in a school corridor. Every memory – afternoons in the long grass, the illegitimate shoots on Brickworth Common, the dreams, the walks, every shared experience – was simultaneously tainted, like the soil of an atomised town. One could not walk there with safety for a long while. While he sat there, looking at his hands and saying nothing, I fetched a precious bottle of whisky out of a cupboard and poured out two large doubles. 'Go on,' I said, 'drink that,' and he obeyed me as though I were his doctor. I poured him out another.

He said slowly, 'Are you certain that he was the real boss?'

'It's as far back as we have got so far.'

'You see, he was always apt to jump before he looked.'

I didn't contradict him, though that wasn't the impression he had before given of Lime. He was searching round for some comfort.

'Suppose,' he said, 'someone had got a line on him, forced him into this racket, as you forced Harbin to double-cross . . . '

'It's possible.'

'And they murdered him in case he talked when he was arrested.'

'It's not impossible.'

'I'm glad they did,' he said. 'I wouldn't have liked to hear Harry squeal.' He made a curious little dusting movement with his hand on his knee as much as to say, 'That's that.' He said, 'I'll be getting back to England.'

'I'd rather you didn't just yet. The Austrian police would make an issue if you tried to leave Vienna at the moment. You see, Cooler's sense of duty made him call them up too.'

'I see,' he said hopelessly.

'When we've found the third man . . . ' I said.

'I'd like to hear *him* squeal,' he said. 'The bastard. The bloody bastard.'

11

After he left me, Martins went straight off to drink himself silly. He chose the Oriental to do it in, the dreary smoky little nightclub that stands behind a sham Eastern façade. The same semi-nude photographs on the stairs, the same half-drunk Americans at the bar, the same bad wine and extraordinary gins – he might have been in any third-rate night haunt in any other shabby capital of a shabby Europe. At one point of the hopeless early hours the International Patrol took a look at the scene, and a Russian soldier made a bolt for the stairs at the sight of them, moving with bent averted head like a small harvest animal. The Americans never stirred and nobody interfered with them. Martins had drink after drink; he would probably have had a woman too, but the cabaret performers had all gone home, and there were practically no women left in the place, except for one beautiful shrewd-looking French journalist who made one remark to her companion and fell contemptuously asleep.

Martins moved on: at Maxim's a few couples were dancing rather gloomily, and at a place called Chez

Victor the heating had failed and people sat in over-coats drinking cocktails. By this time the spots were swimming in front of Martins' eyes, and he was oppressed by a sense of loneliness. His mind reverted to the girl in Dublin, and the one in Amsterdam. That was one thing that didn't fool you – the straight drink, the simple physical act: one didn't expect fidelity from a woman. His mind revolved in circles – from senti-ment to lust and back again from belief to cynicism.

The trams had stopped, and he set out obstinately on foot to find Harry's girl. He wanted to make love to her – just like that: no nonsense, no sentiment. He was in the mood for violence, and the snowy road heaved like a lake and set his mind on a new course towards sorrow, eternal love, renunciation. In the corner of a sheltering wall he was sick in the snow.

It must have been about three in the morning when he climbed the stairs to Anna's room. He was nearly sober by that time and had only one idea in his head, that she must know about Harry too. He felt that somehow this knowledge would pay the mortmain that memory levies on human beings, and he would stand a chance with Harry's girl. If you are in love yourself, it never occurs to you that the girl doesn't know: you believe you have told it plainly in a tone of voice, the touch of a hand. When Anna opened the door to him, with astonishment at the sight of him tousled on the threshold, he never imagined that she was opening the door to a stranger.

He said, 'Anna, I've found out everything.'

'Come in,' she said, 'you don't want to wake the house.' She was in a dressing-gown; the divan had become a bed, the kind of tumbled bed that showed how sleepless the occupant had been.

'Now,' she said, while he stood there, fumbling for words, 'what is it? I thought you were going to keep away. Are the police after you?'

'No.'

'You didn't really kill that man, did you?'

'Of course not.'

'You're drunk, aren't you?'

'I am a bit,' he said sulkily. The meeting seemed to be going on the wrong lines. He said angrily, 'I'm sorry.'

'Why? I would like a drink myself.'

He said, 'I've been with the British police. They are satisfied I didn't do it. But I've learned everything from them. Harry was in a racket – a bad racket.' He said hopelessly, 'He was no good at all. We were both wrong.'

'You'd better tell me,' Anna said. She sat down on the bed and he told her, swaying slightly beside the table where her typescript part still lay open at the first page. I imagine he told it to her pretty confusedly, dwelling chiefly on what had stuck most in his mind, the children dead with meningitis, and the children in the mental ward. He stopped and they were silent. She said, 'Is that all?'

'Yes.'

'You were sober when they told you? They really proved it?'

'Yes.' He added drearily, 'So that, you see, was Harry.'

'I'm glad he's dead now,' she said. 'I wouldn't have wanted him to rot for years in prison.'

'But can you understand how Harry – your Harry, my Harry – could have got mixed up . . . ?' He said hopelessly, 'I feel as though he had never really

99

existed, that we'd dreamed him. Was he laughing at fools like us all the time?'

'He may have been. What does it matter?' she said. 'Sit down. Don't worry.' He had pictured himself comforting *her* – not this other way about. She said, 'If he was alive now, he might be able to explain, but we've got to remember him as he was to us. There are always so many things one doesn't know about a person, even a person one loves – good things, bad things. We have to leave plenty of room for them.'

'Those children – '

She said angrily, 'For God's sake stop making people in *your* image. Harry was real. He wasn't just your hero and my lover. He was Harry. He was in a racket. He did bad things. What about it? He was the man we knew.'

He said, 'Don't talk such bloody wisdom. Don't you see that I love you?'

She looked at him in astonishment. 'You?'

'Yes, me. I don't kill people with fake drugs. I'm not a hypocrite who persuades people that I'm the greatest – I'm just a bad writer who drinks too much and falls in love with girls . . . '

She said, 'But I don't even know what colour your eyes are. If you'd rung me up just now and asked me whether you were dark or fair or wore a moustache, I wouldn't have known.'

'Can't you get him out of your mind?'

'No.'

He said, 'As soon as they've cleared up this Koch murder, I'm leaving Vienna. I can't feel interested any longer in whether Kurtz killed Harry – or the third man. Whoever killed him it was a kind of justice. Maybe I'd kill him myself under these circumstances. But you still love him. You love a cheat, a murderer.'

'I loved a man,' she said. 'I told you – a man doesn't alter because you find out more about him. He's still the same man.'

'I hate the way you talk. I've got a splitting head-ache, and you talk and talk . . . '

'I didn't ask you to come.'

'You make me cross.'

Suddenly she laughed. She said, 'You are so comic. You come here at three in the morning – a stranger – and say you love me. Then you get angry and pick a quarrel. What do you expect me to do – or say?'

'I haven't seen you laugh before. Do it again. I like it.'

'There isn't enough for two laughs,' she said.

He took her by the shoulders and shook her gently. He said, 'I'd make comic faces all day long. I'd stand on my head and grin at you between my legs. I'd learn a lot of jokes from the books on after-dinner speaking.'

'Come away from the window. There are no curtains.'

'There's nobody to see.' But automatically checking his statement, he wasn't quite so sure: a long shadow that had moved, perhaps with the movement of clouds over the moon, was motionless again. He said, 'You still love Harry, don't you?'

'Yes.'

'Perhaps I do. I don't know.' He dropped his hands and said, 'I'll be pushing off.'

He walked rapidly away. He didn't bother to see whether he was being followed, to check up on the shadow. But, passing by the end of a street, he happened to turn, and there just around the corner, pressed against a wall to escape notice, was a thick stocky figure. Martins stopped and stared. There was something familiar about that figure. Perhaps, he thought, I have grown unconsciously used to him during these last twenty-four hours; perhaps he is one of those who have so assiduously checked my movements. Martins stood there, twenty yards away, staring at the silent motionless figure in the dark street who stared back at him. A police spy, perhaps, or an agent of those other men, those men who had corrupted Harry first and then killed him – even possibly the third man?

It was not the face that was familiar, for he could not make out so much as the angle of the jaw; nor a movement, for the body was so still that he began to believe that the whole thing was an illusion caused by shadow. He called sharply, 'Do you want anything?' and there was no reply. He called again with the irascibility of drink, 'Answer, can't you,' and an answer came, for a window curtain was drawn petulantly back by some sleeper he had awakened, and the light fell straight across the narrow street and lit up the features of Harry Lime.

12

'Do you believe in ghosts?' Martins said to me.

'Do you?'

'I do now.'

'I also believe that drunk men see things – sometimes rats, sometimes worse.'

He hadn't come to me at once with his story – only

the danger to Anna Schmidt tossed him back into my office, like something the sea had washed up, tousled, unshaven, haunted by an experience he couldn't understand. He said, 'If it had been just the face, I wouldn't have worried. I'd been thinking about Harry, and I might easily have mistaken a stranger. The light was turned off again at once, you see. I only got one glimpse, and the man made off down the street – if he was a man. There was no turning for a long way, but I was so startled I gave him another thirty yards' start. He came to one of those advertisement kiosks and for a moment moved out of sight. I ran after him. It only took me ten seconds to reach the kiosk, and he must have heard me running, but the strange thing was he never appeared again. I reached the kiosk. There wasn't anybody there. The street was empty. He couldn't have reached a doorway without my seeing him. He simply vanished.'

'A natural thing for ghosts – or illusions.'

'But I can't believe I was as drunk as all that!'

'What did you do then?'

'I had to have another drink. My nerves were all in pieces.'

'Didn't that bring him back?'

'No, but it sent me back to Anna's.'

I think he would have been ashamed to come to me with his absurd story if it had not been for the attempt on Anna Schmidt. My theory, when he did tell me his story, was that there had been a watcher – though it was drink and hysteria that had pasted on the man's face the features of Harry Lime. The watcher had noted his visit to Anna, and the member of the ring – the penicillin ring – had been warned by telephone. Events that night moved fast. You remember that

Kurtz lived in the Russian zone – in the Second Bezirk to be exact, in a wide, empty, desolate street that runs down to the Prater Platz. A man like that had probably obtained his influential contacts. It was ruin for a Russian to be observed on very friendly terms with an American or an Englishman, but the Austrian was a potential ally – and in any case one doesn't fear the influence of the ruined and defeated.

You must understand that at this period cooperation between the Western Allies and the Russians had practically, though not yet completely, broken down.

The original police agreement in Vienna between the Allies confined the military police (who had to deal with crimes involving Allied personnel) to their particular zones, unless permission was given to them to enter the zone of another Power. This agreement worked well enough between the three Western Powers. I only had to get on the phone to my opposite number in the American or French zones before I sent in my men to make an arrest or pursue an investigation. During the first six months of the occupation it had worked reasonably well with the Russians: perhaps forty-eight hours would pass before I received permission, and in practice there are few occasions when it is necessary to work quicker than that. Even at home it is not always possible to obtain a search warrant or permission from one's superiors to detain a suspect with any greater speed. Then the forty-eight hours turned into a week or a fortnight, and I remember my American colleague suddenly taking a look at his records and discovering that there were forty cases dating back more than three months where not even an acknowledgement of his requests had been received. Then the trouble started. We began to turn down, or not to answer, the Russian requests, and sometimes without permission they would send in police, and there were clashes. . . . At the date of this story the Western Powers had more or less ceased to put in applications or reply to the Russian ones. This meant that if I wanted to pick up Kurtz it would be as well to catch him outside the Russian zone, though of course it was always possible his activities might offend the Russians and his punishment be more sudden and severe than any we should inflict. Well, the Anna Schmidt case was one of the clashes: when Rollo Martins went drunkenly back at four o'clock in the morning to tell Anna that he had seen the ghost of Harry, he was told by a frightened porter who had not yet gone back to sleep that she had been taken away by the International Patrol.

What happened was this. Russia, you remember, was in the chair as far as the Innere Stadt was concerned, and when Russia was in the chair, you expected certain irregularities. On this occasion, halfway through the patrol, the Russian policeman pulled a fast one on his colleagues and directed the car to the street where Anna Schmidt lived. The British military policeman that night was new to his job: he didn't realise, till his colleagues told him, that they had entered a British zone. He spoke a little German and no French, and the Frenchman, a cynical hard-bitten Parisian, gave up the attempt to explain to him. The American took on the job. 'It's all right by me,' he said, 'but is it all right by you?' The British MP tapped the Russian's shoulder, who turned his Mongol face and launched a flood of incomprehensible Slav at him. The car drove on.

Outside Anna Schmidt's block the American took

a hand in the game and demanded in German what it was all about. The Frenchman leaned against the bonnet and lit a stinking Caporal. France wasn't concerned, and anything that didn't concern France had no genuine importance to him. The Russian dug out a few words of German and flourished some papers. As far as they could tell, a Russian national wanted by the Russian police was living there without proper papers. They went upstairs and the Russian tried Anna's door. It was firmly bolted, but he put his shoulder to it and tore out the bolt without giving the occupant an opportunity of letting him in. Anna was in bed, though I don't suppose, after Martins' visit, that she was asleep.

There is a lot of comedy in these situations if you are not directly concerned. You need a background of Central European terror, of a father who belonged to a losing side, of house-searches and disappearances, before the fear outweighs the comedy. The Russian, you see, refused to leave the room while Anna dressed: the Englishman refused to remain in the room: the American wouldn't leave a girl unprotected with a Russian soldier, and the Frenchman – well, I think the Frenchman must have thought it was fun. Can't you imagine the scene? The Russian was just doing his duty and watched the girl all the time, without a flicker of sexual interest; the American stood with his back chivalrously turned, but aware, I am sure, of every movement; the Frenchman smoked his cigarette and watched with detached amusement the reflection of the girl dressing in the mirror of the wardrobe; and the Englishman stood in the passage wondering what to do next.

I don't want you to think the English policeman

came too badly out of the affair. In the passage, undistracted by chivalry, he had time to think, and his thoughts led him to the telephone in the next flat. He got straight through to me at my flat and woke me out of that deepest middle sleep. That was why when Martins rang up an hour later I already knew what was exciting him; it gave him an undeserved but very useful belief in my efficiency. I never heard another crack from him about policemen or sheriffs after that night.

I must explain another point of police procedure. If the International Patrol made an arrest, they had to lodge their prisoner for twenty-four hours at the International Headquarters. During that period it would be determined which Power could justifiably claim the prisoner. It was this rule that the Russians were most ready to break. Because so few of us can speak Russian and the Russian is almost debarred from explaining his point of view (try and explain your own point of view on any subject in a language you don't know well – it's not as easy as ordering a meal), we are apt to regard any breach of an agreement by the Russians as deliberate and malign. I think it quite possible that they understood this agreement as referring only to prisoners about whom there was a dispute. It's true that there was a dispute about nearly every prisoner they took, but there was no dispute in their own minds, and no one has a greater sense of self-righteousness than a Russian. Even in his confessions a Russian is self-righteous – he pours out his revelations, but he doesn't excuse himself, he needs no excuse. All this had to form the background of one's decision. I gave my instructions to Corporal Starling.

When he came back to Anna's room a dispute was raging. Anna had told the American that she had Austrian papers (which was true) and that they were quite in order (which was rather stretching the truth). The American told the Russian in bad German that they had no right to arrest an Austrian citizen. He asked Anna for her papers and when she produced them, the Russian snatched them from her hand.

'Hungarian,' he said, pointing at Anna. 'Hungarian,' and then, flourishing the papers, 'bad, bad.'

The American, whose name was O'Brien, said, 'Give the goil back her papers,' which the Russian naturally didn't understand. The American put his hand on his gun, and Corporal Starling said gently, 'Let it go, Pat.'

'If those papers ain't in order we got a right to look.'

'Just let it go. We'll see the papers at HQ.'

'If we get to HQ. You can't trust these Russian drivers. As like as not he'll drive straight through to his zone.'

'We'll see,' Starling said.

'The trouble about you British is you never know when to make a stand.'

'Oh, well,' Starling said; he had been at Dunkirk, but he knew when to be quiet.

They got back into the car with Anna, who sat in the front between the two Russians dumb with fear. After they had gone a little way the American touched the Russian on the shoulder, 'Wrong way,' he said. 'HQ that way.' The Russian chattered back in his own tongue making a conciliatory gesture, while they drove on. 'It's what I said,' O'Brien told Starling. 'They are taking her to the Russian zone.' Anna stared out with terror through the windscreen. 'Don't worry, little goil,' O'Brien said, 'I'll fix them all right.' His hand was fidgeting round his gun again. Starling said, 'Look here, Pat, this is a British case. You don't have to get involved.'

'You are new to this game. You don't know these bastards.'

'It's not worth making an incident about.'

'For Christ's sake,' O'Brien said, 'not worth . . . that little goil's got to have protection.' American chivalry is always, it seems to me, carefully canalised – one still awaits the American saint who will kiss a leper's sores.

The driver put on his brakes suddenly: there was a road block. You see, I knew they would have to pass this military post if they did not make their way to the International HQ in the Inner City. I put my head in at the window and said to the Russian haltingly, in his own tongue, 'What are you doing in the British zone?'

He grumbled that it was 'orders'.

'Whose orders? Let me see them.' I noted the signature – it was useful information. I said, 'This tells you to pick up a certain Hungarian national and war criminal who is living with faulty papers in the British zone. Let me see the papers.'

He started on a long explanation, but I saw the papers sticking in his pocket and I pulled them out. He made a grab at his gun, and I punched his face – I felt really mean at doing so, but it's the conduct they expect from an angry officer and it brought him to reason – that and seeing three British soldiers approaching his headlights. I said, 'These papers look to me quite in order, but I'll investigate them and send a report of the result to your colonel. He can, of course, ask for the extradition of this lady at any time. All we want is proof of her criminal activities. I'm afraid we don't regard Hungarian as Russian nationality.' He goggled at me (my Russian was probably half incomprehensible) and I said to Anna, 'Get out of the car.' She couldn't get by the Russian, so I had to pull him out first. Then I put a packet of cigarettes in his hand, said, 'Have a good smoke,' waved my hand to the others, gave a sigh of relief, and that incident was closed.

13

While Martins told me how he went back to Anna's and found her gone, I did some hard thinking. I wasn't satisfied with the ghost story or the idea that the man with Harry Lime's features had been a drunken illusion. I took out two maps of Vienna and compared them. I rang up my assistant and, keeping Martins silent with a glass of whisky, asked him if he had located Harbin yet. He said no; he understood he'd left Klagenfurt a week ago to visit his family in the adjoining zone. One always wants to do everything oneself; one has to guard against blaming one's juniors. I am convinced that I would never have let Harbin out of our clutches, but then I would probably have made all kinds of mistakes that my junior would have avoided. 'All right,' I said. 'Go on trying to get hold of him.'

'I'm sorry, sir.'

'Forget it. It's just one of those things.'

His young enthusiastic voice – if only one could still feel that enthusiasm for a routine job; how many opportunities, flashes of insight one misses simply because a job has become just a job – tingled up the wire. 'You know, sir, I can't help feeling that we ruled out the possibility of murder too easily. There are one or two points – '

'Put them on paper, Carter.'

'Yes, sir. I think, sir, if you don't mind my saying so' (Carter is a very young man), 'we ought to have him dug up. There's no real evidence that he died just when the others said.'

'I agree, Carter. Get on to the authorities.'

Martins was right. I had made a complete fool of myself, but remember that police work in an occupied city is not like police work at home. Everything is unfamiliar: the methods of one's foreign colleagues, the rules of evidence, even the procedure at inquests. I suppose I had got into the state of mind when one trusts too much to one's personal judgement. I had been immensely relieved by Lime's death. I was satisfied with the accident.

I said to Martins, 'Did you look inside the kiosk or was it locked?'

'Oh, it wasn't a newspaper kiosk,' he said. 'It was one of those solid iron kiosks you see everywhere plastered with posters.'

'You'd better show me the place.'

'But is Anna all right?'

'The police are watching the flat. They won't try anything else yet.'

I didn't want to make a fuss in the neighbourhood with a police car, so we took trams – several trams – changing here and there, and came into the district on foot. I didn't wear my uniform, and I doubted anyway, after the failure of the attempt on Anna, whether they would risk a watcher. 'This is the turning,' Martins said and led me down a side street. We stopped at the kiosk. 'You see, he passed behind here and simply vanished – into the ground.'

'That was exactly where he did vanish to,' I said.

'How do you mean?'

An ordinary passer-by would never have noticed that the kiosk had a door, and of course it had been dark when the man disappeared. I pulled the door open and showed Martins the little curling iron staircase that disappeared into the ground. He said, 'Good God, then I didn't imagine him!'

'It's one of the entrances to the main sewer.'

'And anyone can go down?'

'Anyone. For some reason the Russians object to these being locked.'

'How far can one go?'

'Right across Vienna. People used them in air raids; some of our prisoners hid for two years down there. Deserters have used them – and burglars. If you know your way about you can emerge again almost anywhere in the city through a manhole or a kiosk like this one. The Austrians have to have special police for patrolling these sewers.' I closed the door of the kiosk again. I said, 'So that's how your friend Harry disappeared.'

'You really believe it was Harry?'

'The evidence points that way.'

'Then whom did they bury?'

'I don't know yet, but we soon shall, because we are digging him up again. I've got a shrewd idea, though, that Koch wasn't the only inconvenient man they murdered.'

Martins said, 'It's a bit of a shock.'

'Yes.'

'What are you going to do about it?'

'I don't know. It's no good applying to the Russians, and you can bet he's hiding out now in the Russian zone. We have no line now on Kurtz, for Harbin's blown – he must have been blown or they wouldn't have staged that mock death and funeral.'

'But it's odd, isn't it, that Koch didn't recognise the dead man's face from the window?'

'The window was a long way up and I expect the face had been damaged before they took the body out of the car.'

He said thoughtfully, 'I wish I could speak to him. You see, there's so much I simply can't believe.'

'Perhaps you are the only one who could speak to him. It's risky though, because you know too much.'

'I still can't believe – I only saw the face for a moment.' He said, 'What shall I do?'

'He won't leave the Russian zone now. Perhaps that's why he tried to have the girl taken over – because he loves her? Because he doesn't feel secure? I don't know. I do know that the only person who could persuade him to come over would be you – or her, if he still believes you are his friend. But first you've got to speak to him. I can't see the line.'

'I could go and see Kurtz. I have the address.'

I said, 'Remember. Lime may not want you to leave the Russian zone when once you are there, and I can't protect you there.'

'I want to clear the whole damned thing up,' Martins said, 'but I'm not going to act as a decoy. I'll talk to him. That's all.'

14

Sunday had laid its false peace over Vienna; the wind had dropped and no snow had fallen for twenty-four hours. All the morning trams had been full, going out to Grinzing where the young wine is drunk and to the slopes of snow on the hills outside. Walking over the canal by the makeshift military bridge, Martins was aware of the emptiness of the afternoon: the young were out with their toboggans and their skis, and all around him was the after-dinner sleep of age. A notice-board told him that he was entering the Russian zone, but there were no signs of occupation. You saw more Russian soldiers in the Inner City than here.

Deliberately he had given Kurtz no warning of his visit. Better to find him out than a reception prepared for him. He was careful to carry with him all his papers, including the *laissez-passer* of the Four Powers that on the face of it allowed him to move freely through all the zones of Vienna. It was extraordinarily quiet over here on the other side of the canal, and a melodramatic journalist had painted a picture of silent terror, but the truth was simply the wider streets, the greater shell damage, the fewer people – and Sunday afternoon. There was nothing to fear, but all the same, in this huge empty street where all the time you heard your own feet moving, it was difficult not to look behind.

He had no difficulty in finding Kurtz's block, and when he rang the bell the door was opened quickly, as though Kurtz expected a visitor, by Kurtz himself.

'Oh,' Kurtz said, 'it's you, Mr Martins,' and made

a perplexed motion with his hand to the back of his head. Martins had been wondering why he looked so different, and now he knew. Kurtz was not wearing the toupée, and yet his head was not bald. He had a perfectly normal head of hair cut close. He said, 'It would have been better to have telephoned to me. You nearly missed me; I was going out.'

'May I come in a moment?'

'Of course.'

In the hall a cupboard door stood open, and Martins saw Kurtz's overcoat, his raincoat, a couple of soft hats, and, hanging sedately on a peg like a wrap, Kurtz's toupée. He said, 'I'm glad to see your hair has grown,' and saw, in the mirror on the cupboard door, the hatred flame and blush on Kurtz's face. When he turned Kurtz smiled at him like a conspirator and said vaguely, 'It keeps the head warm.'

'Whose head?' Martins asked, for it had suddenly occurred to him how useful that toupée might have been on the day of the accident. 'Never mind,' he went quickly on, for his errand was not with Kurtz. 'I'm here to see Harry.'

'Harry?'

'I want to talk to him.'

'Are you mad?'

'I'm in a hurry, so let's assume that I am. Just make a note of my madness. If you should see Harry – or his ghost – let him know that I want to talk to him. A ghost isn't afraid of a man, is it? Surely it's the other way round. I'll be waiting in the Prater by the Big Wheel for the next two hours – if you can get in touch with the dead, hurry.' He added, 'Remember, I was Harry's friend.'

Kurtz said nothing, but somewhere, in a room off

the hall, somebody cleared his throat. Martins threw open a door; he had half expected to see the dead rise yet again, but it was only Dr Winkler who rose from a kitchen chair, in front of the kitchen stove, and bowed very stiffly and correctly with the same celluloid squeak.

'Dr Winkle,' Martins said. Dr Winkler looked extraordinarily out of place in a kitchen. The debris of a snack lunch littered the kitchen table, and the unwashed dishes consorted very ill with Dr Winkler's cleanness.

'Winkler,' the doctor corrected him with stony patience.

Martins said to Kurtz, 'Tell the doctor about my madness. He might be able to make a diagnosis. And remember the place – by the Great Wheel. Or do ghosts only rise by night?' He left the flat.

For an hour he waited, walking up and down to keep warm, inside the enclosure of the Great Wheel; the smashed Prater with its bones sticking crudely through the snow was nearly empty. One stall sold thin flat cakes like cartwheels, and the children queued with their coupons. A few courting couples would be packed together in a single car of the Wheel and revolve slowly above the city, surrounded by empty cars. As the car reached the highest point of the Wheel, the revolutions would stop for a couple of minutes and far overhead the tiny faces would press against the glass. Martins wondered who would come for him. Was there enough friendship left in Harry for him to come alone, or would a squad of police arrive? It was obvious from the raid on Anna Schmidt's flat that he had a certain pull. And then as his watch-hand passed the hour, he wondered: Was it all an invention of my mind? Are they digging up Harry's body now in the Central Cemetery?

Somewhere behind the cake stall a man was whistling, and Martins knew the tune. He turned and waited. Was it fear or excitement that made his heart beat – or just the memories that tune ushered in, for life had always quickened when Harry came, came just as he came now, as though nothing much had happened, nobody had been lowered into a grave or found with cut throat in a basement, came with his amused, deprecating, take-it-or-leave-it manner – and of course one always took it.

'Harry.'

'Hello, Rollo.'

Don't picture Harry Lime as a smooth scoundrel. He wasn't that. The picture I have of him on my files is an excellent one: he is caught by a street photographer with his stocky legs apart, big shoulders a little hunched, a belly that has known too much good food for too long, on his face a look of cheerful rascality, a geniality, a recognition that *his* happiness will make the world's day. Now he didn't make the mistake of putting out a hand that might have been rejected, but instead just patted Martins on the elbow and said, 'How are things?'

'We've got to talk, Harry.'

'Of course.'

'Alone.'

'We couldn't be more alone than here.'

He had always known the ropes, and even in the smashed pleasure park he knew them, tipping the woman in charge of the Wheel, so that they might have a car to themselves. He said, 'Lovers used to do this in the old days, but they haven't the money to spare, poor devils, now,' and he looked out of the window of the swaying, rising car at the figures diminishing below with what looked like genuine commiseration.

Very slowly on one side of them the city sank; very slowly on the other the great cross-girders of the Wheel rose into sight. As the horizon slid away the Danube became visible, and the piers of the Reichs-brücke lifted above the houses. 'Well,' Harry said, 'it's good to see you, Rollo.'

'I was at your funeral.'

'That was pretty smart of me, wasn't it?'

'Not so smart for your girl. She was there too – in tears.'

'She's a good little thing,' Harry said. 'I'm very fond of her.'

'I didn't believe the police when they told me about you.'

Harry said, 'I wouldn't have asked you to come if I'd known what was going to happen, but I didn't think the police were on to me.'

'Were you going to cut me in on the spoils?'

'I've never kept you out of anything, old man, yet.' He stood with his back to the door as the car swung upwards, and smiled back at Rollo Martins, who could remember him in just such an attitude in a secluded corner of the school quad, saying, 'I've learned a way to get out at night. It's absolutely safe. You are the only one I'm letting in on it.' For the first time Rollo Martins looked back through the years without admiration, as he thought: He's never grown up. Marlowe's devils wore squibs attached to their tails; evil was like Peter Pan – it carried with it the horrifying and horrible gift of eternal youth.

Martins said, 'Have you ever visited the children's hospital? Have you seen any of your victims?'

Harry took a look at the toy landscape below and came away from the door. 'I never feel quite safe in these things,' he said. He felt the back of the door with his hand, as though he were afraid that it might fly open and launch him into that iron-ribbed space. 'Victims?' he asked. 'Don't be melodramatic, Rollo. Look down there,' he went on, pointing through the window at the people moving like black flies at the base of the Wheel. 'Would you really feel any pity if one of those dots stopped moving – for ever? If I said you can have twenty thousand pounds for every dot that stops, would you really, old man, tell me to keep my money – without hesitation? Or would you calculate how many dots you could afford to spare? Free of income tax, old man. Free of income tax.' He gave his boyish conspiratorial smile. 'It's the only way to save nowadays.'

'Couldn't you have stuck to tyres?'

'Like Cooler? No, I've always been ambitious.'

'You are finished now. The police know everything.'

'But they can't catch me, Rollo, you'll see. I'll pop up again. You can't keep a good man down.'

The car swung to a standstill at the highest point of the curve and Harry turned his back and gazed out of the window. Martins thought: One good shove and I could break the glass, and he pictured the body falling, falling, through the iron struts, a piece of carrion dropping among the flies. He said, 'You know the police are planning to dig up your body. What will they find?'

'Harbin,' Harry replied with simplicity. He turned away from the window and said, 'Look at the sky.'

The car had reached the top of the Wheel and hung there motionless, while the stain of the sunset ran in streaks over the wrinkled papery sky beyond the black girders.

'Why did the Russians try to take Anna Schmidt?'

'She had false papers, old man.'

'Who told them?'

'The price of living in this zone, Rollo, is service. I have to give them a little information now and then.'

'I thought perhaps you were just trying to get her here – because she was your girl? Because you wanted her?'

Harry smiled. 'I haven't all that influence.'

'What would have happened to her?'

'Nothing very serious. She'd have been sent back to Hungary. There's nothing against her really. A year in a labour camp perhaps. She'd be infinitely better off in her own country than being pushed around by the British police.'

'She hasn't told them anything about you.'

'She's a good little thing,' Harry repeated with satisfaction and pride.

'She loves you.'

'Well, I gave her a good time while it lasted.'

'And I love her.'

'That's fine, old man. Be kind to her. She's worth it. I'm glad.' He gave the impression of having arranged everything to everybody's satisfaction. 'And you can help to keep her mouth shut. Not that she knows anything that matters.'

'I'd like to knock you through the window.'

'But you won't, old man. Our quarrels never last long. You remember that fearful one in the Monaco, when we swore we were through. I'd trust you anywhere, Rollo. Kurtz tried to persuade me not to come, but I know you. Then he tried to persuade me to, well, arrange an accident. He told me it would be quite easy in this car.'

'Except that I'm the stronger man.'

'But I've got the gun. You don't think a bullet wound would show when you hit *that* ground?' Again the car began to move, sailing slowly down, until the flies were midgets, were recognisable human beings. 'What fools we are, Rollo, talking like this, as if I'd do that to you – or you to me.' He turned his back and leaned his face against the glass. One thrust . . . 'How much do you earn a year with your Westerns, old man?'

'A thousand.'

'Taxed. I earn thirty thousand free. It's the fashion. In these days, old man, nobody thinks in terms of human beings. Governments don't, so why should we? They talk of the people and the proletariat, and I talk of the mugs. It's the same thing. They have their five-year plans and so have I.'

'You used to be a Catholic.'

'Oh, I still *believe*, old man. In God and mercy and all that. I'm not hurting anybody's soul by what I do. The dead are happier dead. They don't miss much here, poor devils,' he added with that odd touch of genuine pity as the car reached the platform and the faces of the doomed-to-be-victims, the tired pleasure-hoping Sunday faces, peered in at them. 'I could cut you in, you know. It would be useful. I have no one left in the Inner City.'

'Except Cooler? And Winkler?'

'You really mustn't turn policeman, old man.' They passed out of the car and he put his hand again on

Martins' elbow. 'That was a joke: I know you won't. Have you heard anything of old Bracer recently?'

'I had a card at Christmas.'

'Those were the days, old man. Those were the days. I've got to leave you here. We'll see each other sometime. If you are in a jam, you can always get me at Kurtz's.' He moved away and, turning, waved the hand he had had the tact not to offer: it was like the whole past moving off under a cloud. Martins suddenly called after him, 'Don't trust me, Harry,' but there was too great a distance now between them for the words to carry.

15

'Anna was at the theatre,' Martins told me, 'for the Sunday matinée. I had to see the whole dreary comedy through a second time. About a middle-aged composer and an infatuated girl and an under-standing – a terribly understanding – wife. Anna acted very badly – she wasn't much of an actress at the best of times. I saw her afterwards in her dressing-room, but she was badly fussed. I think she thought I was going to make a serious pass at her all the time, and she didn't want a pass. I told her Harry was alive – I thought she'd be glad and that I would hate to see how glad she was, but she sat in front of her make-up mirror and let the tears streak the grease-paint and I wished afterwards that she had been glad. She looked awful and I loved her. Then I told her about my interview with Harry, but she wasn't really paying much attention because when I'd finished she said, "I wish he was dead."

' "He deserves to be," I said.

' "I mean he would be safe then – from everybody." '

I asked Martins, 'Did you show her the photographs I gave you – of the children?'

'Yes. I thought, it's got to be kill or cure this time. She's got to get Harry out of her system. I propped the pictures up among the pots of grease. She couldn't avoid seeing them. I said, "The police can't arrest Harry unless they get him into this zone, and we've got to help."

'She said, "I thought he was your friend." I said, "He *was* my friend." She said, "I'll never help you to get Harry. I don't want to see him again, I don't want to hear his voice. I don't want to be touched by him, but I won't do a thing to harm him."

'I felt bitter – I don't know why, because after all I had done nothing for her. Even Harry had done more for her than I had. I said, "You want him still," as though I were accusing her of a crime. She said, "I don't want him, but he's in me. That's a fact – not like friendship. Why, when I have a sex dream, he's always the man." '

I prodded Martins on when he hesitated. 'Yes?'

'Oh, I just got up and left her then. Now it's your turn to work on me. What do you want me to do?'

'I want to act quickly. You see, it was Harbin's body in the coffin, so we can pick up Winkler and Cooler right away. Kurtz is out of our reach for the time being, and so is the driver. We'll put in a formal request to the Russians for permission to arrest Kurtz and Lime: it makes our files tidy. If we are going to use you as our decoy, your message must go to Lime straight away – not after you've hung around in this zone for twenty-four hours. As I see it, you were brought here for a grilling almost as soon as you got back into the Inner City; you heard then from me about Harbin; you put two and two together and you go and warn Cooler. We'll let Cooler slip for the sake of the bigger game – we have no evidence that he was in on the penicillin racket. He'll escape into the Second Bezirk to Kurtz, and Lime will know you've played the game. Three hours later you send a message that the police are after you: you are in hiding and must see him.'

'He won't come.'

'I'm not so sure. We'll choose our hiding place carefully – where he'll think there's a minimum of risk. It's worth trying. It would appeal to his pride and his sense of humour if he could scoop you out. And it would stop your mouth.'

Martins said, 'He never used to scoop me out – at school.' It was obvious that he had been reviewing the past with care and coming to conclusions.

'That wasn't such serious trouble and there was no danger of your squealing.'

He said, 'I told Harry not to trust me, but he didn't hear.'

'Do you agree?'

He had given me back the photographs of the children and they lay on my desk. I could see him take a long look at them. 'Yes,' he said, 'I agree.'

16

All the first arrangements went according to plan. We delayed arresting Winkler, who had returned from the Second Bezirk, until after Cooler had been warned. Martins enjoyed his short interview with Cooler. Cooler greeted him without embarrassment and with considerable patronage. 'Why, Mr Martins, it's good to see you. Sit down. I'm glad everything went off all right between you and Colonel Calloway. A very straight chap, Calloway.'

'It didn't,' Martins said.

'You don't bear any ill-will, I'm sure, about my letting him know about you seeing Koch. The way I figured it was this – if you were innocent you'd clear yourself right away, and if you were guilty, well, the fact that I liked you oughtn't to stand in the way. A citizen has his duties.'

'Like giving false evidence at an inquest.'

Cooler said, 'Oh, that old story. I'm afraid you are riled at me, Mr Martins. Look at it this way – you as a citizen, owing allegiance – '

'The police have dug up the body. They'll be after you and Winkler. I want you to warn Harry . . . '

'I don't understand.'

'Oh, yes, you do.' And it was obvious that he did. Martins left him abruptly. He wanted no more of that kindly humanitarian face.

It only remained then to bait the trap. After studying the map of the sewer system I came to the conclusion that a café anywhere near the main entrance of the great sewer, which was placed like all the others in an advertisement kiosk, would be the most likely spot to tempt Lime. He had only to rise once again through the ground, walk fifty yards, bring Martins back with him, and sink again into the obscurity of the sewers. He had no idea that this method of evasion was known to us; he probably knew that one patrol of the sewer police ended before midnight, and the next did not start till two, and so at midnight Martins sat in the little cold café in sight of the kiosk, drinking coffee after coffee. I had lent him a revolver; I had men posted as close to the kiosk as I could, and the sewer police were ready when zero hour struck to close the manholes and start sweeping the sewers inwards from the edge of the city. But I intended, if I could, to catch him before he went underground again. It would save trouble – and risk to Martins. So there, as I say, in the café Martins sat.

The wind had risen again, but it had brought no snow; it came icily off the Danube and in the little grassy square by the café it whipped up the snow like the surf on top of a wave. There was no heating in the café, and Martins sat warming each hand in turn on a cup of ersatz coffee – innumerable cups. There was usually one of my men in the café with him, but I changed them every twenty minutes or so irregularly. More than an hour passed. Martins had long given up hope and so had I, where I waited at the end of a phone several streets away, with a party of the sewer police ready to go down if it became necessary. We were luckier than Martins because we were warm in our great boots up to the thighs and our reefer jackets. One man had a small searchlight about half as big again as a car headlight strapped to his breast, and another man carried a brace of Roman candles. The telephone rang. It was Martins. He said, 'I'm perishing with cold. It's a quarter past one. Is there any point in going on with this?'

'You shouldn't telephone. You must stay in sight.'

'I've drunk seven cups of this filthy coffee. My stomach won't stand much more.'

'He can't delay much longer if he's coming. He won't want to run into the two o'clock patrol. Stick it another quarter of an hour, but keep away from the telephone.'

Martins' voice said suddenly, 'Christ, he's here! He's – ' and then the telephone went dead. I said to my assistant, 'Give the signal to guard all manholes,' and to my sewer police, 'We are going down.'

What had happened was this. Martins was still on the telephone to me when Harry Lime came into the café. I don't know what he heard, if he heard anything. The mere sight of a man wanted by the police and without friends in Vienna speaking on the telephone would have been enough to warn him. He was out of the café again before Martins had put down the receiver. It was one of those rare moments when none of my men was in the café. One had just left and another was on the pavement about to come in. Harry Lime brushed by him and made for the kiosk. Martins came out of the café and saw my man. If he had called out then it would have been an easy shot, but I suppose it was not Lime, the penicillin racketeer, who was escaping down the street; it was Harry. Martins hesitated just long enough for Lime to put the kiosk between them; then he called out, 'That's him,' but Lime had already gone to ground.

What a strange world unknown to most of us lies under our feet: we live above a cavernous land of waterfalls and rushing rivers, where tides ebb and flow as in the world above. If you have ever read the adventures of Allan Quatermain and the account of his voyage along the underground river to the city of Milosis, you will be able to picture the scene of Lime's last stand. The main sewer, half as wide as the Thames, rushes by under a huge arch, fed by tributary streams: these streams have fallen in waterfalls from higher levels and have been purified in their fall, so that only in these side channels is the air foul. The main stream smells sweet and fresh with a faint tang of ozone, and everywhere in the darkness is the sound of falling and rushing water. It was just past high tide when Martins and the policeman reached the river: first the curving iron staircase, then a short passage so low they had to stoop, and then the shallow edge of the water lapped at their feet. My man shone his torch along the edge of the current and said, 'He's gone that way,' for just as a deep stream when it shallows at the rim leaves an accumulation of debris, so the sewer left in the quiet water against the wall a scum of orange peel, old cigarette cartons and the like, and in this scum Lime had left his trail as unmistakably as if he had walked in mud. My policeman shone his torch ahead with his left hand, and carried his gun in his right. He said to Martins, 'Keep behind me, sir, the bastard may shoot.'

'Then why the hell should you be in front?'

'It's my job, sir.' The water came halfway up their legs as they walked; the policeman kept his torch pointing down and ahead at the disturbed trail at the sewer's edge. He said, 'The silly thing is the bastard doesn't stand a chance. The manholes are all guarded and we've cordoned off the way into the Russian zone. All our chaps have to do now is to sweep

inwards down the side passages from the manholes.'
He took a whistle out of his pocket and blew, and
very far away, here and again there, came the notes
of a reply. He said, 'They are all down here now.
The sewer police, I mean. They know this place just
as I know the Tottenham Court Road. I wish my old
woman could see me now,' he said, lifting his torch
for a moment to shine it ahead, and at that moment
the shot came. The torch flew out of his hand and
fell in the stream. He said, 'God blast the bastard!'

'Are you hurt?'

'Scraped my hand, that's all. A week off work.
Here, take this other torch, sir, while I tie my hand
up. Don't shine it. He's in one of the side passages.'
For a long time the sound of the shot went on
reverberating; when the last echo died a whistle blew
ahead of them, and Martins' companion blew an
answer.

Martins said, 'It's an odd thing – I don't even know
your name.'

'Bates, sir.' He gave a low laugh in the darkness.
'This isn't my usual beat. Do you know the Horse-
shoe, sir?'

'Yes.'

'And the Duke of Grafton?'

'Yes.'

'Well, it takes a lot to make a world.'

Martins said, 'Let me come in front. I don't think
he'll shoot at me, and I want to talk to him.'

'I had orders to look after you, sir. Careful.'

'That's all right.' He edged round Bates, plunging
a foot deeper in the stream as he went. When he was
in front he called out, 'Harry,' and the name sent up
an echo, 'Harry, Harry, Harry!' that travelled down

the stream and woke a whole chorus of whistles in the darkness. He called again, 'Harry. Come out. It's no use.'

A voice startlingly close made them hug the wall. 'Is that you, old man?' it called. 'What do you want me to do?'

'Come out. And put your hands above your head.'

'I haven't a torch, old man. I can't see a thing.'

'Be careful, sir,' Bates said.

'Get flat against the wall. He won't shoot at me,' Martins said. He called, 'Harry, I'm going to shine the torch. Play fair and come out. You haven't got a chance.' He flashed the torch on, and twenty feet away, at the edge of the light and the water, Harry stepped into view. 'Hands above the head, Harry.' Harry raised his hand and fired. The shot ricocheted against the wall a foot from Martins' head, and he heard Bates cry out. At the same moment a searchlight from fifty yards away lit the whole channel, caught Harry in its beams, then Martins, then the staring eyes of Bates slumped at the water's edge with the sewage washing to his waist. An empty cigarette carton wedged into his armpit and stayed. My party had reached the scene.

Martins stood dithering there above Bates's body, with Harry Lime halfway between us. We couldn't shoot for fear of hitting Martins, and the light of the searchlight dazzled Lime. We moved slowly on, our revolvers trained for a chance, and Lime turned this way and that way like a rabbit dazzled by headlights; then suddenly he took a flying jump into the deep central rushing stream. When we turned the searchlight after him he was submerged, and the current of the sewer carried him rapidly on, past the body of

Bates, out of the range of the searchlight into the dark. What makes a man, without hope, cling to a few more minutes of existence? Is it a good quality or a bad one? I have no idea.

Martins stood at the outer edge of the searchlight beam, staring downstream. He had his gun in his hand now, and he was the only one of us who could fire with safety. I thought I saw a movement and called out to him, 'There. There. Shoot.' He lifted his gun and fired, just as he had fired at the same command all those years ago on Brickworth Common, fired, as he did then, inaccurately. A cry of pain came tearing back like calico down the cavern: a reproach, an entreaty? 'Well done,' I called and halted by Bates's body. He was dead. His eyes remained blankly open as we turned the searchlight on him; somebody stooped and dislodged the carton and threw it in the river, which whirled it on – a scrap of yellow Gold Flake: he was certainly a long way from the Tottenham Court Road.

I looked up and Martins was out of sight in the darkness. I called his name and it was lost in a confusion of echoes, in the rush and the roar of the underground river. Then I heard a third shot.

Martins told me later, 'I walked downstream to find Harry, but I must have missed him in the dark. I was afraid to lift the torch: I didn't want to tempt him to shoot again. He must have been struck by my bullet just at the entrance of a side passage. Then I suppose he crawled up the passage to the foot of the iron stairs. Thirty feet above his head was the manhole, but he wouldn't have had the strength to lift it, and even if he had succeeded the police were waiting above. He must have known all that, but he was in great pain, and just as an animal creeps into the dark to die, so I suppose a man makes for the light. He wants to die at home, and the darkness is never home to *us*. He began to pull himself up the stairs, but then the pain took him and he couldn't go on. What made him whistle that absurd scrap of a tune I'd been fool enough to believe he had written himself? Was he trying to attract attention, did he want a friend with him, even the friend who had trapped him, or was he delirious and had he no purpose at all? Anyway I heard his whistle and came back along the edge of the stream, and felt where the wall ended and found my way up the passage where he lay. I said, "Harry," and the whistling stopped, just above my head. I put my hand on an iron hand-rail, and climbed. I was still afraid he might shoot. Then, only three steps up, my foot stamped down on his hand, and he was there. I shone my torch on him: he hadn't got a gun; he must have dropped it when my bullet hit him. For a moment I thought he was dead, but then he whimpered with pain. I said, "Harry," and he swivelled his eyes with a great effort to my face. He was trying to speak, and I bent down to listen. "Bloody fool," he said – that was all. I don't know whether he meant that for himself – some sort of act of contrition, however inadequate (he was a Catholic) – or was it for me, with my thousand a year taxed and my imaginary cattle-rustlers – who couldn't even shoot a rabbit clean? Then he began to whimper again. I couldn't bear it any more and I put a bullet through him.'

'We'll forget that bit,' I said.

Martins said, 'I never shall.'

17

A thaw set in that night, and all over Vienna the snow melted, and the ugly ruins came to light again; steel rods hanging like stalactites, and rusty girders thrusting like bones through the grey slush. Burials were much simpler than they had been a week before, when electric drills had been needed to break the frozen ground. It was almost as warm as a spring day when Harry Lime had his second funeral. I was glad to get him under the earth again, but it had taken two men's deaths. The group by the grave was smaller now: Kurtz wasn't there, nor Winkler – only the girl and Rollo Martins and myself. And there weren't any tears.

After it was over the girl walked away without a word to either of us down the long avenue of trees that led to the main entrance and the tram stop, splashing through the melted snow. I said to Martins, 'I've got transport. Can I give you a lift?'

'No,' he said, 'I'll take a tram back.'

'You win. You've proved me a bloody fool.'

'I haven't won,' he said. 'I've lost.' I watched him striding off on his overgrown legs after the girl. He caught her up and they walked side by side. I don't think he said a word to her: it was like the end of a story except that before they turned out of my sight her hand was through his arm – which is how a story usually begins. He was a very bad shot and a very bad judge of character, but he had a way with Westerns (a trick of tension) and with girls (I wouldn't know what). And Crabbin? Oh, Crabbin is still arguing with the British Council about Dexter's expenses. They say they can't pass simultaneous payments in Stockholm and Vienna. Poor Crabbin. Poor all of us, when you come to think of it.

MAY WE BORROW YOUR HUSBAND?
and Other Comedies of the Sexual Life

*Cling to the virtues normally
manifested by all Lebanese*

PRIME MINISTER SAMI-AS-SULH

May We Borrow Your Husband?

I never heard her called anything else but Poopy, either by her husband or by the two men who became their friends. Perhaps I was a little in love with her (absurd though that may seem at my age), because I found that I resented the name. It was unsuited to someone so young and so open – too open; she belonged to the age of trust just as I belonged to the age of cynicism. 'Good old Poopy' – I even heard her called that by the elder of the two interior-decorators (who had known her no longer than I had): a sobriquet which might have been good enough for some vague bedraggled woman of middle age who drank a bit too much but who was useful to drag around as a kind of blind – and those two certainly needed a blind. I once asked the girl her real name, but all she said was, 'Everyone calls me Poopy,' as though that finished it, and I was afraid of appearing too square if I pursued the question further – too middle-aged perhaps as well, so though I hate the name whenever I write it down, Poopy she has to remain: I have no other.

I had been at Antibes working on a book of mine, a biography of the seventeenth-century poet, the Earl of Rochester, for more than a month before Poopy and her husband arrived. I had come there as soon as the full season was over, to a small ugly hotel by the sea not far from the ramparts, and I was able to watch the season depart with the leaves in the Boulevard Général Leclerc. At first, even before the trees had begun to drop, the foreign cars were on the move homeward. A few weeks earlier, I had counted cars from fourteen nations, including Morocco, Turkey, Sweden and Luxembourg, between the sea and the Place de Gaulle, to which I walked every day for the English papers. Now all the foreign number-plates had gone, except for the Belgian and the German and an occasional English one, and, of course, the ubiquitous number-plates of the State of Monaco. The cold weather had come early and Antibes catches only the morning sun – good enough for breakfast on the terrace, but it was safer to lunch indoors or the shadow might overtake the coffee. A cold and solitary Algerian was always there, leaning over the ramparts, looking for something, perhaps safety.

It was the time of year I liked best, when Juan les Pins becomes as squalid as a closed funfair, with Lunar Park boarded up and cards marked *Fermeture Annuelle* outside the Pam-Pam and Maxim's and the Concours International Amateur de Striptease at the Vieux Colombiers over for another season. Then Antibes comes into its own as a small country town with the Auberge de Provence full of local people and old men sit indoors drinking beer or pastis at the *glacier* in the Place de Gaulle. The small garden, which forms a roundabout on the ramparts, looks a little sad with the short stout palms bowing their brown fronds; the sun in the morning shines without any glare, and the few white sails move gently on the unblinding sea.

You can always trust the English to stay on longer than others into the autumn. We have a blind faith in the southern sun and we are taken by surprise when the wind blows icily over the Mediterranean. Then a bickering war develops with the hotel-keeper over the heating on the third floor, and the tiles strike cold underfoot. For a man who has reached the age when all he wants is some good wine and some good cheese and a little work, it is the best season of all. I know how I resented the arrival of the interior-decorators just at the moment when I had hoped to be the only foreigner left, and I prayed that they were birds of passage. They arrived before lunch in a scarlet Sprite – a car much too young for them, and they wore elegant sports clothes more suited to spring at the Cap. The elder man was nearing fifty and the grey hair that waved over his ears was too uniform to be true; the younger had passed thirty and his hair was as black as the other's was grey. I knew their names were Stephen and Tony before they even reached the reception desk, for they had clear, penetrating yet superficial voices, like their gaze, which had quickly lighted on me where I sat with a Ricard on the terrace and registered that I had nothing of interest for them and passed on. They were not arrogant: it was simply that they were more concerned with each other, and yet perhaps, like a married couple of some years' standing, not very profoundly.

I soon knew a great deal about them. They had rooms side by side in my passage, though I doubt if both rooms were often occupied, for I used to hear voices from one room or the other most evenings when I went to bed. Do I seem too curious about other people's affairs? But in my own defence I have to say that the events of this sad little comedy were forced by all the participants on my attention. The balcony where I worked every morning on my life of Rochester overhung the terrace where the interior-decorators took their coffee, and even when they occupied a table out of sight those clear elocutionary voices mounted up to me. I didn't want to hear them; I wanted to work. Rochester's relations with the actress, Mrs Barry, were my concern at the moment, but it is almost impossible in a foreign land not to listen to one's own tongue. French I could have accepted as a kind of background noise, but I could not fail to overhear English.

'My dear, guess who's written to me now?'

'Alec?'

'No, Mrs Clarenty.'

'What does the old hag want?'

'She objects to the mural in her bedroom.'

'But, Stephen, it's divine. Alec's never done anything better. The dead faun . . . '

'I think she wants something more nubile and less necrophilous.'

'The old lecher.'

They were certainly hardy, those two. Every morning around eleven they went bathing off the little rocky peninsula opposite the hotel – they had the autumnal Mediterranean, so far as the eye could see, entirely to themselves. As they walked briskly back in their elegant bikinis, or sometimes ran a little way for warmth, I had the impression that they took their bathes less for pleasure than for exercise – to preserve the slim legs, the flat stomachs, the narrow hips for more recondite and Etruscan pastimes.

Idle they were not. They drove the Sprite to Cagnes, Vence, St Paul, to any village where an antique store was to be rifled, and they brought back with them objects of olive wood, spurious old lanterns, painted religious figures which in the shop would have seemed to me ugly or banal, but which I suspect already fitted in their imaginations some scheme of decoration the reverse of commonplace. Not that their minds were altogether on their profession. They relaxed.

I encountered them one evening in a little sailors' bar in the old port of Nice. Curiosity this time had led me in pursuit, for I had seen the scarlet Sprite standing outside the bar. They were entertaining a boy of about eighteen who, from his clothes, I imagine worked as a hand on the boat to Corsica which was at the moment in harbour. They both looked very sharply at me when I entered, as though they were thinking, 'Have we misjudged him?' I drank a glass of beer and left, and the younger said 'Good-evening' as I passed the table. After that we had to greet each other every day in the hotel. It was as though I had been admitted to an intimacy.

Time for a few days was hanging as heavily on my hands as on Lord Rochester's. He was staying at Mrs Fourcard's baths in Leather Lane, receiving mercury treatment for the pox, and I was awaiting a whole section of my notes which I had inadvertently left in London. I couldn't release him till they came, and my sole distraction for a few days was those two. As they packed themselves into the Sprite of an afternoon or an evening I liked to guess from their clothes the nature of their excursion. Always elegant, they were yet successful, by the mere exchange of one *tricot* for another, in indicating their mood: they were just as well dressed in the sailors' bar, but a shade more simply; when dealing with a Lesbian antique dealer at St Paul, there was a masculine dash about their handkerchiefs. Once they disappeared altogether for the inside of a week in what I took to be their oldest clothes, and when they returned the older man had a contusion on his right cheek. They told me they had been over to Corsica. Had they enjoyed it? I asked.

'Quite barbaric,' the young man Tony said, but not, I thought, in praise.

He saw me looking at Stephen's cheek, and he added quickly, 'We had an accident in the mountains.'

It was two days after that, just at sunset, that Poopy arrived with her husband. I was back at work on Rochester, sitting in an overcoat on my balcony, when a taxi drove up – I recognised the driver as someone who plied regularly from Nice airport. What I noticed first, because the passengers were still hidden, was the luggage, which was bright blue and of an astonishing newness. Even the initials – rather absurdly PT – shone like newly minted coins. There were a large suitcase and a small suitcase and a hat-box, all of the same cerulean hue, and after that a respectable old leather case totally unsuited to air travel, the kind one inherits from a father, with half a label still left from Shepheard's Hotel or the Valley of the Kings. Then the passengers emerged and I saw Poopy for the first time. Down below, the interior-decorators were watching too, and drinking Dubonnet.

She was a very tall girl, perhaps five feet nine, very slim, very young, with hair the colour of conkers, and her costume was as new as the luggage. She said, 'Finalmente,' looking at the undistinguished façade with an air of rapture – or perhaps it was only the shape of her eyes. When I saw the young man I felt certain they were just married; it wouldn't have surprised me if confetti had fallen out from the seams of their clothes. They were like a photograph in the *Tatler*; they had camera smiles for each other and an underlying nervousness. I was sure they had come straight from the reception, and that it had been a smart one, after a proper church wedding.

They made a very handsome couple as they hesitated a moment before going up the steps to the reception. The long beam of the Phare de la Garoupe brushed the water behind them, and the floodlighting went suddenly on outside the hotel as if the manager had been waiting for their arrival to turn it up. The two decorators sat there without drinking, and I noticed that the elder one had covered the contusion on his cheek with a very clean white handkerchief. They were not, of course, looking at the girl but at the boy. He was over six feet tall and as slim as the girl, with a face that might have been cut on a coin, completely handsome and completely dead – but perhaps that was only an effect of his nerves. His clothes, too, I thought, had been bought for the occasion, the sports-jacket with a double slit and the grey trousers cut a little narrowly to show off the long legs. It seemed to me that they were both too young to marry – I doubt if they had accumulated forty-five years between them – and I had a wild impulse to lean over the balcony and warn them away – 'Not this hotel. Any hotel but this.' Perhaps I could have told them that the heating was insufficient or the hot water erratic or the food terrible, not that the English care much about food, but of course they would have paid me no attention – they were so obviously 'booked', and what an ageing lunatic I should have appeared in their eyes. ('One of those eccentric English types one finds abroad' – I could imagine the letter home.) This was the first time I wanted to interfere, and I didn't know them at all. The second time it was already too late, but I think I shall always regret that I did not give way to that madness . . .

It had been the silence and attentiveness of those two down below which had frightened me, and the patch of white handkerchief hiding the shameful contusion. For the first time I heard the hated name: 'Shall we see the room, Poopy, or have a drink first?'

They decided to see the room, and the two glasses of Dubonnet clicked again into action.

I think she had more idea of how a honeymoon should be conducted than he had, because they were not seen again that night.

2

I was late for breakfast on the terrace, but I noticed that Stephen and Tony were lingering longer than usual. Perhaps they had decided at last that it was too cold for a bathe; I had the impression, however, that they were lying in wait. They had never been so friendly to me before, and I wondered whether perhaps they regarded me as a kind of cover, with my distressingly normal appearance. My table for some reason that day had been shifted and was out of the sun, so Stephen suggested that I should join theirs: they would be off in a moment, after one more cup . . . The contusion was much less noticeable today, but I think he had been applying powder.

'You staying here long?' I asked them, conscious of how clumsily I constructed a conversation compared with their easy prattle.

'We had meant to leave tomorrow,' Stephen said, 'but last night we changed our minds.'

'Last night?'

'It was such a beautiful day, wasn't it? "Oh," I said to Tony, "surely we can leave poor dreary old London a little longer?" It has an awful staying power – like a railway sandwich.'

'Are your clients so patient?'

'My dear, the clients? You never in your life saw such atrocities as we get from Brompton Square. It's always the same. People who pay others to decorate for them have ghastly taste themselves.'

'You do the world a service then. Think what we might suffer without you. In Brompton Square.'

Tony giggled, 'I don't know how we'd stand it if we had not our private jokes. For example, in Mrs Clarenty's case, we've installed what we call the Loo of Lucullus.'

'She was enchanted,' Stephen said.

'The most obscene vegetable forms. It reminded me of a harvest festival.'

They suddenly became very silent and attentive, watching somebody over my shoulder. I looked back. It was Poopy, all by herself. She stood there, waiting for the boy to show her which table she could take, like a new girl at school who doesn't know the rules. She even seemed to be wearing a school uniform: very tight trousers, slit at the ankle – but she hadn't realised that the summer term was over. She had dressed up like that, I felt certain, so as not to be noticed, in order to hide herself, but there were only two other women on the terrace and they were both wearing sensible tweed skirts. She looked at them nostalgically as the waiter led her past our table to one nearer the sea. Her long legs moved awkwardly in the pants as though they felt exposed.

'The young bride,' Tony said.

'Deserted already,' Stephen said with satisfaction.

'Her name is Poopy Travis, you know.'

'It's an extraordinary name to choose. She couldn't have been *christened* that way, unless they found a very liberal vicar.'

'He is called Peter. Of an undefined occupation. Not Army, I think, do you?'

'Oh no, not Army. Something to do with land perhaps – there's an agreeable *herbal* smell about him.'

'You seem to know nearly all there is to know,' I said.

'We looked at their police *carnet* before dinner.'

'I have an idea,' Tony said, 'that PT hardly represents their activities last night.' He looked across the tables at the girl with an expression extraordinarily like hatred.

'We were both taken,' Stephen said, 'by the air of innocence. One felt he was more used to horses.'

'He mistook the yearnings of the rider's crotch for something quite different.'

Perhaps they hoped to shock me, but I don't think it was that. I really believe they were in a state of extreme sexual excitement; they had received a *coup de foudre* last night on the terrace and were quite incapable of disguising their feelings. I was an excuse to talk, to speculate about the desired object. The sailor had been a stopgap: this was the real thing. I was inclined to be amused, for what could this absurd pair hope to gain from a young man newly married to the girl who now sat there patiently waiting, wearing her beauty like an old sweater she had forgotten to change? But that was a bad simile to use: she would have been afraid to wear an old sweater, except secretly, by herself, in the playroom. She had no idea that she was one of those who can afford to disregard the fashion of their clothes. She caught my eye and, because I was so obviously English, I suppose, gave me half a timid smile. Perhaps I too would have received the *coup de foudre* if I had not been thirty years older and twice married.

Tony detected the smile. 'A regular body-snatcher,' he said. My breakfast and the young man arrived at the same moment before I had time to reply. As he passed the table I could feel the tension.

'Cuir de Russie,' Stephen said, quivering a nostril. 'A mistake of inexperience.'

The youth caught the words as he went past and turned with an astonished look to see who had spoken, and they both smiled insolently back at him as though they really believed they had the power to take him over . . .

For the first time I felt disquiet.

3

Something was not going well; that was sadly obvious. The girl nearly always came down to breakfast ahead of her husband – I have an idea he spent a long time bathing and shaving and applying his Cuir de Russie. When he joined her he would give her a courteous brotherly kiss as though they had not spent the night together in the same bed. She began to have those shadows under the eyes which come from lack of sleep – for I couldn't believe that they were 'the lineaments of gratified desire'. Sometimes from my balcony I saw them returning from a walk – nothing, except perhaps a pair of horses, could have been more handsome. His gentleness towards her might have reassured her mother, but it made a man impatient to see him squiring her across the undangerous road, holding open doors, following a pace behind her like the husband of a princess. I longed to see some outbreak of irritation caused by the sense of satiety, but they never seemed to be in conversation when they returned from their walk, and at table I caught only the kind of phrases people use who are dining together for the sake of politeness. And yet I could swear that she loved him, even by the way she avoided watching him. There was nothing avid or starved about her; she stole her quick glances when she was quite certain that his attention was absorbed elsewhere – they were tender, anxious perhaps, quite undemanding. If one enquired after him when he wasn't there, she glowed with the pleasure of using his name. 'Oh, Peter overslept this morning.' 'Peter cut himself. He's staunching the blood now.' 'Peter's mislaid his tie. He thinks the floor-waiter has purloined it.' Certainly she loved him; I was far less certain of what his feelings were.

And you must imagine how all the time those other two were closing in. It was like a medieval siege: they dug their trenches and threw up their earthworks. The difference was that the besieged didn't notice what they were at – at any rate, the girl didn't; I don't know about him. I longed to warn her, but what could I have said that wouldn't have shocked her or

angered her? I believe the two would have changed
their floor if that would have helped to bring them
closer to the fortress; they probably discussed the
move together and decided against it as too overt.

Because they knew that I could do nothing against
them, they regarded me almost in the role of an ally.
After all, I might be useful one day in distracting the
girl's attention – and I suppose they were not quite
mistaken in that; they could tell from the way I
looked at her how interested I was, and they
probably calculated that my interests might in the
long run coincide with theirs. It didn't occur to them
that, perhaps, I was a man with scruples. If one
really wanted a thing scruples were obviously, in
their eyes, out of place. There was a tortoiseshell star
mirror at St Paul they were plotting to obtain for half
the price demanded (I think there was an old mother
who looked after the shop when her daughter was
away at a *boîte* for women of a certain taste);
naturally, therefore, when I looked at the girl, as
they saw me so often do, they considered I would be
ready to join in any 'reasonable' scheme.

'When I looked at the girl' – realise that I have
made no real attempt to describe her. In writing a
biography one can, of course, just insert a portrait
and the affair is done: I have the prints of Lady
Rochester and Mrs Barry in front of me now. But
speaking as a professional novelist (for biography
and reminiscence are both new forms to me), one
describes a woman not so much that the reader
should see her in all the cramping detail of colour
and shape (how often Dickens's elaborate portraits
seem like directions to the illustrator which might
well have been left out of the finished book), but to

convey an emotion. Let the reader make his own image of a wife, a mistress, some passer-by 'sweet and kind' (the poet required no other descriptive words), if he has a fancy to. If I were to describe the girl (I can't bring myself at this moment to write her hateful name), it would be not to convey the colour of her hair, the shape of her mouth, but to express the pleasure and the pain with which I recall her – I, the writer, the observer, the subsidiary character, what you will. But if I didn't bother to convey them to her, why should I bother to convey them to you, *hypocrite lecteur*?

How quickly those two tunnelled. I don't think it was more than four mornings after the arrival that, when I came down to breakfast, I found they had moved their table next to the girl's and were entertaining her in her husband's absence. They did it very well; it was the first time I had seen her relaxed and happy – and she was happy because she was talking about Peter. Peter was agent for his father, somewhere in Hampshire – there were three thousand acres to manage. Yes, he was fond of riding and so was she. It all tumbled out – the kind of life she dreamed of having when she returned home. Stephen just dropped in a word now and then, of a rather old-fashioned courteous interest, to keep her going. Apparently he had once decorated some hall in their neighbourhood and knew the names of some people Peter knew – Winstanley, I think – and that gave her immense confidence.

'He's one of Peter's best friends,' she said, and the two flickered their eyes at each other like lizards' tongues.

'Come and join us, William,' Stephen said, but

only when he had noticed that I was within earshot. 'You know Mrs Travis?'

How could I refuse to sit at their table? And yet in doing so I seemed to become an ally.

'Not *the* William Harris?' the girl asked. It was a phrase which I hated, and yet she transformed even that with her air of innocence. For she had a capacity to make everything new: Antibes became a discovery and we were the first foreigners to have made it. When she said, 'Of course, I'm afraid I haven't actually *read* any of your books,' I heard the over-familiar remark for the first time; it even seemed to me a proof of her honesty – I nearly wrote her virginal honesty. 'You must know an awful lot about people,' she said, and again I read into the banality of the remark an appeal – for help against whom, those two or the husband who at that moment appeared on the terrace? He had the same nervous air as she, even the same shadows under the lids, so that they might have been taken by a stranger, as I wrote before, for brother and sister. He hesitated a moment when he saw all of us there and she called across to him, 'Come and meet these nice people, darling.' He didn't look any too pleased, but he sat glumly down and asked whether the coffee was still hot.

'I'll order some more, darling. They know the Winstanleys, and this is *the* William Harris.'

He looked at me blankly; I think he was wondering if I had anything to do with tweeds.

'I hear you like horses,' Stephen said, 'and I was wondering whether you and your wife would come to lunch with us at Cagnes on Saturday. That's tomorrow, isn't it? There's a very good racecourse at Cagnes . . .'

'I don't know,' he said dubiously, looking to his wife for a clue.

'But, darling, of course we must go. You'd love it.'

His face cleared instantly. I really believe he had been troubled by a social scruple: the question whether one accepts invitations on a honeymoon. 'It's very good of you,' he said, 'Mr . . . '

'Let's start as we mean to go on. I'm Stephen and this is Tony.'

'I'm Peter.' He added a trifle gloomily, 'And this is Poopy.'

'Tony, you take Poopy in the Sprite, and Peter and I will go by autobus.' (I had the impression, and I think Tony had too, that Stephen had gained a point.)

'You'll come too, Mr Harris?' the girl asked, using my surname as though she wished to emphasise the difference between me and them.

'I'm afraid I can't. I'm working against time.'

I watched them that evening from my balcony as they returned from Cagnes and, hearing the way they all laughed together, I thought, 'The enemy are within the citadel: it's only a question of time.' A lot of time, because they proceeded very carefully, those two. There was no question of a quick grab which I suspect had caused the contusion in Corsica.

4

It became a regular habit with the two of them to entertain the girl during her solitary breakfast before her husband arrived. I never sat at their table again, but scraps of the conversation would come over to me, and it seemed to me that she was never quite so cheerful again. Even the sense of novelty had gone. I heard her say once, 'There's so little to do here,' and it struck me as an odd observation for a honeymooner to make.

Then one evening I found her in tears outside the Musée Grimaldi. I had been fetching my papers, and, as my habit was, I made a round by the Place Nationale with the pillar erected in 1819 to celebrate – a remarkable paradox – the loyalty of Antibes to the monarchy and her resistance to the Troupes Etrangères, who were seeking to re-establish the monarchy. Then, according to rule, I went on by the market and the old port and Lou-Lou's restaurant up the ramp towards the cathedral and the Musée, and there in the grey evening light, before the street-lamps came on, I found her crying under the cliff of the château.

I noticed too late what she was at or I wouldn't have said, 'Good-evening, Mrs Travis.' She jumped a little as she turned and dropped her handkerchief, and when I picked it up I found it soaked with tears – it was like holding a small drowned animal in my hand. I said, 'I'm sorry,' meaning that I was sorry to have startled her, but she took it in quite another sense. She said, 'Oh, I'm being silly, that's all. It's just a mood. Everybody has moods, don't they?'

'Where's Peter?'

'He's in the museum with Stephen and Tony looking at the Picassos. I don't understand them a bit.'

'That's nothing to be ashamed of. Lots of people don't.'

'But Peter doesn't understand them either. I know he doesn't. He's just pretending to be interested.'

'Oh well . . .'

'And it's not that either. I pretended for a time too, to please Stephen. But he's pretending just to get away from me.'

'You are imagining things.'

Punctually at five o'clock the *phare* lit up, but it was still too light to see the beam.

I said, 'The museum will be closing now.'

'Walk back with me to the hotel.'

'Wouldn't you like to wait for Peter?'

'I don't smell, do I?' she asked miserably.

'Well, there's a trace of Arpège. I've always liked Arpège.'

'How terribly experienced you sound.'

'Not really. It's just that my first wife used to buy Arpège.'

We began walking back, and the mistral bit our ears and gave her an excuse when the time came for the reddened eyes.

She said, 'I think Antibes so sad and grey.'

'I thought you enjoyed it here.'

'Oh, for a day or two.'

'Why not go home?'

'It would look odd, wouldn't it, returning early from a honeymoon?'

'Or go on to Rome – or somewhere. You can get a plane to most places from Nice.'

'It wouldn't make any difference,' she said. 'It's not the place that's wrong, it's me.'

'I don't understand.'

'He's not happy with me. It's as simple as that.'

She stopped opposite one of the little rock houses by the ramparts. Washing hung down over the street below and there was a cold-looking canary in a cage.

'You said yourself . . . a mood . . . '

'It's not his fault,' she said. 'It's me. I expect it seems very stupid to you, but I never slept with anyone before I married.' She gulped miserably at the canary.

'And Peter?'

'He's terribly sensitive,' she said, and added quickly, 'That's a good quality. I wouldn't have fallen in love with him if he hadn't been.'

'If I were you, I'd take him home – as quickly as possible.' I couldn't help the words sounding sinister, but she hardly heard them. She was listening to the voices that came nearer down the ramparts – to Stephen's gay laugh. 'They're very sweet,' she said. 'I'm glad he's found friends.'

How could I say that they were seducing Peter before her eyes? And in any case wasn't her mistake already irretrievable? Those were two of the questions which haunted the hours, dreary for a solitary man, of the middle afternoon when work is finished and the exhilaration of the wine at lunch, and the time for the first evening drink has not yet come and the winter heating is at its feeblest. Had she no idea of the nature of the young man she had married? Had he taken her on as a blind or as a last desperate throw for normality? I couldn't bring myself to believe that. There was a sort of innocence about the boy which seemed to justify her love, and I preferred to think that he was not yet fully formed, that he had married honestly and it was only now that he found himself on the brink of a different experience. And yet if that were the case the comedy was all the crueller. Would everything have gone normally well if some conjunction of the planets had not crossed their honeymoon with that hungry pair of hunters?

I longed to speak out, and in the end I did speak, but not, so it happened, to her. I was going to my room and the door of one of theirs was open and I heard again Stephen's laugh – a kind of laugh which is sometimes with unintentional irony called infectious; it maddened me. I knocked and went in. Tony was stretched on a double bed and Stephen was 'doing' his hair, holding a brush in each hand and meticulously arranging the grey waves on either side. The dressing-table had as many pots on it as a woman's.

'You really mean he told you that?' Tony was saying. 'Why, how are you, William? Come in. Our young friend has been confiding in Stephen. Such really fascinating things.'

'Which of your young friends?' I asked.

'Why, Peter, of course. Who else? The secrets of married life.'

'I thought it might have been your sailor.'

'Naughty!' Tony said. 'But *touché* too, of course.'

'I wish you'd leave Peter alone.'

'I don't think he'd like that,' Stephen said. 'You can see that he hasn't quite the right tastes for this sort of honeymoon.'

'Now you happen to like women, William,' Tony said. 'Why not go after the girl? It's a grand opportunity. She's not getting what I believe is vulgarly called her greens.' Of the two he was easily the more brutal. I wanted to hit him, but this is not the century for that kind of romantic gesture, and anyway he was stretched out flat upon the bed. I said feebly enough – I ought to have known better than to have entered into a debate with those two – 'She happens to be in love with him.'

'I think Tony is right and she would find more satisfaction with you, William dear,' Stephen said, giving a last flick to the hair over his right ear – the contusion was quite gone now. 'From what Peter has said to me, I think you'd be doing a favour to both of them.'

'Tell him what Peter said, Stephen.'

'He said that from the very first there was a kind of hungry femininity about her which he found frightening and repulsive. Poor boy – he was really trapped into this business of marriage. His father wanted heirs – he breeds horses too, and then her mother – there's quite a lot of lucre with that lot. I don't think he had any idea of – of the Shape of Things to Come.' Stephen shuddered into the glass and then regarded himself with satisfaction.

Even today I have to believe for my own peace of mind that the young man had not really said those monstrous things. I believe, and hope, that the words were put into his mouth by that cunning dramatiser, but there is little comfort in the thought, for Stephen's inventions were always true to character. He even saw through my apparent indifference to the girl and realised that Tony and he had gone too far; it would suit their purpose, if I were driven to the wrong kind of action, or if, by their crudities, I lost my interest in Poopy.

'Of course,' Stephen said, 'I'm exaggerating. Undoubtedly he felt a bit amorous before it came to the point. His father would describe her, I suppose, as a fine filly.'

'What do you plan to do with him?' I asked. 'Do you toss up, or does one of you take the head and the other the tail?'

Tony laughed. 'Good old William. What a clinical mind you have.'

'And suppose,' I said, 'I went to her and recounted this conversation?'

'My dear, she wouldn't even understand. She's incredibly innocent.'

'Isn't he?'

'I doubt it – knowing our friend Colin Winstanley. But it's still a moot point. He hasn't given himself away yet.'

'We are planning to put it to the test one day soon,' Stephen said.

'A drive in the country,' Tony said. 'The strain's telling on him, you can see that. He's even afraid to take a siesta for fear of unwanted attentions.'

'Haven't you *any* mercy?' It was an absurd old-fashioned word to use to those two sophisticates. I felt more than ever square. 'Doesn't it occur to you that you may ruin her life – for the sake of your little game?'

'We can depend on you, William,' Tony said, 'to give her creature comforts.'

Stephen said, 'It's no game. You should realise we are saving *him*. Think of the life that he would lead – with all those soft contours lapping him around.' He added, 'Women always remind me of a damp salad – you know, those faded bits of greenery positively swimming . . .'

'Every man to his taste,' Tony said. 'But Peter's not cut out for that sort of life. He's very sensitive,' he said, using the girl's own words. There wasn't any more I could think of to say.

5

You will notice that I play a very unheroic part in this comedy. I could have gone direct, I suppose, to the girl and given her a little lecture on the facts of life, beginning gently with the regime of an English public school – he had worn a scarf of old-boy colours, until Tony had said to him one day at breakfast that he thought the puce stripe was an error of judgement. Or perhaps I could have protested to the boy himself, but, if Stephen had spoken the truth and he was under a severe nervous strain, my intervention would hardly have helped to ease it. There was no move I could make. I had just to sit there and watch while they made the moves carefully and adroitly towards the climax.

It came three days later at breakfast when, as usual, she was sitting alone with them, while her husband was upstairs with his lotions. They had never been more charming or more entertaining. As I arrived at my table they were giving her a really funny description of a house in Kensington that they had decorated for a dowager duchess who was passionately interested in the Napoleonic Wars. There was an ashtray, I remember, made out of a horse's hoof, guaranteed – so the dealer said – by Apsley House to have belonged to a grey ridden by Wellington at the Battle of Waterloo; there was an umbrella stand made out of a shell case found on the field of Austerlitz; a fire-escape made of a scaling ladder from Badajoz. She had lost half that sense of strain listening to them. She had forgotten her rolls and coffee; Stephen had her complete attention. I wanted to say to her, 'You little owl.' I wouldn't have been insulting her – she *had* got rather large eyes.

And then Stephen produced the master-plan. I could tell it was coming by the way his hands stiffened on his coffee-cup, by the way Tony lowered his eyes and appeared to be praying over his croissant. 'We were wondering, Poopy – may we borrow your husband?' I have never heard words spoken with more elaborate casualness.

She laughed. She hadn't noticed a thing. 'Borrow my husband?'

'There's a little village in the mountains behind Monte Carlo – Peille it's called – and I've heard rumours of a devastatingly lovely old bureau there – not for sale, of course, but Tony and I, we have our winning ways.'

'I've noticed that,' she said, 'myself.'

Stephen for an instant was disconcerted, but she meant nothing by it, except perhaps a compliment.

'We were thinking of having lunch at Peille and passing the whole day on the road so as to take a look at the scenery. The only trouble is there's no room in the Sprite for more than three, but Peter was saying the other day that you wanted some time to have a hair-do, so we thought . . .'

I had the impression that he was talking far too much to be convincing, but there wasn't any need for him to worry: she saw nothing at all. 'I think it's a marvellous idea,' she said. 'You know, he needs a little holiday from me. He's had hardly a moment to himself since I came up the aisle.' She was magnificently sensible, and perhaps even relieved. Poor girl. She needed a little holiday, too.

'It's going to be excruciatingly uncomfortable. He'll have to sit on Tony's knee.'

'I don't suppose he'll mind that.'

'And, of course, we can't guarantee the quality of food *en route*.'

For the first time I saw Stephen as a stupid man. Was there a shade of hope in that?

In the long run, of the two, notwithstanding his brutality, Tony had the better brain. Before Stephen had time to speak once more, Tony raised his eyes from the croissant and said decisively, 'That's fine. All's settled, and we'll deliver him back in one piece by dinner-time.'

He looked challengingly across at me. 'Of course, we hate to leave you alone for lunch, but I am sure William will look after you.'

'William?' she asked, and I hated the way she looked at me as if I didn't exist. 'Oh, you mean Mr Harris?'

I invited her to have lunch with me at Lou-Lou's in the old port – I couldn't very well do anything else – and at that moment the laggard Peter came out on to the terrace. She said quickly, 'I don't want to interrupt your work . . .'

'I don't believe in starvation,' I said. 'Work has to be interrupted for meals.'

Peter had cut himself again shaving and had a large blob of cottonwool stuck on his chin: it reminded me of Stephen's contusion. I had the impression, while he stood there waiting for someone to say something to him, that he knew all about the conversation; it had been carefully rehearsed by all three, the parts allotted, the unconcerned manner practised well beforehand, even the bit about the food . . . Now somebody had missed a cue, so I spoke.

'I've asked your wife to lunch at Lou-Lou's,' I said. 'I hope you don't mind.'

I would have been amused by the expression of quick relief on all three faces if I had found it possible to be amused by anything at all in the situation.

6

'And you didn't marry again after she left?'

'By that time I was getting too old to marry.'

'Picasso does it.'

'Oh, I'm not quite as old as Picasso.'

The silly conversation went on against a background of fishing-nets draped over a wallpaper with a design of wine-bottles – interior decoration again. Sometimes I longed for a room which had simply grown that way like the lines on a human face. The fish soup steamed away between us, smelling of garlic. We were the only guests there. Perhaps it was the solitude, perhaps it was the directness of her question, perhaps it was only the effect of the rosé, but quite suddenly I had the comforting sense that we were intimate friends. 'There's always work,' I said, 'and wine and a good cheese.'

'I couldn't be that philosophical if I lost Peter.'

'That's not likely to happen, is it?'

'I think I'd die,' she said, 'like someone in Christina Rossetti.'

'I thought nobody of your generation read her.'

If I had been twenty years older, perhaps, I could have explained that nothing is quite as bad as that, that at the end of what is called 'the sexual life' the only love which has lasted is the love that has accepted everything, every disappointment, every failure and every betrayal, which has accepted even the sad fact that in the end there is no desire so deep as the simple desire for companionship.

She wouldn't have believed me. She said, 'I used to weep like anything at that poem "Passing Away". Do you write sad things?'

'The biography I am writing now is sad enough. Two people tied together by love and yet one of them incapable of fidelity. The man dead of old age, burnt-out, at less than forty, and a fashionable preacher lurking by the beside to snatch his soul. No privacy even for a dying man; the bishop wrote a book about it.'

An Englishman who kept a chandler's shop in the old port was talking at the bar, and two old women who were part of the family knitted at the end of the room. A dog trotted in and looked at us and went away again with its tail curled.

'How long ago did all that happen?'

'Nearly three hundred years.'

'It sounded quite contemporary. Only now it would be the man from the *Mirror* and not a bishop.'

'That's why I wanted to write it. I'm not really interested in the past. I don't like costume-pieces.'

Winning someone's confidence is rather like the way some men set about seducing a woman; they circle a long way from their true purpose, they try to interest and amuse until finally the moment comes to strike. It came, so I wrongly thought, when I was adding up the bill. She said, 'I wonder where Peter is at this moment,' and I was quick to reply, 'What's going wrong between the two of you?'

She said, 'Let's go.'

'I've got to wait for my change.'

It was always easier to get served at Lou-Lou's than to pay the bill. At that moment everyone always had a habit of disappearing: the old woman (her knitting abandoned on the table), the aunt who helped to serve, Lou-Lou herself, her husband in his blue sweater. If the dog hadn't gone already he would have left at that moment.

I said, 'You forget – you told me that he wasn't happy.'

'Please, please find someone and let's go.'

So I disinterred Lou-Lou's aunt from the kitchen and paid. When we left, everyone seemed to be back again, even the dog.

Outside I asked her whether she wanted to return to the hotel.

'Not just yet – but I'm keeping you from your work.'

'I never work after drinking. That's why I like to start early. It brings the first drink nearer.'

She said that she had seen nothing of Antibes but the ramparts and the beach and the lighthouse, so I walked her around the small narrow back-streets where the washing hung out of the windows as in Naples and there were glimpses of small rooms overflowing with children and grandchildren; stone scrolls were carved over the ancient doorways of what had once been noblemen's houses; the pavements were blocked by barrels of wine and the streets by children playing at ball. In a low room on a ground floor a man sat painting the horrible ceramics which would later go to Vallauris to be sold to tourists in Picasso's old stamping-ground – spotted pink frogs and mauve fish and pigs with slits for coins.

She said, 'Let's go back to the sea.' So we returned

to a patch of hot sun on the bastion, and again I was tempted to tell her what I feared, but the thought that she might watch me with the blankness of ignorance deterred me. She sat on the wall and her long legs in the tight black trousers dangled down like Christmas stockings. She said, 'I'm not sorry that I married Peter,' and I was reminded of a song Edith Piaf used to sing, 'Je ne regrette rien'. It is typical of such a phrase that it is always sung or spoken with defiance.

I could only say again, 'You ought to take him home,' but I wondered what would have happened if I had said, 'You are married to a man who only likes men and he's off now picnicking with his boy friends. I'm thirty years older than you, but at least I have always preferred women and I've fallen in love with you and we could still have a few good years together before the time comes when you want to leave me for a younger man.' All I said was, 'He probably misses the country – and the riding.'

'I wish you were right, but it's really worse than that.'

Had she, after all, realised the nature of her problem? I waited for her to explain her meaning. It was a little like a novel which hesitates on the verge between comedy and tragedy. If she recognised the situation it would be a tragedy; if she were ignorant it was a comedy, even a farce – a situation between an immature girl too innocent to understand and a man too old to have the courage to explain. I suppose I have a taste for tragedy. I hoped for that.

She said, 'We didn't really know each other much before we came here. You know, weekend parties and the odd theatre – and riding, of course.'

I wasn't sure where her remarks tended. I said,

'These occasions are nearly always a strain. You are picked out of ordinary life and dumped together after an elaborate ceremony – almost like two animals shut in a cage who haven't seen each other before.'

'And now he sees me he doesn't like me.'

'You are exaggerating.'

'No.' She added, with anxiety, 'I won't shock you, will I, if I tell you things? There's nobody else I can talk to.'

'After fifty years I'm guaranteed shockproof.'

'We haven't made love – properly – once, since we came here.'

'What do you mean – properly?'

'He starts, but he doesn't finish; nothing happens.'

I said uncomfortably, 'Rochester wrote about that. A poem called "The Imperfect Enjoyment".' I don't know why I gave her this shady piece of literary information; perhaps, like a psychoanalyst, I wanted her not to feel alone with her problem. 'It can happen to anybody.'

'But it's not his fault,' she said. 'It's mine. I know it is. He just doesn't like my body.'

'Surely it's a bit late to discover that.'

'He'd never seen me naked till I came here,' she said with the candour of a girl to her doctor – that was all I meant to her, I felt sure.

'There are nearly always first-night nerves. And then if a man worries (you must realise how much it hurts his pride) he can get stuck in the situation for days – weeks even.' I began to tell her about a mistress I once had – we stayed together a very long time and yet for two weeks at the beginning I could do nothing at all. 'I was too anxious to succeed.'

'That's different. You didn't hate the sight of her.'

'You are making such a lot of so little.'

'That's what he tries to do,' she said with sudden schoolgirl coarseness and giggled miserably.

'We went away for a week and changed the scene, and everything after that was all right. For ten days it had been a flop, and for ten years afterwards we were happy. Very happy. But worry can get established in a room, in the colour of the curtains – it can hang itself up on coat-hangers; you find it smoking away in the ashtray marked Pernod, and when you look at the bed it pokes its head out from underneath like the toes of a pair of shoes.' Again I repeated the only charm I could think of, 'Take him home.'

'It wouldn't make any difference. He's disappointed, that's all it is.' She looked down at her long black legs; I followed the course of her eyes because I was finding now that I really wanted her and she said with sincere conviction, 'I'm just not pretty enough when I'm undressed.'

'You are talking real nonsense. You don't know what nonsense you are talking.'

'Oh, no, I'm not. You see – it started all right, but then he touched me' – she put her hands on her breasts – 'and it all went wrong. I always knew they weren't much good. At school we used to have dormitory inspection – it was awful. Everybody could grow them big except me. I'm no Jayne Mansfield, I can tell you.' She gave again that mirthless giggle. 'I remember one of the girls told me to sleep with a pillow on top – they said they'd struggle for release and what they needed was exercise. But of course it didn't work. I doubt if the idea was very scientific.' She added, 'I remember it was awfully hot at night like that.'

'Peter doesn't strike me,' I said cautiously, 'as a man who would want a Jayne Mansfield.'

'But you understand, don't you, that if he finds me ugly, it's all so hopeless.'

I wanted to agree with her – perhaps this reason which she had thought up would be less distressing than the truth, and soon enough there would be someone to cure her distrust. I had noticed before that it is often the lovely women who have the least confidence in their looks, but all the same I couldn't pretend to her that I understood it her way. I said, 'You must trust me. There's nothing at all wrong with you and that's why I'm talking to you the way I am.'

'You are very sweet,' she said, and her eyes passed over me rather as the beam from the lighthouse which at night went past the Musée Grimaldi and after a certain time returned and brushed all our windows indifferently on the hotel front. She continued, 'He said they'd be back by cocktail-time.'

'If you want a rest first' – for a little time we had been close, but now again we were getting further and further away. If I pressed her now she might in the end be happy – does conventional morality demand that a girl remains tied as she was tied? They'd been married in church; she was probably a good Christian, and I knew the ecclesiastical rules: at this moment of her life she could be free of him, the marriage could be annulled, but in a day or two it was only too probable that the same rules would say, 'He's managed well enough, you are married for life.'

And yet I couldn't press her. Wasn't I after all assuming far too much? Perhaps it was only a question of first-night nerves; perhaps in a little while the three of them would be back, silent, embarrassed, and Tony in his turn would have a contusion on his cheek. I would have been very glad to see it there; egotism fades a little with the passions which engender it, and I would have been content, I think, just to see her happy.

So we returned to the hotel, not saying much, and she went to her room and I to mine. It was in the end a comedy and not a tragedy, a farce even, which is why I have given this scrap of reminiscence a farcical title.

7

I was woken from my middle-aged siesta by the telephone. For a moment, surprised by the darkness, I couldn't find the light-switch. Scrambling for it, I knocked over my bedside lamp – the telephone went on ringing, and I tried to pick up the holder and knocked over a tooth-glass in which I had given myself a whisky. The little illuminated dial of my watch gleamed up at me marking 8.30. The telephone continued to ring. I got the receiver off, but this time it was the ashtray which fell over. I couldn't get the cord to extend up to my ear, so I shouted in the direction of the telephone, 'Hello!'

A tiny sound came up from the floor which I interpreted as 'Is that William?'

I shouted, 'Hold on,' and now that I was properly awake I realised the light-switch was just over my head (in London it was placed over the bedside table). Little petulant noises came up from the floor as I put on the light, like the creaking of crickets.

'Who's that?' I said rather angrily, and then I recognised Tony's voice.

'William, whatever's the matter?'

'Nothing's the matter. Where are you?'

'But there was quite an enormous crash. It hurt my eardrum.'

'An ashtray,' I said.

'Do you usually hurl ashtrays around?'

'I was asleep.'

'At 8.30? William! William!'

I said, 'Where are you?'

'A little bar in what Mrs Clarenty would call Monty.'

'You promised to be back by dinner,' I said.

'That's why I'm telephoning you. I'm being, *responsible*, William. Do you mind telling Poopy that we'll be a little late? Give her dinner. Talk to her as only you know how. We'll be back by ten.'

'Has there been an accident?'

I could hear him chuckling up the phone. 'Oh, I wouldn't call it an accident.'

'Why doesn't Peter call her himself?'

'He says he's not in the mood.'

'But what shall I tell her?' The telephone went dead.

I got out of bed and dressed and then I called her room. She answered very quickly; I think she must have been sitting by the telephone. I relayed the message, asked her to meet me in the bar, and rang off before I had to face answering any questions.

But I found it was not so difficult as I feared to cover up; she was immensely relieved that somebody had telephoned. She had sat there in her room from half-past seven onwards thinking of all the dangerous turns and ravines on the Grande Corniche, and when I rang she was half afraid that it might be the police or a hospital. Only after she had drunk two dry Martinis and laughed quite a lot at her fears did she say, 'I wonder why Tony rang you and not Peter me?'

I said (I had been working the answer out), 'I gather he suddenly had an urgent appointment – in the loo.'

It was as though I had said something enormously witty.

'Do you think they are a bit tight?' she asked.

'I wouldn't wonder.'

'Darling Peter,' she said, 'he deserved the day off,' and I couldn't help wondering in what direction his merit lay.

'Do you want another Martini?'

'I'd better not,' she said, 'you've made me tight too.'

I had become tired of the thin cold *rosé* so we had a bottle of real wine at dinner and she drank her full share and talked about literature. She had, it seemed, a nostalgia for Dornford Yates, had graduated in the sixth form as far as Hugh Walpole, and now she talked respectfully about Sir Charles Snow, who she obviously thought had been knighted, like Sir Hugh, for his services to literature. I must have been very much in love or I would have found her innocence almost unbearable – or perhaps I was a little tight as well. All the same, it was to interrupt her flow of critical judgements that I asked her what her real name was and she replied, 'Everyone calls me Poopy.' I remembered the PT stamped on her bags, but the only real names that I could think of at the moment were Patricia and Prunella. 'Then I shall simply call you You,' I said.

After dinner I had brandy and she had a kümmel. It was past 10.30 and still the three had not returned, but she didn't seem to be worrying any more about them. She sat on the floor of the bar beside me and every now and then the waiter looked in to see if he could turn off the lights. She leant against me with her hand on my knee and she said such things as, 'It must be wonderful to be a writer,' and in the glow of brandy and tenderness I didn't mind them a bit. I even began to tell her again about the Earl of Rochester. What did I care about Dornford Yates, Hugh Walpole or Sir Charles Snow? I was even in the mood to recite to her, hopelessly inapposite to the situation though the lines were:

> Then talk not of Inconstancy,
> False Hearts, and broken Vows;
> If I, by Miracle, can be
> This live-long Minute true to thee,
> 'Tis all that Heav'n allows . . .

when the noise – what a noise! – of the Sprite approaching brought us both to our feet. It was only too true that all that heaven allowed was the time in the bar at Antibes.

Tony was singing; we heard him all the way up the Boulevard Général Leclerc; Stephen was driving with the greatest caution, most of the time in second gear, and Peter, as we saw when we came out on to the terrace, was sitting on Tony's knee – nestling would be a better description – and joining in the refrain. All I could make out was:

> 'Round and white
> On a winter's night,
> The hope of the Queen's Navee.'

If they hadn't seen us on the steps I think they would have driven past the hotel without noticing.

'You *are* tight,' the girl said with pleasure. Tony put his arm round her and ran her up to the top of the steps. 'Be careful,' she said, 'William's made me tight too.'

'Good old William.'

Stephen climbed carefully out of the car and sank down on the nearest chair.

'All well?' I asked, not knowing what I meant.

'The children have been very happy,' he said, 'and very, very relaxed.'

'Got to go to the loo,' Peter said (the cue was in the wrong place), and made for the stairs. The girl gave him a helping hand and I heard him say, 'Wonderful day. Wonderful scenery. Wonderful . . . ' She turned at the top of the stairs and swept us with her smile, gay, reassured, happy. As on the first night, when they had hesitated about the cocktail, they didn't come down again. There was a long silence and then Tony chuckled. 'You seem to have had a wonderful day,' I said.

'Dear William, we've done a very good action. You've never seen him so *détendu*.'

Stephen sat saying nothing; I had the impression that today hadn't gone quite so well for him. Can people ever hunt quite equally in couples or is there always a loser? The too-grey waves of hair were as immaculate as ever, there was no contusion on the cheek, but I had the impression that the fear of the future had cast a long shadow.

'I suppose you mean you got him drunk?'

'Not with alcohol,' Tony said. 'We aren't vulgar seducers, are we, Stephen?' But Stephen made no reply.

'Then what was your good action?'

'Le pauvre petit Pierre. He was in such a state. He had quite convinced himself – or perhaps she had convinced him – that he was *impuissant*.'

'You seem to be making a lot of progress in French.'

'It sounds more delicate in French.'

'And with your help he found he wasn't?'

'After a little virginal timidity. Or near virginal. School hadn't left him quite unmoved. Poor Poopy. She just hadn't known the right way to go about things. My dear, he has a superb virility. Where are you going, Stephen?'

'I'm going to bed,' Stephen said flatly, and went up the steps alone. Tony looked after him, I thought with a kind of tender regret, a very light and superficial sorrow. 'His rheumatism came back very badly this afternoon,' he said. 'Poor Stephen.'

I thought it was well then to go to bed before I should become 'Poor William' too. Tony's charity tonight was all-embracing.

8

It was the first morning for a long time that I found myself alone on the terrace for breakfast. The women in tweed skirts had been gone for some days, and I had never before known 'the young men' to be absent. It was easy enough, while I waited for my coffee, to speculate about the likely reasons. There was, for example, the rheumatism . . . though I couldn't quite picture Tony in the character of a bedside companion. It was even remotely possible that they felt some shame and were unwilling to be confronted by their victim. As for the victim, I wondered sadly what painful revelation the night would certainly have brought. I blamed myself more than ever for not speaking in time. Surely she would have learned the truth more gently from me than from some tipsy uncontrolled outburst of her husband. All the same – such egoists are we in our passions – I was glad to be there in attendance . . . to staunch the tears . . . to take her tenderly in my arms, comfort her . . . oh, I had quite a romantic daydream on the terrace before she came down the steps and I saw that she had never had less need of a comforter.

She was just as I had seen her the first night: shy, excited, gay, with a long and happy future established in her eyes. 'William,' she said, 'can I sit at your table? Do you mind?'

'Of course not.'

'You've been so patient with me all the time I was in the doldrums. I've talked an awful lot of nonsense to you. I know you told me it was nonsense, but I didn't believe you and you were right all the time.'

I couldn't have interrupted her even if I had tried. She was a Venus at the prow sailing through sparkling seas. She said, 'Everything's all right. Everything. Last night – he loves me, William. He really does. He's not a bit disappointed with me. He was just tired and strained, that's all. He needed a day off alone – *détendu*.' She was even picking up Tony's French expressions second-hand. 'I'm afraid of nothing now, nothing at all. Isn't it strange how black life seemed only two days ago? I really believe if it hadn't been for you I'd have thrown in my hand. How lucky I was to meet you and the others too. They're such wonderful friends for Peter. We are all going home next week –

175

and we've made a lovely plot together. Tony's going to come down almost immediately we get back and decorate our house. Yesterday, driving in the country, they had a wonderful discussion about it. You won't know our house when you see it – oh, I forgot, you never *have* seen it, have you? You must come down when it's all finished – with Stephen.'

'Isn't Stephen going to help?' I just managed to slip in.

'Oh, he's too busy at the moment, Tony says, with Mrs Clarenty. Do you like riding? Tony does. He adores horses, but he has so little chance in London. It will be wonderful for Peter – to have someone like that because, after all, I can't be riding with Peter all day long, there will be a lot of things to do in the house, especially now, when I'm not accustomed. It's wonderful to think that Peter won't have to be lonely. He says there are going to be Etruscan murals in the bathroom – whatever Etruscan means; the drawing-room *basically* will be eggshell green and the dining-room walls Pompeian red. They really did an awful lot of work yesterday afternoon – I mean in their heads, while we were glooming around. I said to Peter, "As things are going now we'd better be prepared for a nursery," but Peter said Tony was content to leave all that side to me. Then there are the stables: they were an old coach-house once, and Tony feels we could restore a lot of the ancient character and there's a lamp he bought in St Paul which will just fit . . . it's endless the things there are to be done – a good six months' work, so Tony says, but luckily he can leave Mrs Clarenty to Stephen and concentrate on us. Peter asked him about the garden, but he's not a specialist in gardens. He said,

"Everyone to his own *métier*," and he's quite content if I bring in a man who knows all about roses.

'He knows Colin Winstanley too, of course, so there'll be quite a band of us. It's a pity the house won't be all ready for Christmas, but Peter says he's certain to have wonderful ideas for a really original tree. Peter thinks . . . '

She went on and on like that; perhaps I ought to have interrupted her even then; perhaps I should have tried to explain to her why her dream wouldn't last. Instead, I sat there silent, and presently I went to my room and packed – there was still one hotel open in the abandoned funfair of Juan between Maxim's and the boarded-up Striptease.

If I had stayed . . . who knows whether he could have kept on pretending for a second night? But I was just as bad for her as he was. If he had the wrong hormones, I had the wrong age. I didn't see any of them again before I left. She and Peter and Tony were out somewhere in the Sprite, and Stephen – so the receptionist told me – was lying late in bed with his rheumatism.

I planned a note for her, explaining rather feebly my departure, but when I came to write it I realised I had still no other name with which to address her than Poopy.

Beauty

The woman wore an orange scarf which she had so twisted around her forehead that it looked like a toque of the twenties, and her voice bulldozed through all opposition – the speech of her two companions, the young motorcyclist revving outside, even the clatter of soup plates in the kitchen of the small Antibes restaurant which was almost empty now that autumn had truly set in. Her face was familiar to me; I had seen it looking down from the balcony of one of the reconditioned houses on the ramparts, while she called endearments to someone or something invisible below. But I hadn't seen her since the summer sun had gone, and I thought she had departed with the other foreigners. She said, 'I'll be in Vienna for Christmas. I just love it there. Those lovely white horses – and the little boys singing Bach.'

Her companions were English; the man was struggling still to maintain the appearance of a summer visitor, but he shivered in secret every now and then in his blue cotton sports-shirt. He asked throatily, 'We won't see you then in London?' and his wife, who was much younger than either of them, said, 'Oh, but you simply must come.'

'There are difficulties,' she said. 'But if you two dear people are going to be in Venice in the spring . . . '

'I don't suppose we'll have enough money, will we, darling, but we'd love to show you London. Wouldn't we, darling?'

'Of course,' he said gloomily.

'I'm afraid that's quite, quite impossible, because of Beauty, you see.'

I hadn't noticed Beauty until then because he was so well behaved. He lay flat on the window-still as inert as a cream bun on a counter. I think he was the most perfect Pekinese I have ever seen – although I can't pretend to know the points a judge ought to look for. He would have been as white as milk if a little coffee had not been added, but that was hardly an imperfection – it enhanced his beauty. His eyes from where I sat seemed deep black, like the centre of a flower, and they were completely undisturbed by thought. This was not a dog to respond to the word 'rat' or to show a youthful enthusiasm if someone suggested a walk. Nothing less than his own image in a glass would rouse him, I imagined, to a flicker of interest. He was certainly well fed enough to ignore the meal that the others had left unfinished, though perhaps he was accustomed to something richer than langouste.

'You couldn't leave him with a friend?' the younger woman asked.

'Leave Beauty?' The question didn't rate a reply. She ran her fingers through the long café-au-lait hair, but the dog made no motion with his tail as a common dog might have done. He gave a kind of grunt like an old man in a club who has been disturbed by the waiter. 'All these laws of quarantine – why don't your congressmen do something about them?'

'We call them MPs,' the man said with what I thought was hidden dislike.

'I don't care what you call them. They live in the Middle Ages. I can go to Paris, to Vienna, Venice –

why, I could go to Moscow if I wanted, but I can't go to London without leaving Beauty in a horrible prison. With all kinds of undesirable dogs.'

'I think he'd have,' he hesitated with what I thought was admirable English courtesy as he weighed in the balance the correct term – cell? kennel? – 'a room of his own.'

'Think of the diseases he might pick up.' She lifted him from the window-sill as easily as she might have lifted a stole of fur and pressed him resolutely against her left breast; he didn't even grunt. I had the sense of something completely possessed. A child at least would have rebelled . . . for a time. Poor child. I don't know why I couldn't pity the dog. Perhaps he was too beautiful.

She said, 'Poor Beauty's thirsty.'

'I'll get him some water,' the man said.

'A half-bottle of Evian if you don't mind. I don't trust the tap-water.'

It was then that I left them, because the cinema in the Place de Gaulle opened at nine.

It was after eleven that I emerged again, and, since the night was fine, except for a cold wind off the Alps, I made a circuit from the Place and, as the ramparts would be too exposed, I took the narrow dirty streets off the Place Nationale – the Rue de Sade, the Rue des Bains . . . The dustbins were all out and dogs had made ordure on the pavements and children had urinated in the gutters. A patch of white, which I first took to be a cat, moved stealthily along the house-fronts ahead of me, then paused, and as I approached snaked behind a dustbin. I stood amazed and watched. A pattern of light through the slats of a shutter striped the road in yellow tigerish bars and presently Beauty slid out again and looked at me with his pansy face and black expressionless eyes. I think he expected me to lift him up, and he showed his teeth in warning.

'Why, Beauty,' I exclaimed. He gave his clubman grunt again and waited. Was he cautious because he found that I knew his name or did he recognise in my clothes and my smell that I belonged to the same class as the woman in the toque, that I was one who would disapprove of his nocturnal ramble? Suddenly he cocked an ear in the direction of the house on the ramparts; it was possible that he had heard a woman's voice calling. Certainly he looked dubiously up at me as though he wanted to see whether I had heard it too, and perhaps because I made no move he considered he was safe. He began to undulate down the pavement with a purpose, like the feather boa in the cabaret act which floats around seeking a top-hat. I followed at a discreet distance.

Was it memory or a keen sense of smell which affected him? Of all the dustbins in the mean street there was only one which had lost its cover – indescribable tendrils drooped over the top. Beauty – he ignored me as completely now as he would have ignored an inferior dog – stood on his hind legs with two delicately feathered paws holding the edge of the bin. He turned his head and looked at me, without expression, two pools of ink in which a soothsayer perhaps could have read an infinite series of predictions. He gave a scramble like an athlete raising himself on a parallel bar, and he was within the dustbin, and the feathered forepaws – I am sure I have read somewhere that the feathering is very important in a contest of Pekinese – were rooting and delving among the old vegetables, the empty cartons, the squashy fragments in the bin. He became excited and his nose went down like a pig after truffles. Then his back paws got into play, discarding the rubbish behind – old fruit-skins fell on the pavement and rotten figs, fish-heads . . . At last he had what he had come for – a long tube of intestine belonging to God knows what animal; he tossed it in the air, so that it curled round the milk-white throat. Then he abandoned the dustbin, and he galumphed down the street like a harlequin, trailing behind him the intestine which might have been a string of sausages.

I must admit I was wholly on his side. Surely any-thing was better than the embrace of a flat breast.

Round a turning he found a dark corner obviously more suited than all the others to gnawing an intestine because it contained a great splash of ordure. He tested the ordure first, like the clubman he was, with his nostrils, and then he rolled lavishly back on it, paws in the air, rubbing the café-au-lait fur in the dark shampoo, the intestines trailing from his mouth, while the satin eyes gazed imperturbably up at the great black Midi sky.

Curiosity took me back home, after all, by way of the ramparts, and there over the balcony the woman leant, trying, I suppose, to detect her dog in the shadows of the street below. 'Beauty!' I heard her call wearily, 'Beauty!' And then with growing impatience, 'Beauty! Come home! You've done your wee-wee, Beauty. Where are you, Beauty, Beauty?' Such small things ruin our sense of compassion, for surely, if it had not been for that hideous orange toque, I would have felt some pity for the old sterile thing, perched up there, calling for lost Beauty.

Chagrin in Three Parts

It was February in Antibes. Gusts of rain blew along the ramparts, and the emaciated statues on the terrace of the Château Grimaldi dripped with wet, and there was a sound absent during the flat blue days of summer, the continual rustle below the ramparts of the small surf. All along the Côte the summer restaurants were closed, but lights shone in Félix au Port and one Peugeot of the latest model stood in the parking-rank. The bare masts of the abandoned yachts stuck up like toothpicks and the last plane in the winter-service dropped, in a flicker of green, red and yellow lights, like Christmas-tree baubles, towards the airport of Nice. This was the Antibes I always enjoyed; and I was disappointed to find I was not alone in the restaurant as I was most nights of the week.

Crossing the road I saw a very powerful lady dressed in black who stared out at me from one of the window-tables, as though she were willing me not to enter, and when I came in and took my place before the other window, she regarded me with too evident distaste. My raincoat was shabby and my shoes were muddy and in any case I was a man. Momentarily, while she took me in, from balding top to shabby toe, she interrupted her conversation with the *patronne* who addressed her as Madame Dejoie.

Madame Dejoie continued her monologue in a tone of firm disapproval: it was unusual for Madame Volet to be late, but she hoped nothing had happened to her on the ramparts. In winter there were always Algerians about, she added with mysterious apprehension, as though she were talking of wolves, but none the less Madame Volet had refused Madame Dejoie's offer to be fetched from her home. 'I did not press her under the circumstances. Poor Madame Volet.' Her hand clutched a huge pepper-mill like a bludgeon and I pictured Madame Volet as a weak timid old lady, dressed too in black, afraid even of protection by so formidable a friend.

How wrong I was. Madame Volet blew suddenly in with a gust of rain through the side door beside my table, and she was young and extravagantly pretty, in her tight black pants, and with a long neck emerging from a wine-red polo-necked sweater. I was glad when she sat down side by side with Madame Dejoie, so that I need not lose the sight of her while I ate.

'I am late,' she said, 'I know that I am late. So many little things have to be done when you are alone, and I am not yet accustomed to being alone,' she added with a pretty little sob which reminded me of a cut-glass Victorian tear-bottle. She took off thick winter gloves with a wringing gesture which made me think of handkerchiefs wet with grief, and her hands looked suddenly small and useless and vulnerable.

'Pauvre cocotte,' said Madame Dejoie, 'be quiet here with me and forget awhile. I have ordered a bouillabaisse with langouste.'

'But I have no appetite, Emmy.'

'It will come back. You'll see. Now here is your porto and I have ordered a bottle of blanc de blancs.'

'You will make me *tout à fait saoule*.'

'We are going to eat and drink and for a little while we are both going to forget everything. I know exactly how you are feeling, for I too lost a beloved husband.'

'By death,' little Madame Volet said. 'That makes a great difference. Death is quite bearable.'

'It is more irrevocable.'

'Nothing can be more irrevocable than my situation. Emmy, he loves the little bitch.'

'All I know of her is that she has deplorable taste – or a deplorable hairdresser.'

'But that was exactly what I told him.'

'You were wrong. I should have told him, not you, for he might have believed me and in any case my criticism would not have hurt his pride.'

'I love him,' Madame Volet said, 'I cannot be prudent,' and then suddenly became aware of my presence. She whispered something to her companion, and I heard the reassurance, 'Un anglais.' I watched her as covertly as I could – like most of my fellow writers I have the spirit of a *voyeur* – and I wondered at how stupid married men could be. I was temporarily free, and I very much wanted to console her, but I didn't exist in her eyes, now she knew that I was English, nor in the eyes of Madame Dejoie. I was less than human – I was only a reject from the Common Market.

I ordered a small rouget and a half bottle of Pouilly and tried to be interested in the Trollope I had brought with me. But my attention strayed.

'I adored my husband,' Madame Dejoie was saying, and her hand again grasped the pepper-mill, but this time it looked less like a bludgeon.

'I still do, Emmy. That is the worst of it. I know that if he came back . . . '

'Mine can never come back,' Madame Dejoie retorted, touching the corner of one eye with her handkerchief and then examining the smear of black left behind.

In a gloomy silence they both drained their *portos*. Then Madame Dejoie said with determination, 'There is no turning back. You should accept that as I do. There remains for us only the problem of adaptation.'

'After such a betrayal I could never look at another man,' Madame Volet replied. At that moment she looked right through me. I felt invisible. I put my hand between the light and the wall to prove that I had a shadow, and the shadow looked like a beast with horns.

'I would never suggest another man,' Madame Dejoie said. 'Never.'

'What then?'

'When my poor husband died from an infection of the bowels I thought myself quite inconsolable, but I said to myself, Courage, courage. You must learn to laugh again.'

'To laugh,' Madame Volet exclaimed. 'To laugh at what?' But before Madame Dejoie could reply, Monsieur Félix had arrived to perform his neat surgical operation upon the fish for the bouillabaisse. Madame Dejoie watched with real interest; Madame Volet, I thought, watched for politeness' sake while she finished a glass of blanc de blancs.

When the operation was over Madame Dejoie filled the glasses and said, 'I was lucky enough to have *une amie* who taught me not to mourn for the past.' She raised her glass and cocking a finger as I had seen men do, she added, 'Pas de mollesse.'

'Pas de mollesse,' Madame Volet repeated with a wan enchanting smile.

I felt decidedly ashamed of myself – a cold literary observer of human anguish. I was afraid of catching poor Madame Volet's eyes (what kind of a man was capable of betraying her for a woman who took the wrong sort of rinse?) and I tried to occupy myself with sad Mr Crawley's courtship as he stumped up the muddy lane in his big clergyman's boots. In any case the two of them had dropped their voices; a gentle smell of garlic came to me from the bouillabaisse, the bottle of blanc de blancs was nearly finished, and, in spite of Madame Volet's protestation, Madame Dejoie had called for another. 'There are no half bottles,' she said. 'We can always leave something for the gods.' Again their voices sank to an intimate murmur as Mr Crawley's suit was accepted (though how he was to support an inevitably large family would not appear until the succeeding volume). I was startled out of my forced concentration by a laugh: a musical laugh: it was Madame Volet's.

'*Cochon*,' she exclaimed. Madame Dejoie regarded her over her glass (the new bottle had already been broached) under beetling brows. 'I am telling you the truth,' she said. 'He would crow like a cock.'

'But what a joke to play!'

'It began as a joke, but he was really proud of himself. Après seulement deux coups . . .'

'Jamais trois?' Madame Volet asked and she giggled and splashed a little of her wine down her polo-necked collar.

'Jamais.'

'Je suis saoule.'

'Moi aussi, cocotte.'

Madame Volet said, 'To crow like a cock – at least it was a fantaisie. My husband has no fantaisies. He is strictly classical.'

'Pas de vices?'

'Hélas, pas de vices.'

'And yet you miss him?'

'He worked hard,' Madame Volet said and giggled. 'To think that at the end he must have been working hard for both of us.'

'You found it a little boring?'

'It was a habit – how one misses a habit. I wake now at five in the morning.'

'At five?'

'It was the hour of his greatest activity.'

'My husband was a very small man,' Madame Dejoie said. 'Not in height, of course. He was two metres high.'

'Oh, Paul is big enough – but always the same.'

'Why do you continue to love that man?' Madame Dejoie sighed and put her large hand on Madame Volet's knee. She wore a signet-ring which perhaps had belonged to her late husband. Madame Volet sighed too and I thought melancholy was returning to the table, but then she hiccuped and both of them laughed.

'Tu es vraiment saoule, cocotte.'

'Do I truly miss Paul, or is it only that I miss his habits?' She suddenly met my eye and blushed right down into the wine-coloured wine-stained polo-necked collar.

Madame Dejoie repeated reassuringly, 'Un anglais – ou un américain.' She hardly bothered to lower her voice at all. 'Do you know how limited my experience was when my husband died? I loved him when he crowed like a cock. I was glad he was so pleased. I only wanted him to be pleased. I adored him, and yet in those days – j'ai peut-être joui trois fois par semaine. I did not expect more. It seemed to me a natural limit.'

'In my case it was three times a day,' Madame Volet said and giggled again. 'Mais toujours d'une façon classique.' She put her hands over her face and gave a little sob. Madame Dejoie put an arm round her shoulders. There was a long silence while the remains of the bouillabaisse were cleared away.

2

'Men are curious animals,' Madame Dejoie said at last. The coffee had come and they divided one *marc* between them, in turn dipping lumps of sugar which they inserted into one another's mouths. 'Animals too lack imagination. A dog has no *fantaisie*.'

'How bored I have been sometimes,' Madame Volet said. 'He would talk politics continually and turn on the news at eight in the morning. At eight! What do I care for politics? But if I asked his advice about anything important he showed no interest at all. With you I can talk about anything, about the whole world.'

'I adored my husband,' Madame Dejoie said, 'yet it was only after his death I discovered my capacity for love. With Pauline. You never knew Pauline. She died five years ago. I loved her more than I ever loved Jacques, and yet I felt no despair when she died. I

knew that it was not the end, for I knew by then my
capacity.'

'I have never loved a woman,' Madame Volet said.

'Chérie, then you do not know what love can mean.
With a woman you do not have to be content with
une façon classique three times a day.'

'I love Paul, but he is so different from me in every
way . . .'

'Unlike Pauline, he is a man.'

'Oh Emmy, you describe him so perfectly. How
well you understand. A man!'

'When you really think of it, how comic that little
object is. Hardly enough to crow about, one would
think.'

Madame Volet giggled and said, '*Cochon.*'

'Perhaps smoked like an eel one might enjoy it.'

'Stop it. Stop it.' They rocked up and down with
little gusts of laughter. They were drunk, of course,
but in the most charming way.

3

How distant now seemed Trollope's muddy lane, the
heavy boots of Mr Crawley, his proud shy courtship.
In time we travel a space as vast as any astronaut's.
When I looked up Madame Volet's head rested on
Madame Dejoie's shoulder. 'I feel so sleepy,' she said.

'Tonight you shall sleep, chérie.'

'I am so little good to you. I know nothing.'

'In love one learns quickly.'

'But am I in love?' Madame Volet asked, sitting
up very straight and staring into Madame Dejoie's
sombre eyes.

'If the answer were no, you wouldn't ask the question.'

'But I thought I could never love again.'

'Not another man,' Madame Dejoie said. 'Chérie, you are almost asleep. Come.'

'The bill?' Madame Volet asked as though perhaps she were trying to delay the moment of decision.

'I will pay tomorrow. What a pretty coat this is – but not warm enough, chérie, in February. You need to be cared for.'

'You've given me back my courage,' Madame Volet said. 'When I came in here I was *si démoralisée* . . . '

'Soon – I promise – you will be able to laugh at the past . . . '

'I have already laughed,' Madame Volet said. 'Did he really crow like a cock?'

'Yes.'

'I shall never be able to forget what you said about smoked eel. Never. If I saw one now . . . ' She began to giggle again and Madame Dejoie steadied her a little on the way to the door.

I watched them cross the road to the car-park. Suddenly Madame Volet gave a little hop and skip and flung her arms around Madame Dejoie's neck, and the wind, blowing through the archway of the port, carried the faint sound of her laughter to me where I sat alone *chez* Félix. I was glad she was happy again. I was glad that she was in the kind reliable hands of Madame Dejoie. What a fool Paul had been, I reflected, feeling chagrin myself now for so many wasted opportunities.

The Overnight Bag

The little man who came to the information desk in
Nice airport when they demanded 'Henry Cooper,
passenger on BEA flight 105 for London' looked like
a shadow cast by the brilliant glitter of the sun. He
wore a grey town-suit and black shoes; he had a grey
skin which carefully matched his suit, and since it was
impossible for him to change his skin, it was possible
that he had no other suit.

'Are you Mr Cooper?'

'Yes.' He carried a BOAC overnight bag and he
laid it tenderly on the ledge of the information desk as
though it contained something precious and fragile
like an electric razor.

'There is a telegram for you.'

He opened it and read the message twice over.

Bon voyage. Much missed. You will be welcome
home, dear boy. Mother.

He tore the telegram once across and left it on the
desk, from which the girl in the blue uniform, after a
discreet interval, picked the pieces and with natural
curiosity joined them together. Then she looked for
the little grey man among the passengers who were
now lining up at the tourist gate to join the Trident.
He was among the last, carrying his blue BOAC bag.

Near the front of the plane Henry Cooper found a
window-seat and placed the bag on the central seat
beside him. A large woman in pale blue trousers too

tight for the size of her buttocks took the third seat.
She squeezed a very large handbag in beside the other
on the central seat, and she laid a large fur coat on
top of both. Henry Cooper said, 'May I put it on the
rack, please?'

She looked at him with contempt. 'Put what?'

'Your coat.'

'If you want to. Why?'

'It's a very heavy coat. It's squashing my overnight
bag.'

He was so small he could stand nearly upright
under the rack. When he sat down he fastened the
seat-belt over the two bags before he fastened his
own. The woman watched him with suspicion. 'I've
never seen anyone do that before,' she said.

'I don't want it shaken about,' he said. 'There are
storms over London.'

'You haven't got an animal in there, have you?'

'Not exactly.'

'It's cruel to carry an animal shut up like that,' she
said, as though she disbelieved him.

As the Trident began its run he laid his hand on
the bag as if he were reassuring something within.
The woman watched the bag narrowly. If she saw
the least movement of life she had made up her
mind to call the stewardess. Even if it were only a
tortoise . . . A tortoise needed air, or so she supposed,
in spite of hibernation. When they were safely
airborne he relaxed and began to read a *Nice-Matin*
– he spent a good deal of time on each story as
though his French were not very good. The woman
struggled angrily to get her big cavernous bag from
under the seat-belt. She muttered 'Ridiculous' twice
for his benefit. Then she made up, put on thick

horn-rimmed glasses and began to reread a letter which began 'My darling Tiny' and ended 'Your own cuddly Bertha'. After a while she grew tired of the weight of the bag on her knees and dropped it on to the BOAC overnight bag.

The little man leapt in distress. 'Please,' he said, 'please.' He lifted her bag and pushed it quite rudely into a corner of the seat. 'I don't want it squashed,' he said. 'It's a matter of respect.'

'What have you got in your precious bag?' she asked him angrily.

'A dead baby,' he said. 'I thought I had told you.'

'On the left of the aircraft,' the pilot announced through the loudspeaker, 'you will see Montélimar. We shall be passing Paris in – '

'You are not serious,' she said.

'It's just one of those things,' he replied in a tone that carried conviction.

'But you can't take dead babies – like that – in a bag – in the economy class.'

'In the case of a baby it is so much cheaper than freight. Only a week old. It weighs so little.'

'But it should be in a coffin, not an overnight bag.'

'My wife didn't trust a foreign coffin. She said the materials they use are not durable. She's rather a conventional woman.'

'Then it's *your* baby?' Under the circumstances she seemed almost prepared to sympathise.

'My wife's baby,' he corrected her.

'What's the difference?'

He said sadly, 'There could well be a difference,' and turned the page of *Nice-Matin*.

'Are you suggesting . . . ?' But he was deep in a column dealing with a Lions Club meeting in Antibes and the rather revolutionary suggestion made there by a member from Grasse. She read over again her letter from 'cuddly Bertha', but it failed to hold her attention. She kept on stealing a glance at the overnight bag.

'You don't anticipate trouble with the customs?' she asked him after a while.

'Of course I shall have to declare it,' he said. 'It was acquired abroad.'

When they landed, exactly on time, he said to her with old-fashioned politeness, 'I have enjoyed our flight.' She looked for him with a certain morbid curiosity in the customs – Channel 10 – but then she saw him in Channel 12, for passengers carrying hand-baggage only. He was speaking, earnestly, to the officer who was poised, chalk in hand, over the overnight bag. Then she lost sight of him as her own inspector insisted on examining the contents of her cavernous bag, which yielded up a number of un-declared presents for Bertha.

Henry Cooper was the first out of the arrivals door and he took a hired car. The charge for taxis rose every year when he went abroad and it was his one extravagance not to wait for the airport-bus. The sky was overcast and the temperature only a little above freezing, but the driver was in a mood of euphoria. He had a dashing comradely air – he told Henry Cooper that he had won fifty pounds on the pools. The heater was on full blast, and Henry Cooper opened the window, but an icy current of air from Scandinavia flowed round his shoulders. He closed the window again and said, 'Would you mind turning off the heater?' It was as hot in the car as in a New York hotel during a blizzard.

'It's cold outside,' the driver said.

'You see,' Henry Cooper said, 'I have a dead baby in my bag.'

'Dead baby?'

'Yes.'

'Ah well,' the driver said, 'he won't feel the heat, will he? It's a he?'

'Yes. A he. I'm anxious he shouldn't – deteriorate.'

'They keep a long time,' the driver said. 'You'd be surprised. Longer than old people. What did you have for lunch?'

Henry Cooper was a little surprised. He had to cast his mind back. He said, 'Carré d'agneau à la provençale.'

'Curry?'

'No, not curry, lamb chops with garlic and herbs. And then an apple-tart.'

'And you drank something I wouldn't be surprised?'

'A half bottle of rosé. And a brandy.'

'There you are, you see.'

'I don't understand.'

'With all that inside you, *you* wouldn't keep so well.'

Gillette Razors were half hidden in icy mist. The driver had forgotten or had refused to turn down the heat, but he remained silent for quite a while, perhaps brooding on the subject of life and death.

'How did the little perisher die?' he asked at last.

'They die so easily,' Henry Cooper answered.

'Many a true word's spoken in jest,' the driver said, a little absent-mindedly because he had swerved to avoid a car which braked too suddenly, and Henry Cooper instinctively put his hand on the overnight bag to steady it.

'Sorry,' the driver said. 'Not my fault. Amateur drivers! Anyway, you don't need to worry – they can't bruise after death, or can they? I read something about it once in *The Cases of Sir Bernard Spilsbury*, but I don't remember now exactly what. That's always the trouble about reading.'

'I'd be much happier,' Henry Cooper said, 'if you would turn off the heat.'

'There's no point in your catching a chill, is there? Or me either. It won't help *him* where he's gone – if anywhere at all. The next thing you know you'll be in the same position yourself. Not in an overnight bag, of course. That goes without saying.'

The Knightsbridge tunnel as usual was closed because of flooding. They turned north through the park. The trees dripped on empty benches. The pigeons blew out their grey feathers the colour of soiled city snow.

'Is he yours?' the driver asked. 'If you don't mind my enquiring.'

'Not exactly.' Henry Cooper added briskly and brightly, 'My wife's, as it happens.'

'It's never the same if it's not your own,' the driver said thoughtfully. 'I had a nephew who died. He had a split palate – that wasn't the reason, of course, but it made it easier to bear for the parents. Are you going to an undertaker's now?'

'I thought I would take it home for the night and see about the arrangements tomorrow.'

'A little perisher like that would fit easily into the fridge. No bigger than a chicken. As a precaution only.'

They entered the large whitewashed Bayswater square. The houses resembled the above-ground tombs you find in continental cemeteries, except that, unlike the tombs, they were divided into flatlets and there were rows and rows of bell-pushes to wake the inmates. The driver watched Henry Cooper get out with the overnight bag at a portico entitled Stare House. 'Bloody orful aircraft company,' he said mechanically when he saw the letters BOAC – without ill-will, it was only a Pavlov response.

Henry Cooper went up to the top floor and let himself in. His mother was already in the hall to greet him. 'I saw your car draw up, dear.' He put the overnight bag on a chair so as to embrace her better.

'You've come quickly. You got my telegram at Nice?'

'Yes, mother. With only an overnight bag I walked straight through the customs.'

'So clever of you to travel light.'

'It's the drip-dry shirt that does it,' Henry Cooper said. He followed his mother into their sitting-room. He noticed she had changed the position of his favourite picture – a reproduction from *Life* magazine of a painting by Hieronymus Bosch. 'Just so that I don't see it from *my* chair, dear,' his mother explained, interpreting his glance. His slippers were laid out by his armchair and he sat down with an air of satisfaction at being home again.

'And now, dear,' his mother said, 'tell me how it was. Tell me everything. Did you make some new friends?'

'Oh yes, mother, wherever I went I made friends.' Winter had fallen early on the House of Stare. The overnight bag disappeared in the darkness of the hall like a blue fish into blue water.

'And adventures? What adventures?'

Once, while he talked, his mother got up and tip-toed to draw the curtains and to turn on a reading-lamp, and once she gave a little gasp of horror. 'A little toe? In the marmalade?'

'Yes, mother.'

'It wasn't English marmalade?'

'No, mother, foreign.'

'I could have understood a finger – an accident slicing the orange – but a toe!'

'As I understood it,' Henry Cooper said, 'in those parts they use a kind of guillotine worked by the bare foot of a peasant.'

'You complained, of course?'

'Not in words, but I put the toe very conspicuously at the edge of the plate.'

After one more story it was time for his mother to go and put the shepherd's pie into the oven and Henry Cooper went into the hall to fetch the overnight bag. 'Time to unpack,' he thought. He had a tidy mind.

Mortmain

How wonderfully secure and peaceful a genuine marriage seemed to Carter, when he attained it at the age of forty-two. He even enjoyed every moment of the church service, except when he saw Josephine wiping away a tear as he conducted Julia down the aisle. It was typical of this new frank relationship that Josephine was there at all. He had no secrets from Julia; they had often talked together of his ten tormented years with Josephine, of her extravagant jealousy, of her well-timed hysterics. 'It was her insecurity,' Julia argued with understanding, and she was quite convinced that in a little while it would be possible to form a friendship with Josephine.

'I doubt it, darling.'

'Why? I can't help being fond of anyone who loved you.'

'It was a rather cruel love.'

'Perhaps at the end when she knew she was losing you, but, darling, there *were* happy years.'

'Yes.' But he wanted to forget that he had ever loved anyone before Julia.

Her generosity sometimes staggered him. On the seventh day of their honeymoon, when they were drinking retsina in a little restaurant on the beach by Sunion, he accidentally took a letter from Josephine out of his pocket. It had arrived the day before and he had concealed it, for fear of hurting Julia. It was typical of Josephine that she could not leave him alone for the brief period of the honeymoon. Even her handwriting was now abhorrent to him – very neat, very small, in black ink the colour of her hair. Julia was platinum-fair. How had he ever thought that black hair was beautiful? Or been impatient to read letters in black ink?

'What's the letter, darling? I didn't know there had been a post.'

'It's from Josephine. It came yesterday.'

'But you haven't even opened it!' she exclaimed without a word of reproach.

'I don't want to think about her.'

'But, darling, she may be ill.'

'Not she.'

'Or in distress.'

'She earns more with her fashion-designs than I do with my stories.'

'Darling, let's be kind. We can afford to be. We are so happy.'

So he opened the letter. It was affectionate and uncomplaining and he read it with distaste.

DEAR PHILIP – I didn't want to be a death's head at the reception, so I had no chance to say goodbye and wish you both the greatest possible happiness. I thought Julia looked terribly beautiful and so very, very young. You must look after her carefully. I know how well you can do that, Philip dear. When I saw her, I couldn't help wondering why you took such a long time to make up your mind to leave me. Silly Philip. It's much less painful to act quickly.

I don't suppose you are interested to hear about my activities now, but just in case you are worrying a little about me – you know what an old worrier you are – I want you to know that I'm working *very* hard at a whole series for – guess, the French *Vogue*. They are paying me a fortune in francs, and I simply have no time for unhappy thoughts. I've been back once – I hope you don't mind – to our apartment (slip of the tongue) because I'd lost a key sketch. I found it at the back of our communal drawer – the ideas-bank, do you remember? I thought I'd taken all my stuff away, but there it was between the leaves of the story you started that heavenly summer, and never finished, at Napoule. Now I'm rambling on when all I really wanted to say was: Be happy both of you.

    Love,

                         JOSEPHINE

Carter handed the letter to Julia and said, 'It could have been worse.'

'But would she like me to read it?'

'Oh, it's meant for both of us.' Again he thought how wonderful it was to have no secrets. There had been so many secrets during the last ten years, even innocent secrets, for fear of misunderstanding, of Josephine's rage or silence. Now he had no fear of anything at all: he could have trusted even a guilty secret to Julia's sympathy and comprehension. He said, 'I was a fool not to show you the letter yesterday. I'll never do anything like that again.' He tried to recall Spenser's line – ' . . . port after stormie seas'.

When Julia had finished reading the letter she said, 'I think she's a wonderful woman. How very, very sweet of her to write like that. You know I was – only now and then, of course – just a little worried about her. After all *I* wouldn't like to lose you after ten years.'

When they were in the taxi going back to Athens she said, 'Were you very happy at Napoule?'

'Yes, I suppose so. I don't remember, it wasn't like this.'

With the antennae of a lover he could feel her moving away from him, though their shoulders still touched. The sun was bright on the road from Sunion, the warm sleepy loving siesta lay ahead, and yet . . . 'Is anything the matter, darling?' he asked.

'Not really . . . It's only . . . do you think one day you'll say the same about Athens as about Napoule? "I don't remember, it wasn't like this." '

'What a dear fool you are,' he said and kissed her. After that they played a little in the taxi going back to Athens, and when the streets began to unroll she sat up and combed her hair. 'You aren't really a cold man, are you?' she asked, and he knew that all was right again. It was Josephine's fault that – momentarily – there had been a small division.

When they got out of bed to have dinner, she said, 'We must write to Josephine.'

'Oh no!'

'Darling, I know how you feel, but really it was a wonderful letter.'

'A picture-postcard then.'

So they agreed on that.

Suddenly it was autumn when they arrived back in London – if not winter already, for there was ice in the rain falling on the tarmac, and they had quite forgotten how early the lights came on at home – passing Gillette and Lucozade and Smith's Crisps, and no view of the Parthenon anywhere. The BOAC posters seemed more than usually sad – 'BOAC takes you there and brings you back.'

'We'll put on all the electric fires as soon as we get in,' Carter said, 'and it will be warm in no time at all.' But when they opened the door of the apartment they found the fires were already alight. Little glows greeted them in the twilight from the depths of the living-room and the bedroom.

'Some fairy has done this,' Julia said.

'Not a fairy of any kind,' Carter said. He had already seen the envelope on the mantelpiece addressed in black ink to 'Mrs Carter'.

DEAR JULIA – you won't mind my calling you Julia, will you? I feel we have so much in common, having loved the same man. Today was so icy that I could not help thinking of how you two were returning from the sun and the warmth to a cold flat. (I know how cold the flat can be. I used to catch a chill every year when we came back from the South of France.) So I've done a very presumptuous thing. I've slipped in and put on the fires, but to show you that I'll never do such a thing again, I've hidden my key under the mat outside the front door. That's just in case your plane is held up in Rome or some-where. I'll telephone the airport and if by some unlikely chance you haven't arrived, I'll come back and turn out the fires for safety (and economy! the rates are awful). Wishing you a very warm evening in your new home, love from

JOSEPHINE

PS. I did notice that the coffee jar was empty, so I've left a packet of Blue Mountain in the kitchen. It's the only coffee Philip really cares for.

'Well,' Julia said laughing, 'she does think of every-thing.'

'I wish she'd just leave us alone,' Carter said.

'We wouldn't be warm like this, and we wouldn't have any coffee for breakfast.'

'I feel that she's lurking about the place and she'll walk in at any moment. Just when I'm kissing you.' He kissed Julia with one careful eye on the door.

'You *are* a bit unfair, darling. After all, she's left her key under the mat.'

'She might have had a duplicate made.'

She closed his mouth with another kiss.

'Have you noticed how erotic an aeroplane makes you after a few hours?' Carter asked.

'Yes.'

'I suppose it's the vibration.'

'Let's do something about it, darling.'

'I'll just look under the mat first. To make sure she wasn't lying.'

He enjoyed marriage – so much that he blamed himself for not having married before, forgetting that in that case he would have been married to Josephine. He found Julia, who had no work of her own, almost miraculously available. There was no maid to mar their relationship with habits. As they were always together, at cocktail parties, in restaurants, at small dinner parties, they had only to meet each other's eyes . . . Julia soon earned the reputation of being delicate and easily tired, it occurred so often that they left a cocktail party after a quarter of an hour or abandoned a dinner after the coffee – 'Oh dear, I'm so sorry, such a vile headache, so stupid of me. Philip, *you* must stay . . .'

'Of course I'm not going to stay.'

Once they had a narrow escape from discovery on the stairs while they were laughing uncontrollably.

Their host had followed them out to ask them to post a letter. Julia in the nick of time changed her laughter into what seemed to be a fit of hysterics . . . Several weeks went by. It was a really successful marriage . . . They liked – between whiles – to discuss its success, each attributing the main merit to the other. 'When I think you might have married Josephine,' Julia said. 'Why didn't you marry Josephine?'

'I suppose at the back of our minds we knew it wasn't going to be permanent.'

'Are we going to be permanent?'

'If we aren't, nothing will ever be.'

It was early in November that the time-bombs began to go off. No doubt they had been planned to explode earlier, but Josephine had not taken into account the temporary change in his habits. Some weeks passed before he had occasion to open what they used to call the ideas-bank in the days of their closest companionship – the drawer in which he used to leave notes for stories, scraps of overheard dialogue and the like, and she would leave roughly sketched ideas for fashion advertisements.

Directly he opened the drawer he saw her letter. It was labelled heavily 'Top Secret' in black ink with a whimsically drawn exclamation mark in the form of a girl with big eyes (Josephine suffered in an elegant way from exophthalmic goitre) rising genie-like out of a bottle. He read the letter with extreme distaste:

Dear – you didn't expect to find me here, did you? But after ten years I can't not now and then say good-night or good-morning, how are you? Bless you. Lots of love (really and truly).
  Your
                                              JOSEPHINE

The threat of 'now and then' was unmistakable. He slammed the drawer shut and said 'Damn' so loudly that Julia looked in. 'Whatever is it, darling?'

'Josephine again.'

She read the letter and said, 'You know, I can understand the way she feels. Poor Josephine. Are you tearing it up, darling?'

'What else do you expect me to do with it? Keep it for a collected edition of her letters?'

'It just seems a bit unkind.'

'Me unkind to *her*? Julia, you've no idea of the sort of life that we led those last years. I can show you scars: when she was in a rage she would stub her cigarettes *anywhere*.'

'She felt she was losing you, darling, and she got desperate. They are my fault really, those scars, every one of them.' He could see growing in her eyes that soft amused speculative look which always led to the same thing.

Only two days passed before the next time-bomb went off. When they got up Julia said, 'We really ought to change the mattress. We both fall into a kind of hole in the middle.'

'I hadn't noticed.'

'Lots of people change the mattress every week.'

'Yes. Josephine always did.'

They stripped the bed and began to roll the mattress. Lying on the springs was a letter addressed to Julia. Carter saw it first and tried to push it out of sight, but Julia saw him.

'What's that?'

'Josephine, of course. There'll soon be too many letters for one volume. We shall have to get them properly edited at Yale like George Eliot's.'

'Darling, this is addressed to me. What were you planning to do with it?'

'Destroy it in secret.'

'I thought we were going to have no secrets.'

'I had counted without Josephine.'

For the first time she hesitated before opening the letter. 'It's certainly a bit bizarre to put a letter here. Do you think it got there accidentally?'

'Rather difficult, I should think.'

She read the letter and then gave it to him. She said with relief, 'Oh, she explains why. It's quite natural really.' He read:

DEAR JULIA – how I hope you are basking in a really Greek sun. Don't tell Philip (Oh, but of course you wouldn't have secrets yet) but I never really cared for the South of France. Always that mistral, drying the skin. I'm glad to think you are not suffering there. We always planned to go to Greece when we could afford it, so I know Philip will be happy. I came in today to find a sketch and then remembered that the mattress hadn't been turned for at least a fortnight. We were rather distracted, you know, the last weeks we were together. Anyway I couldn't bear the thought of your coming back from the lotus islands and finding bumps in your bed the first night, so I've turned it for you. I'd advise you to turn it every week: otherwise a hole always develops in the middle. By the way I've put up the winter curtains and sent the summer ones to the cleaners at 153 Brompton Road.

Love,

JOSEPHINE

'If you remember, she wrote to me that Napoule

had been heavenly,' he said. 'The Yale editor will have to put in a cross-reference.'

'You *are* a bit cold-blooded,' Julia said. 'Darling, she's only trying to be helpful. After all I never knew about the curtains or the mattress.'

'I suppose you are going to write a long cosy letter in reply, full of household chat.'

'She's been waiting weeks for an answer. This is an *ancient* letter.'

'And I wonder how many more ancient letters there are waiting to pop out. By God, I'm going to search the flat through and through. From attic to basement.'

'We don't have either.'

'You know very well what I mean.'

'I only know you are getting fussed in an exaggerated way. You really behave as though you are frightened of Josephine.'

'Oh hell!'

Julia left the room abruptly and he tried to work. Later that day a squib went off – nothing serious, but it didn't help his mood. He wanted to find the dialling number for overseas telegrams and he discovered inserted in volume one of the directory a complete list in alphabetical order, typed on Josephine's machine on which O was always blurred, a complete list of the numbers he most often required. John Hughes, his oldest friend, came after Harrods; and there were the nearest taxi-rank, the chemist's the butcher's, the bank, the dry-cleaner's, the greengrocer's, the fishmonger's, his publisher and agent, Elizabeth Arden's and the local hairdresser's – marked in brackets ('For J please note, quite reliable and very inexpensive') – it was the first time he noticed they had the same initials.

Julia, who saw him discover the list, said, 'The angel-woman. We'll pin it up over the telephone. It's really terribly complete.'

'After the crack in her last letter I'd have expected her to include Cartier's.'

'Darling, it wasn't crack. It was a bare statement of fact. If I hadn't had a little money, we would have gone to the South of France too.'

'I suppose you think I married you to get to Greece.'

'Don't be an owl. You don't see Josephine clearly, that's all. You twist every kindness she does.'

'Kindness?'

'I expect it's the sense of guilt.'

After that he really began a search. He looked in cigarette-boxes, drawers, filing-cabinets, he went through all the pockets of the suits he had left behind, he opened the back of the television-cabinet, he lifted the lid of the lavatory-cistern, and even changed the roll of toilet-paper (it was quicker than unwinding the whole thing). Julia came to look at him, as he worked in the lavatory, without her usual sympathy. He tried the pelmets (who knew what they mightn't discover when next the curtains were sent for cleaning?), he took their dirty clothes out of the basket in case something had been overlooked at the bottom. He went on hands-and-knees through the kitchen to look under the gas-stove, and once, when he found a piece of paper wrapped around a pipe, he exclaimed in a kind of triumph, but it was nothing at all – a plumber's relic. The afternoon post rattled through the letter-box and Julia called to him from the hall – 'Oh, good, you never told me you took in the French *Vogue*.'

'I don't.'

'Sorry, there's a kind of Christmas card in another

envelope. A subscription's been taken out for us by Miss Josephine Heckstall-Jones. I do call that sweet of her.'

'She's sold a series of drawings to them. I won't look at it.'

'Darling, you are being childish. Do you expect her to stop reading your books?'

'I only want to be left alone with you. Just for a few weeks. It's not so much to ask.'

'You're a bit of an egoist, darling.'

He felt quiet and tired that evening, but a little relieved in mind. His search had been very thorough. In the middle of dinner he had remembered the wedding-presents, still crated for lack of room, and insisted on making sure between the courses that they were still nailed down – he knew Josephine would never have used a screwdriver for fear of injuring her fingers, and she was terrified of hammers. The peace of a solitary evening at last descended on them: the delicious calm which they knew either of them could alter at any moment with a touch of the hand. Lovers cannot postpone as married people can. 'I am grown peaceful as old age tonight,' he quoted to her.

'Who wrote that?'

'Browning.'

'I don't know Browning. Read me some.'

He loved to read Browning aloud – he had a good voice for poetry, it was his small harmless Narcissism. 'Would you really like it?'

'Yes.'

'I used to read to Josephine,' he warned her.

'What do I care? We can't help doing *some* of the same things, can we, darling?'

'There is something I never read to Josephine. Even though I was in love with her, it wasn't suitable. We weren't – permanent.' He began:

'How well I know what I mean to do
    When the long dark autumn evenings come . . . '

He was deeply moved by his own reading. He had never loved Julia so much as at this moment. Here was home – nothing else had been other than a caravan.

' . . . I will speak now,
    No longer watch you as you sit
Reading by firelight, that great brow
    And the spirit-small hand propping it,
Mutely, my heart knows how.'

He rather wished that Julia had really been reading, but then of course she wouldn't have been listening to him with such adorable attention.

' . . . If two lives join, there is oft a scar.
    They are one and one, with a shadowy third;
One near one is too far.'

He turned the page and there lay a sheet of paper (he would have discovered it at once, before reading, if she had put it in an envelope) with the black neat handwriting.

DEAREST PHILIP – only to say good-night to you between the pages of your favourite book – and mine. We are so lucky to have ended in the way we have. With memories in common we shall for ever be a little in touch.
    Love,
                                            JOSEPHINE

He flung the book and the paper on the floor. He said, 'The bitch. The bloody bitch.'

'I won't have you talk of her like that,' Julia said with surprising strength. She picked up the paper and read it.

'What's wrong with that?' she demanded. 'Do you hate memories? What's going to happen to our memories?'

'But don't you see the trick she's playing? Don't you understand? Are you an idiot, Julia?'

That night they lay in bed on opposite sides, not even touching with their feet. It was the first night since they had come home that they had not made love. Neither slept much. In the morning Carter found a letter in the most obvious place of all, which he had somehow neglected: between the leaves of the unused single-lined foolscap on which he always wrote his stories. It began, 'Darling, I'm sure you won't mind my using the old term . . .'

Cheap in August

It was cheap in August: the essential sun, the coral reefs, the bamboo bar and the calypsos – they were all of them at cut prices, like the slightly soiled slips in a bargain-sale. Groups arrived periodically from Philadelphia in the manner of school-treats and departed with less *bruit*, after an exact exhausting week, when the picnic was over. Perhaps for twenty-four hours the swimming-pool and the bar were almost deserted, and then another school-treat would arrive, this time from St Louis. Everyone knew everyone else; they had bussed together to an airport, they had flown together, together they had faced an alien customs; they would separate during the day and greet each other noisily and happily after dark, exchanging impressions of 'shooting the rapids', the botanic gardens, the Spanish fort. 'We are doing that tomorrow.'

Mary Watson wrote to her husband in Europe, 'I had to get away for a bit and it's so cheap in August.' They had been married ten years and they had only been separated three times. He wrote to her every day and the letters arrived twice a week in little bundles. She arranged them like newspapers by the date and read them in the correct order. They were tender and precise; what with his research, with preparing lectures and writing letters, he had little time to *see* Europe – he insisted on calling it 'your Europe' as though to assure her that he had not forgotten the sacrifice which she must have made by marrying an American professor from New England, but sometimes little criticisms of 'her Europe' escaped him: the food was too rich, cigarettes too expensive, wine too often served and milk very difficult to obtain at lunchtime – which might indicate that, after all, she ought not to exaggerate her sacrifice. Perhaps it would have been a good thing if James Thomson, who was his special study at the moment, had written *The Seasons* in America – an American fall, she had to admit, was more beautiful than an English autumn.

Mary Watson wrote to him every other day, but sometimes a postcard only, and she was apt to forget if she had repeated the postcard. She wrote in the shade of the bamboo bar where she could see everyone who passed on the way to the swimming-pool. She wrote truthfully, 'It's so cheap in August; the hotel is not half full, and the heat and the humidity are very tiring. But, of course, it's a change.' She had no wish to appear extravagant; the salary, which to her European eyes had seemed astronomically large for a professor of literature, had long dwindled to its proper proportions, relative to the price of steaks and salads – she must justify with a little enthusiasm the money she was spending in his absence. So she wrote also about the flowers in the botanic gardens – she had ventured that far on one occasion – and with less truth of the beneficial changes wrought by the sun and the lazy life on her friend Margaret who from 'her England' had written and demanded her company: a Margaret, she admitted frankly to herself, who was not visible to any eye but the eye of faith. But then Charlie had complete faith. Even good qualities become with the erosion of time a reproach. After ten years of being happily married, she thought, one undervalues security and tranquillity.

She read Charlie's letters with great attention. She longed to find in them one ambiguity, one evasion, one time-gap which he had ill-explained. Even an unusually strong expression of love would have pleased her, for its strength might have been there to counterweigh a sense of guilt. But she couldn't deceive herself that there was any sense of guilt in Charlie's facile flowing informative script. She calculated that if he had been one of the poets he was now so closely studying, he would have completed already a standard-sized epic during his first two months in 'her Europe', and the letters, after all, were only a spare-time occupation. They filled up the vacant hours, and certainly they could have left no room for any other occupation. 'It is ten o'clock at night, it is raining outside and the temperature is rather cool for August, not above fifty-six degrees. When I have said good-night to you, my dear one, I shall go happily to bed with the thought of you. I have a long day tomorrow at the museum and dinner in the evening with the Henry Wilkinsons who are passing through on their way from Athens – you remember the Henry Wilkinsons, don't you?' (Didn't she just?) She had wondered whether, when Charlie returned, she might perhaps detect some small unfamiliar note in his lovemaking which would indicate that a stranger had passed that way. Now she disbelieved in the possibility, and anyway the evidence would arrive too late – it was no good to her now that she might be justified later. She wanted her justification immediately, a justification not alas! for any act that she had committed but only for an intention, for the intention of betraying Charlie, of having, like so many of her friends, a holiday affair. (The idea had come to her immediately the dean's wife had said, 'It's so cheap in Jamaica in August.')

The trouble was that, after three weeks of calypsos in the humid evenings, the rum punches (for which she could no longer disguise from herself a repugnance), the warm Martinis, the interminable red snappers, and tomatoes with everything, there had been no affair, not even the hint of one. She had discovered with disappointment the essential morality of a holiday resort in the cheap season; there were no opportunities for infidelity, only for writing postcards – with great brilliant blue skies and seas – to Charlie. Once a woman from St Louis had taken too obvious pity on her, when she sat alone in the bar writing postcards, and invited her to join their party which was about to visit the botanic gardens – 'We are an awfully jolly bunch,' she had said with a big turnip smile. Mary exaggerated her English accent to repel her better and said that she didn't much care for flowers. It had shocked the woman as deeply as if she had said she did not care for television. From the motion of the heads at the other end of the bar, the agitated clinking of the Coca-Cola glasses, she could tell that her words were being repeated from one to another. Afterwards, until the jolly bunch had taken the airport limousine on the way back to St Louis, she was aware of averted heads. She was English, she had taken a superior attitude to flowers, and as she preferred even warm Martinis to Coca-Cola, she was probably in their eyes an alcoholic.

It was a feature common to most of these jolly bunches that they contained no male attachment, and perhaps that was why the attempt to look attractive was completely abandoned. Huge buttocks were exposed in their full horror in tight large-patterned Bermuda shorts. Heads were bound in scarves to cover rollers which were not removed even by lunchtime – they stuck out like small molehills. Daily she watched the bums lurch by like hippos on the way to the water. Only in the evening would the women change from the monstrous shorts into monstrous cotton frocks, covered with mauve or scarlet flowers, in order to take dinner on the terrace where formality was demanded in the book of rules, and the few men who appeared were forced to wear jackets and ties though the thermometer stood at close on eighty degrees after sunset. The market in femininity being such, how could one hope to see any male foragers? Only old and broken husbands were sometimes to be seen towed towards an Issa store advertising freeport prices.

She had been encouraged during the first week by the sight of three men with crew-cuts who went past the bar towards the swimming-pool wearing male bikinis. They were far too young for her, but in her present mood she would have welcomed altruistically the sight of another's romance. Romance is said to be contagious, and if in the candle-lit evenings the 'informal' coffee-tavern had contained a few young amorous couples, who could say what men of maturer years might not eventually arrive to catch the infection? But her hopes dwindled. The young men came and went without a glance at the Bermuda shorts or the pinned hair. Why should they stay?

They were certainly more beautiful than any girl there and they knew it.

By nine o'clock most evenings Mary Watson was on her way to bed. A few evenings of calypsos, of quaint false impromptus and the hideous jangle of rattles, had been enough. Outside the closed windows of the hotel annexe the boxes of the air-conditioners made a continuous rumble in the starred and palmy night like over-fed hotel guests. Her room was full of dried air which bore no more resemblance to fresh air than the dried figs to the newly picked fruit. When she looked in the glass to brush her hair she often regretted her lack of charity to the jolly bunch from St Louis. It was true she did not wear Bermuda shorts nor coil her hair in rollers, but her hair was streaky none the less with heat and the mirror reflected more plainly than it seemed to do at home her thirty-nine years. If she had not paid in advance for a four-weeks *pension* on her individual round-trip tour, with tickets exchangeable for a variety of excursions, she would have turned tail and returned to the campus. Next year, she thought, when I am forty, I must feel grateful that I have preserved the love of a good man.

She was a woman given to self-analysis, and perhaps because it is a great deal easier to direct questions to a particular face rather than to a void (one has the right to expect some kind of a response even from eyes one sees many times a day in a compact), she posed the questions to herself with a belligerent direct stare into the looking-glass. She was an honest woman, and for that reason the questions were all the cruder. She would say to herself, I have slept with no one other than Charlie (she wouldn't admit as sexual experiences the small exciting halfway points that she had reached before marriage); why am I now seeking to find a strange body, which will probably give me less pleasure than the body I already know? It had been more than a month before Charlie brought her real pleasure. Pleasure, she learnt, grew with habit, so that if it were not really pleasure that she now looked for, what was it? The answer could only be the unfamiliar. She had friends, even on the respectable campus, who had admitted to her, in the frank admirable American way, their adventures. These had usually been in Europe – a momentary marital absence had given the opportunity for a momentary excitement, and then with what a sigh of relief they had found themselves safely at home. All the same they felt afterwards that they had enlarged their experience; they understood something that their husbands did not really understand – the real character of a Frenchman, an Italian, even – there were such cases – of an Englishman.

Mary Watson was painfully aware, as an English-woman, that her experience was confined to one American. They all, on the campus, believed her to be European, but all she knew was confined to one man and he was a citizen of Boston who had no curiosity for the great Western regions. In a sense she was more American by choice than he was by birth. Perhaps she was less European even than the wife of the Professor of Romance Languages, who had confided to her that once – overwhelmingly – in Antibes . . . it had happened only once because the sabbatical year was over . . . her husband was up in Paris checking manuscripts before they flew home . . .

Had she herself, Mary Watson sometimes wondered, been just such a European adventure which Charlie mistakenly had domesticated? (She couldn't pretend to be a tigress in a cage, but they kept smaller creatures in cages, white mice, lovebirds.) And, to be fair, Charlie too was her adventure, her American adventure, the kind of man whom at twenty-seven she had not before encountered in frowsy London. Henry James had described the type, and at that moment in her history she had been reading a great deal of Henry James: 'A man of intellect whose body was not much to him and its senses and appetites not importunate.' All the same for a while she had made the appetites importunate.

That was her private conquest of the American continent, and when the Professor's wife had spoken of the dancer of Antibes (no, that was a Roman inscription – the man had been a *marchand de vin*) she had thought, The lover I know and admire is American and I am proud of it. But afterwards came the thought: American or New England? Yet to know a country must one know every region sexually?

It was absurd at thirty-nine not to be content. She had her man. The book on James Thomson would be published by the University Press, and Charlie had the intention afterwards of making a revolutionary break from the romantic poetry of the eighteenth century into a study of the American image in European literature – it was to be called *The Double Reflection*: the effect of Fenimore Cooper on the European scene; the image of America presented by Mrs Trollope – the details were not yet worked out. The study might possibly end with the first arrival of Dylan Thomas on the shores of America – at the Cunard quay or at Idlewild? That was a point for later research. She examined herself again closely in the glass – the new decade of the forties stared frankly back at her – an Englander who had become a New Englander. After all she hadn't travelled very far – Kent to Connecticut. This was not just the physical restlessness of middle age, she argued; it was the universal desire to see a little bit farther, before one surrendered to old age and the blank certitude of death.

2

Next day she picked up her courage and went as far as the swimming-pool. A strong wind blew and whipped up the waves in the almost land-girt harbour – the hurricane season would soon be here. All the world creaked around her: the wooden struts of the shabby harbour, the jalousies of the small hopeless houses which looked as though they had been knocked together from a make-it-yourself kit, the branches of the palms – a long, weary, worn-out creaking. Even the water of the swimming-pool imitated in miniature the waves of the harbour.

She was glad that she was alone in the swimming-pool, at least for all practical purposes alone, for the old man splashing water over himself, like an elephant, in the shallow end hardly counted. He was a solitary elephant and not one of the hippo band. They would have called her with merry cries to join them – and it's difficult to be stand-offish in a swimming-pool which is common to all as a table is not. They might even in their resentment have ducked her – pretending like schoolchildren that it was all a merry game; there was nothing she put beyond those thick thighs, whether they were encased in bikinis or Bermuda shorts. As she floated in the pool her ears were alert for their approach. At the first sound she would get well away from the water, but today they were probably making an excursion to Tower Isle on the other side of the island, or had they done that yesterday? Only the old man watched her, pouring water over his head to keep away sunstroke. She was safely alone, which was the next best thing to the adventure she had come here to find. All the same, as she sat on the rim of the pool, and let the sun and wind dry her, she realised the extent of her solitude. She had spoken to no one but black waiters and Syrian receptionists for more than two weeks. Soon, she thought, I shall even begin to miss Charlie – it would be an ignoble finish to what she had intended to be an adventure.

A voice from the water said to her, 'My name's Hickslaughter – Henry Hickslaughter.' She couldn't have sworn to the name in court, but that was how it had sounded at the time and he never repeated it. She looked down at a polished mahogany crown surrounded by white hair; perhaps he resembled Neptune more than an elephant. Neptune was always outsize, and as he had pulled himself a little out of the water to speak, she could see the rolls of fat folding over the blue bathing-slip, with tough hair lying like weeds along the ditches. She replied with amusement, 'My name is Watson. Mary Watson.'

'You're English?'

'My husband's American,' she said in extenuation.

'I haven't seen him around, have I?'

'He's in England,' she said with a small sigh, for the geographical and national situation seemed too complicated for casual explanation.

'You like it here?' he asked and lifting a hand-cup of water he distributed it over his bald head.

'So so.'

'Got the time on you?'

She looked in her bag and told him, 'Eleven fifteen.'

'I've had my half hour,' he said and trod heavily away towards the ladder at the shallow end.

An hour later, staring at her lukewarm Martini with its great green unappetising olive, she saw him looming down at her from the other end of the bamboo bar. He wore an ordinary shirt open at the neck and a brown leather belt; his type of shoes in her childhood had been known as co-respondent, but one seldom saw them today. She wondered what Charlie would think of her pick-up; unquestionably she had landed him, rather as an angler struggling with a heavy catch finds that he has hooked nothing better than an old boot. She was no angler; she didn't know whether a boot would put an ordinary hook out of action altogether, but she knew that *her* hook could be irremediably damaged. No one would approach her if she were in his company. She drained the Martini in one gulp and even attacked the olive so as to have no excuse to linger in the bar.

'Would you do me the honour,' Mr Hickslaughter asked, 'of having a drink with me?' His manner was completely changed; on dry land he seemed unsure of himself and spoke with an old-fashioned propriety.

'I'm afraid I've only just finished one. I have to be off.' Inside the gross form she thought she saw a tousled child with disappointed eyes. 'I'm having lunch early today.' She got up and added rather stupidly, for the bar was quite empty, 'You can have my table.'

'I don't need a drink that much,' he said solemnly. 'I was just after company.'

She knew that he was watching her as she moved to the adjoining coffee tavern, and she thought with guilt, at least I've got the old boot off the hook. She refused the shrimp cocktail with tomato ketchup and fell back as was usual with her on a grapefruit, with grilled trout to follow. 'Please no tomato with the trout,' she implored, but the black waiter obviously didn't understand her. While she waited she began with amusement to picture a scene between Charlie and Mr Hickslaughter, who happened for the purpose of her story to be crossing the campus. 'This is Henry Hickslaughter, Charlie. We used to go bathing together when I was in Jamaica.' Charlie, who always wore English clothes, was very tall, very thin, very concave. It was a satisfaction to know that he would never lose his figure – his nerves would see to that and his extreme sensibility. He hated anything gross; there was no grossness in *The Seasons*, not even in the lines on spring.

She heard slow footsteps coming up behind her and panicked. 'May I share your table?' Mr Hickslaughter asked. He had recovered his terrestrial politeness, but only so far as speech was concerned, for he sat firmly down without waiting for her reply. The chair was too small for him; his thighs overlapped like a double mattress on a single bed. He began to study the menu.

'They copy American food; it's worse than the reality,' Mary Watson said.

'You don't like American food?'

'Tomatoes even with the trout!'

'Tomatoes? Oh, you mean tomatoes,' he said,

correcting her accent. 'I'm very fond of tomatoes myself.'

'And fresh pineapple in the salad.'

'There's a lot of vitamins in fresh pineapple.' Almost as if he wished to emphasise their disagreement, he ordered shrimp cocktail, grilled trout and a sweet salad. Of course, when her trout arrived, the tomatoes were there. 'You can have mine if you want to,' she said and he accepted with pleasure. 'You are very kind. You are really very kind.' He held out his plate like Oliver Twist.

She began to feel oddly at ease with the old man. She would have been less at ease, she was certain, with a possible adventure: she would have been wondering about her effect on him, while now she could be sure that she gave him pleasure – with the tomatoes. He was perhaps less the old anonymous boot than an old shoe comfortable to wear. And curiously enough, in spite of his first approach and in spite of his correcting her over the pronunciation of tomatoes, it was not really an old American shoe of which she was reminded. Charlie wore English clothes over his English figure, he studied English eighteenth-century literature, his book would be published in England by the Cambridge University Press who would buy sheets, but she had the impression that he was far more fashioned as an American shoe than Hickslaughter. Even Charlie, whose manners were perfect, if they had met for the first time today at the swimming-pool, would have interrogated her more closely. Interrogation had always seemed to her a principal part of American social life – an inheritance perhaps from the Indian smoke-fires: 'Where are you from? Do you know the

so and so's? Have you been to the botanic gardens?'
It came over her that Mr Hickslaughter, if that were
really his name, was perhaps an American reject –
not necessarily more flawed than the pottery rejects
of famous firms you find in bargain-basements.

She found herself questioning *him*, with circum-
locutions, while he savoured the tomatoes. 'I was
born in London. I couldn't have been born more
than six hundred miles from there without drowning,
could I? But you belong to a continent thousands of
miles wide and long. Where were you born?' (She
remembered a character in a Western movie directed
by John Ford who asked, 'Where do you hail from,
stranger?' The question was more frankly put than
hers.)

He said, 'St Louis.'

'Oh, then there are lots of your people here – you
are not alone.' She felt a slight disappointment that
he might belong to the jolly bunch.

'I'm alone,' he said. 'Room 63.' It was in her own
corridor on the third floor of the annexe. He spoke
firmly as though he were imparting information for
future use. 'Five doors down from you.'

'Oh.'

'I saw you come out your first day.'

'I never noticed you.'

'I keep to myself unless I see someone I like.'

'Didn't you see anyone you liked from St Louis?'

'I'm not all that fond of St Louis, and St Louis can
do without me. I'm not a favourite son.'

'Do you come here often?'

'In August. It's cheap in August.' He kept on surprising her. First there was his lack of local patriotism,
and now his frankness about money or rather about

the lack of it, a frankness that could almost be classed as an un-American activity.

'Yes.'

'I have to go where it's reasonable,' he said, as though he were exposing his bad hand to a partner at gin.

'You've retired?'

'Well – I've been retired.' He added, 'You ought to take salad . . . It's good for you.'

'I feel quite well without it.'

'You could do with more weight.' He added appraisingly, 'A couple of pounds.' She was tempted to tell him that he could do with less. They had both seen each other exposed.

'Were you in business?' She was being driven to interrogate. He hadn't asked her a personal question since his first at the pool.

'In a way,' he said. She had a sense that he was supremely uninterested in his own doings; she was certainly discovering an America which she had not known existed.

She said, 'Well, if you'll excuse me . . . '

'Aren't you taking any dessert?'

'No, I'm a light luncher.'

'It's all included in the price. You ought to eat some fruit.' He was looking at her under his white eyebrows with an air of disappointment which touched her.

'I don't care much for fruit and I want a nap. I always have a nap in the afternoon.'

Perhaps, after all, she thought, as she moved away through the formal dining-room, he is disappointed only because I'm not taking full advantage of the cheap rate.

She passed his room going to her own: the door was

231

open and a big white-haired mammy was making the bed. The room was exactly like her own; the same pair of double beds, the same wardrobe, the same dressing-table in the same position, the same heavy breathing of the air-conditioner. In her own room she looked in vain for the thermos of iced water; then she rang the bell and waited for several minutes. You couldn't expect good service in August. She went down the passage; Mr Hickslaughter's door was still open and she went in to find the maid. The door of the bathroom was open too and a wet cloth lay on the tiles.

How bare the bedroom was. At least she had taken the trouble to add a few flowers, a photograph and half a dozen books on a bedside table which gave her room a lived-in air. Beside his bed there was only a literary digest lying open and face down; she turned it over to see what he was reading – as she might have expected it was something to do with calories and proteins. He had begun writing a letter at his dressing-table and with the simple unscrupulousness of an intellectual she began to read it with her ears cocked for any sound in the passage.

DEAR JOE – the draft was two weeks late last month and I was in real difficulties. I had to borrow from a Syrian who runs a tourist junk-shop in Curaçao and pay him interest. You owe me a hundred dollars for the interest. It's your own fault. Mum never gave us lessons on how to live with an empty stomach. Please add it to the next draft and be sure to do that, you wouldn't want me coming back to collect. I'll be here till the end of August. It's cheap in August, and a man gets tired of nothing but Dutch, Dutch, Dutch. Give my love to Sis.

The letter broke off unfinished. Anyway she would have had no opportunity to read more because someone was approaching down the passage. She went to the door in time to see Mr Hickslaughter on the threshold. He said, 'You looking for me?'

'I was looking for the maid. She was in here a minute ago.'

'Come in and sit down.'

He looked through the bathroom door and then at the room in general. Perhaps it was only an uneasy conscience which made her think that his eyes strayed a moment to the unfinished letter.

'She's forgotten my iced water.'

'You can have mine if it's filled.' He shook his thermos and handed it to her.

'Thanks a lot.'

'When you've had your sleep . . . ' he began and looked away from her. Was he looking at the letter?

'Yes?'

'We might have a drink.'

She was, in a sense, trapped. She said, 'Yes.'

'Give me a ring when you wake up.'

'Yes.' She said nervously, 'Have a good sleep yourself.'

'Oh, I don't sleep.' He didn't wait for her to leave the room before turning away, swinging that great elephantine backside of his towards her. She had walked into a trap baited with a flask of iced water, and in her room she drank the water gingerly as though it might have a flavour different from hers.

She found it difficult to sleep: the old fat man had become an individual now that she had read his letter. She couldn't help comparing his style with Charlie's. 'When I have said good-night to you, my dear one, I shall go happily to bed with the thought of you.' In Mr Hickslaughter's there was an ambiguity, a hint of menace. Was it possible that the old man could be dangerous?

At half-past five she rang up room 63. It was not the kind of adventure she had planned, but it was an adventure none the less. 'I'm awake,' she said.

'You coming for a drink?' he asked.

'I'll meet you in the bar.'

'Not the bar,' he said. 'Not at the prices they charge for bourbon. I've got all we need here.' She felt as though she were being brought back to the scene of a crime, and she needed a little courage to knock on the door.

He had everything prepared: a bottle of Old Walker, a bucket of ice, two bottles of soda. Like books, drinks can make a room inhabited. She saw him as a man fighting in his own fashion against the sense of solitude.

'Siddown,' he said, 'make yourself comfortable,' like a character in a movie. He began to pour out two highballs.

She said, 'I've got an awful sense of guilt. I did come in here for iced water, but I was curious too. I read your letter.'

'I knew someone had touched it,' he said.

'I'm sorry.'

'Who cares? It was only to my brother.'

'I had no business . . .'

'Look,' he said, 'if I came into your room and found a letter open I'd read it, wouldn't I? Only your letter would be more interesting.'

'Why?'

'I don't write love letters. Never did and I'm too old now.' He sat down on a bed – she had the only easy chair. His belly hung in heavy folds under his sports-shirt, and his flies were a little open. Why was it always fat men who left them unbuttoned? He said, 'This is good bourbon,' taking a drain of it. 'What does your husband do?' he asked – it was his first personal question since the pool and it took her by surprise.

'He writes about literature. Eighteenth-century poetry,' she added, rather inanely under the circumstances.

'Oh.'

'What did you do? I mean when you worked.'

'This and that.'

'And now?'

'I watch what goes on. Sometimes I talk to someone like you. Well, no, I don't suppose I've ever talked to anyone like you before.' It might have seemed a compliment if he had not added, 'A professor's wife.'

'And you read the *Digest*?'

'Ye-eh. They make books too long – I haven't the patience. Eighteenth-century poetry. So they wrote poetry back in those days, did they?'

She said, 'Yes,' not sure whether or not he was mocking her.

'There was a poem I liked at school. The only one that ever stuck in my head. By Longfellow, I think.

You ever read Longfellow?'

'Not really. They don't read him much in school any longer.'

'Something about "Spanish sailors with bearded lips and the something and mystery of the ships and the something of the sea." It hasn't stuck all that well, after all, but I suppose I learned it sixty years ago and even more. Those were the days.'

'The 1900s?'

'No, no. I meant pirates, Kidd and Bluebeard and those fellows. This was their stamping ground, wasn't it? The Caribbean. It makes you kind of sick to see those women going around in their shorts here.' His tongue had been tingled into activity by the bourbon.

It occurred to her that she had never really been curious about another human being; she had been in love with Charlie, but he hadn't aroused her curiosity except sexually, and she had satisfied that only too quickly. She asked him, 'Do you love your sister?'

'Yes, of course, why? How do you know I've got a sister?'

'And Joe?'

'You certainly read my letter. Oh, he's OK.'

'OK?'

'Well, you know how it is with brothers. I'm the eldest in my family. There was one that died. My sister's twenty years younger than I am. Joe's got the means. He looks after her.'

'You haven't got the means?'

'I had the means. I wasn't good at managing them though. We aren't here to talk about myself.'

'I'm curious. That's why I read your letter.'

'You? Curious about me?'

'It could be, couldn't it?'

She had confused him, and now that she had the upper hand, she felt that she was out of the trap; she was free, she could come and go as she pleased, and if she chose to stay a little longer, it was her own choice.

'Have another bourbon?' he said. 'But you're English. Maybe you'd prefer Scotch?'

'Better not mix.'

'No.' He poured her another glass. He said, 'I was wondering – sometimes I want to get away from this joint for a little. What about having dinner down the road?'

'It would be stupid,' she said. 'We've both paid our *pension* here, haven't we? And it would be the same dinner in the end. Red snapper. Tomatoes.'

'I don't know what you have against tomatoes.' But he did not deny the good sense of her economic reasoning: he was the first unsuccessful American she had ever had a drink with. One must have seen them in the street . . . But even the young men who came to the house were not yet unsuccessful. The Professor of Romance Languages had perhaps hoped to be head of a university – success is relative, but it remains success.

He poured out another glass. She said, 'I'm drinking all your bourbon.'

'It's in a good cause.'

She was a little drunk by now and things – which only *seemed* relevant – came to her mind. She said, 'That thing of Longfellow's. It went on – something about "the thoughts of youth are long, long thoughts". I must have read it somewhere. That was the refrain, wasn't it?'

'Maybe. I don't remember.'

'Did you want to be a pirate when you were a boy?'

He gave an almost happy grin. He said, 'I succeeded. That's what Joe called me once – "pirate".'

'But you haven't any buried treasure?'

He said, 'He knows me well enough not to send me a hundred dollars. But if he feels scared enough that I'll come back – he might send fifty. And the interest was only twenty-five. He's not mean, but he's stupid.'

'How?'

'He ought to know I wouldn't go back. I wouldn't do one thing to hurt Sis.'

'Would it be any good if I asked you to have dinner with me?'

'No. It wouldn't be right.' In some ways he was obviously very conservative. 'It's as you said – you don't want to go throwing money about.' When the bottle of Old Walker was half empty, he said, 'You'd better have some food even if it is red snapper and tomatoes.'

'Is your name really Hickslaughter?'

'Something like that.'

They went downstairs, following rather carefully in each other's footsteps like ducks. In the formal restaurant open to all the heat of the evening, the men sat and sweated in their jackets and ties. They passed, the two of them, through the bamboo bar into the coffee tavern, which was lit by candles that increased the heat. Two young men with crew-cuts sat at the next table – they weren't the same young men she had seen before, but they came out of the same series. One of them said, 'I'm not denying that he has a certain style, but even if you *adore* Tennessee Williams . . . '

'Why did he call you a pirate?'

'It was just one of those things.'

When it came to the decision there seemed nothing

to choose except red snapper and tomatoes, and again she offered him her tomatoes; perhaps he had grown to expect it and already she was chained by custom. He was an old man, he had made no pass which she could reasonably reject – how could a man of his age make a pass at a woman of hers? – and yet all the same she had a sense that she had landed on a conveyor belt . . . The future was not in her hands, and she was a little scared. She would have been more frightened if it had not been for her unusual consumption of bourbon.

'It was good bourbon,' she commented for something to say, and immediately regretted it. It gave him an opening.

'We'll have another glass before bed.'

'I think I've drunk enough.'

'A good bourbon won't hurt you. You'll sleep well.'

'I always sleep well.' It was a lie – the kind of unimportant lie one tells a husband or a lover in order to keep some privacy. The young man who had been talking about Tennessee Williams rose from his table. He was very tall and thin and he wore a skin-tight black sweater; his small elegant buttocks were outlined in skin-tight trousers. It was easy to imagine him a degree more naked. Would he have looked at her, she wondered, with interest if she had not been sitting there in the company of a fat old man so horribly clothed? It was unlikely; his body was not designed for a woman's caress.

'I don't.'

'You don't what?'

'I don't sleep well.' The unexpected self-disclosure after all his reticences came as a shock. It was as though he had put out one of his square brick-like hands and pulled her to him. He had been aloof, he had evaded her personal questions, he had lulled her into a sense of security, but now every time she opened her mouth, she seemed doomed to commit an error, to invite him nearer. Even her harmless remark about the bourbon . . . She said stupidly, 'Perhaps it's the change of climate.'

'What change of climate?'

'Between here and . . . and . . . '

'Curaçao? I guess there's no great difference. I don't sleep there either.'

'I've got some very good pills . . . ' she said rashly.

'I thought you said you slept well.'

'Oh, there are always times. It's sometimes just a question of digestion.'

'Yes, digestion. You're right there. A bourbon will be good for that. If you've finished dinner . . . '

She looked across the coffee tavern to the bamboo bar, where the young man stood *déhanché*, holding a glass of crème-de-menthe between his face and his companion's like an exotically coloured monocle.

Mr Hickslaughter said in a shocked voice, 'You don't care for that type, do you?'

'They're often good conversationalists.'

'Oh, conversation . . . If that's what you want.' It was as though she had expressed an un-American liking for snails or frogs' legs.

'Shall we have our bourbon in the bar? It's a little cooler tonight.'

'And pay and listen to their chatter? No, we'll go upstairs.'

He swung back again in the direction of old-fashioned courtesy and came behind her to pull out her chair – even Charlie was not so polite, but was it politeness or the determination to block her way of escape to the bar?

They entered the lift together. The black attendant had a radio turned on, and from the small brown box came the voice of a preacher talking about the Blood of the Lamb. Perhaps it was a Sunday, and that would explain the temporary void around them – between one jolly bunch and another. They stepped out into the empty corridor like undesirables marooned. The boy followed them out and sat down upon a chair beside the elevator to wait for another signal, while the voice continued to talk about the Blood of the Lamb. What was she afraid of? Mr Hickslaughter began to unlock his door. He was much older than her father would have been if he had been still alive; he could be her grandfather – the excuse, 'What will the boy think?' was inadmissible – it was even shocking, for his manner had never ceased to be correct. He might be old, but what right had she to think of him as 'dirty'?

'Damn the hotel key . . . ' he said. 'It won't open.'

She turned the handle for him. 'The door wasn't locked.'

'I can sure do with a bourbon after those nancies . . . '

But now she had her excuse ready on the lips. 'I've had one too many already, I'm afraid. I've got to sleep it off.' She put her hand on his arm. 'Thank you so much . . . It was a lovely evening.' She was aware how insulting her English accent sounded as she walked quickly down the corridor leaving it behind her like a mocking presence, mocking all the things she liked best in him: his ambiguous character, his memory of Longfellow, his having to make ends meet.

241

She looked back when she reached her room: he was standing in the passage as though he couldn't make up his mind to go in. She was reminded of an old man whom she had passed one day on the campus leaning on his broom among the unswept autumn leaves.

4

In her room she picked up a book and tried to read. It was Thomson's *Seasons*. She had carried it with her, so that she could understand any reference to his work that Charlie might make in a letter. This was the first time she had opened it, and she was not held:

And now the mounting Sun dispels the Fog:
The rigid Hoar-Frost melts! before his Beam;
And hung on every Spray, on every Blade
Of Grass, the myriad Dew-Drops twinkle round.

If she could be so cowardly, she thought, with a harmless old man like that, how could she have faced the real decisiveness of an adventure? One was not, at her age, 'swept off the feet'. Charlie had been proved just as sadly right to trust her as she was right to trust Charlie. Now with the difference in time he would be leaving the Museum, or rather, if this were a Sunday as the Blood of the Lamb seemed to indicate, he would probably have just quit writing in his hotel room. After a successful day's work he always resembled an advertisement for a new shaving-cream: a kind of glow . . . She found it irritating, like living with a halo. Even his voice had a different timbre and he would call her 'old girl' and pat her bottom patronisingly. She preferred him when he was touchy with failure: only temporary failure, of course, the failure of an idea which hadn't worked out, the touchiness of a child's disappointment at a party which has not come up to his expectations, not the failure of the old man – the rusted framework of a ship transfixed once and for all upon the rock where it had struck.

She felt ignoble. What earthly risk could the old man represent to justify refusing him half an hour's companionship? He could no more assault her than the boat could detach itself from the rock and steam out to sea for the Fortunate Islands. She pictured him sitting alone with his half-empty bottle of bourbon seeking unconsciousness. Or was he perhaps finishing the crude blackmailing letter to his brother? What a story she would make of it one day, she thought with self-disgust as she took off her dress, her evening with a blackmailer and 'pirate'.

There was one thing she could do for him: she could give him her bottle of pills. She put on her dressing-gown and retrod the corridor, room by room, until she arrived at 63. His voice told her to come in. She opened the door and in the light of the bedside lamp saw him sitting on the edge of the bed wearing a crumpled pair of cotton pyjamas with broad mauve stripes. She began, 'I've brought you . . . ' and then she saw to her amazement that he had been crying. His eyes were red and the evening darkness of his cheeks sparkled with points like dew. She had only once before seen a man cry – Charlie, when the University Press had decided against his first volume of literary essays.

'I thought you were the maid,' he said. 'I rang for her.'

'What did you want?'

'I thought she might take a glass of bourbon,' he said.

'Did you want so much . . . ? I'll take a glass.' The bottle was still on the dressing-table where they had left it and the two glasses – she identified hers by the smear of lipstick. 'Here you are,' she said, 'drink it up. It will make you sleep.'

He said, 'I'm not an alcoholic.'

'Of course you aren't.'

She sat on the bed beside him and took his left hand in hers. It was cracked and dry, and she wanted to clean back the cuticle until she remembered that was something she did for Charlie.

'I wanted company,' he said.

'I'm here.'

'You'd better turn off the bell-light or the maid will come.'

'She'll never know what she missed in the way of Old Walker.'

When she returned from the door he was lying back against the pillows in an odd twisted position, and she thought again of the ship broken-backed upon the rocks. She tried to pick up his feet to lay them on the bed, but they were like heavy stones at the bottom of a quarry.

'Lie down,' she said, 'you'll never be sleepy that way. What do you do for company in Curaçao?'

'I manage,' he said.

'You've finished the bourbon. Let me put out the lights.'

'It's no good pretending to you,' he said.

'Pretending?'

'I'm afraid of the dark.'

She thought, I'll smile later when I think of who it

was I feared. She said, 'Do the old pirates you fought come back to haunt you?'

'I've done some bad things,' he said, 'in my time.'

'Haven't we all?'

'Nothing extraditable,' he explained as though that were an extenuation.

'If you take one of my pills . . . '

'You won't go – not yet?'

'No, no. I'll stay till you're sleepy.'

'I've been wanting to talk to you for days.'

'I'm glad you did.'

'Would you believe it – I hadn't got the nerve.' If she had shut her eyes it might have been a very young man speaking. 'I don't know your sort.'

'Don't you have my sort in Curaçao?'

'No.'

'You haven't taken the pill yet.'

'I'm afraid of not waking up.'

'Have you so much to do tomorrow?'

'I mean ever.' He put out his hand and touched her knee, searchingly, without sensuality, as if he needed support from the bone. 'I'll tell you what's wrong. You're a stranger, so I can tell you. I'm afraid of dying, with nobody around, in the dark.'

'Are you ill?'

'I wouldn't know. I don't see doctors. I don't like doctors.'

'But why should you think . . . ?'

'I'm over seventy. The Bible age. It could happen any day now.'

'You'll live to a hundred,' she said with an odd conviction.

'Then I'll have to live with fear the hell of a long time.'

'Was that why you were crying?'

'No. I thought you were going to stay awhile, and then suddenly you went. I guess I was disappointed.'

'Are you never alone in Curaçao?'

'I pay not to be alone.'

'As you'd have paid the maid?'

'Ye-eh. Sort of.'

It was as though she were discovering for the first time the interior of the enormous continent on which she had elected to live. America had been Charlie, it had been New England; through books and movies she had been aware of the wonders of nature like some great cineramic film with Lowell Thomas cheapening the Painted Desert and the Grand Canyon with his clichés. There had been no mystery anywhere from Miami to Niagara Falls, from Cape Cod to the Pacific Palisades; tomatoes were served on every plate and Coca-Cola in every glass. Nobody anywhere admitted failure or fear; they were like sins 'hushed up' – worse perhaps than sins, for sins have glamour – they were bad taste. But here stretched on the bed, dressed in striped pyjamas which Brooks Brothers would have disowned, failure and fear talked to her without shame, and in an American accent. It was as though she were living in the remote future, after God knew what catastrophe.

She said, 'I wasn't for sale? There was only the Old Walker to tempt *me*.'

He raised his antique Neptune head a little way from the pillow and said, 'I'm not afraid of death. Not sudden death. Believe me, I've looked for it here and there. It's the certain-sure business, closing in on you, like tax-inspectors . . .'

She said, 'Sleep now.'

'I can't.'

'Yes, you can.'

'If you'd stay with me awhile . . . '

'I'll stay with you. Relax.' She lay down on the bed beside him on the outside of the sheet. In a few minutes he was deeply asleep and she turned off the light. He grunted several times and spoke only once, when he said, 'You've got me wrong,' and after that he became for a little while like a dead man in his immobility and his silence, so that during that period she fell asleep. When she woke she was aware from his breathing that he was awake too. He was lying away from her so that their bodies wouldn't touch. She put out her hand and felt no repulsion at all at his excitement. It was as though she had spent many nights beside him in the one bed, and when he made love to her, silently and abruptly in the darkness, she gave a sigh of satisfaction. There was no guilt; she would be going back in a few days, resigned and tender, to Charlie and Charlie's loving skill, and she wept a little, but not seriously, at the temporary nature of this meeting.

'What's wrong?' he asked.

'Nothing. Nothing. I wish I could stay.'

'Stay a little longer. Stay till it's light.' That would not be very long. Already they could distinguish the grey masses of the furniture standing around them like Caribbean tombs.

'Oh yes, I'll stay till it's light. That wasn't what I meant.' His body began to slip out of her, and it was as though he were carrying away her unknown child, away in the direction of Curaçao, and she tried to hold him back, the fat old frightened man whom she almost loved.

He said, 'I never had this in mind.'

'I know. Don't say it. I understand.'

'I guess after all we've got a lot in common,' he said, and she agreed in order to quieten him. He was fast asleep by the time the light came back, so she got off the bed without waking him and went to her room. She locked the door and began with resolution to pack her bag: it was time for her to leave, it was time for term to start again. She wondered afterwards, when she thought of him, what it was they could have had in common, except the fact, of course, that for both of them Jamaica was cheap in August.

A Shocking Accident

I

Jerome was called into his housemaster's room in the break between the second and the third classes on a Thursday morning. He had no fear of trouble, for he was a warden – the name that the proprietor and headmaster of a rather expensive preparatory school had chosen to give to approved, reliable boys in the lower forms (from a warden one became a guardian and finally before leaving, it was hoped for Marlborough or Rugby, a crusader). The housemaster, Mr Wordsworth, sat behind his desk with an appearance of perplexity and apprehension. Jerome had the odd impression when he entered that he was a cause of fear.

'Sit down, Jerome,' Mr Wordsworth said. 'All going well with the trigonometry?'

'Yes, sir.'

'I've had a telephone call, Jerome. From your aunt. I'm afraid I have bad news for you.'

'Yes, sir?'

'Your father has had an accident.'

'Oh.'

Mr Wordsworth looked at him with some surprise. 'A serious accident.'

'Yes, sir?'

Jerome worshipped his father: the verb is exact. As man recreates God, so Jerome recreated his father –

from a restless widowed author into a mysterious adventurer who travelled in far places – Nice, Beirut, Majorca, even the Canaries. The time had arrived about his eighth birthday when Jerome believed that his father either 'ran guns' or was a member of the British Secret Service. Now it occurred to him that his father might have been wounded in 'a hail of machine-gun bullets'.

Mr Wordsworth played with the ruler on his desk. He seemed at a loss how to continue. He said, 'You know your father was in Naples?'

'Yes, sir.'

'Your aunt heard from the hospital today.'

'Oh.'

Mr Wordsworth said with desperation, 'It was a street accident.'

'Yes, sir?' It seemed quite likely to Jerome that they would call it a street accident. The police of course had fired first; his father would not take human life except as a last resort.

'I'm afraid your father was very seriously hurt indeed.'

'Oh.'

'In fact, Jerome, he died yesterday. Quite without pain.'

'Did they shoot him through the heart?'

'I beg your pardon. What did you say, Jerome?'

'Did they shoot him through the heart?'

'Nobody shot him, Jerome. A pig fell on him.' An inexplicable convulsion took place in the nerves of Mr Wordsworth's face; it really looked for a moment as though he were going to laugh. He closed his eyes, composed his features and said rapidly, as though it were necessary to expel the story as rapidly as possible, 'Your father was walking along a street in Naples when a pig fell on him. A shocking accident. Apparently in the poorer quarters of Naples they keep pigs on their balconies. This one was on the fifth floor. It had grown too fat. The balcony broke. The pig fell on your father.'

Mr Wordsworth left his desk rapidly and went to the window, turning his back on Jerome. He shook a little with emotion.

Jerome said, 'What happened to the pig?'

2

This was not callousness on the part of Jerome, as it was interpreted by Mr Wordsworth to his colleagues (he even discussed with them whether, perhaps, Jerome was yet fitted to be a warden). Jerome was only attempting to visualise the strange scene to get the details right. Nor was Jerome a boy who cried; he was a boy who brooded, and it never occurred to him at his preparatory school that the circumstances of his father's death were comic – they were still part of the mystery of life. It was later, in his first term at his public school, when he told the story to his best friend, that he began to realise how it affected others. Naturally after that disclosure he was known, rather unreasonably, as Pig.

Unfortunately his aunt had no sense of humour. There was an enlarged snapshot of his father on the piano: a large sad man in an unsuitable dark suit posed in Capri with an umbrella (to guard him against sunstroke), the Faraglione rocks forming the back-ground. By the age of sixteen Jerome was well aware that the portrait looked more like the author of *Sunshine and Shade* and *Rambles in the Balearics* than an agent of the Secret Service. All the same he loved the memory of his father: he still possessed an album fitted with picture-postcards (the stamps had been soaked off long ago for his other collection), and it pained him when his aunt embarked with strangers on the story of his father's death.

'A shocking accident,' she would begin, and the stranger would compose his or her features into the correct shape for interest and commiseration. Both reactions, of course, were false, but it was terrible for Jerome to see how suddenly, midway in her rambling discourse, the interest would become genuine. 'I can't think how such things can be allowed in a civilised country,' his aunt would say. 'I suppose one has to regard Italy as civilised. One is prepared for all kinds of things abroad, of course, and my brother was a great traveller. He always carried a water-filter with him. It was far less expensive, you know, than buying all those bottles of mineral water. My brother always said that his filter paid for his dinner wine. You can see from that what a careful man he was, but who could possibly have expected when he was walking along the Via Dottore Manuele Panucci on his way to the Hydrographic Museum that a pig would fall on him?' That was the moment when the interest became genuine.

Jerome's father had not been a very distinguished writer, but the time always seems to come, after an author's death, when somebody thinks it worth his while to write a letter to the *Times Literary Supplement* announcing the preparation of a biography and asking to see any letters or documents or receive any anecdotes from friends of the dead man. Most of the biographies, of course, never appear – one wonders whether the whole thing may not be an obscure form of blackmail and whether many a potential writer of a biography or thesis finds the means in this way to finish his education at Kansas or Nottingham. Jerome, however, as a chartered accountant, lived far from the literary world. He did not realise how small the menace really was, or that the danger period for someone of his father's obscurity had long passed. Sometimes he rehearsed the method of recounting his father's death so as to reduce the comic element to its smallest dimensions – it would be of no use to refuse information, for in that case the biographer would undoubtedly visit his aunt who was living to a great old age with no sign of flagging.

It seemed to Jerome that there were two possible methods – the first led gently up to the accident, so that by the time it was described the listener was so well prepared that the death came really as an anti-climax. The chief danger of laughter in such a story was always surprise. When he rehearsed this method Jerome began boringly enough.

'You know Naples and those high tenement buildings? Somebody once told me that the Neapolitan always feels at home in New York just as the man from Turin feels at home in London because the river runs in much the same way in both cities. Where was I? Oh, yes. Naples, of course. You'd be surprised in the poorer quarters what things they keep on the balconies of those sky-scraping tenements – not washing, you know, or bedding, but things like livestock, chickens or even pigs. Of course the pigs get no exercise whatever and fatten all the quicker.'

He could imagine how his hearer's eyes would have glazed by this time. 'I've no idea, have you, how heavy a pig can be, but these old buildings are all badly in need of repair. A balcony on the fifth floor gave way under one of those pigs. It struck the third floor balcony on its way down and sort of ricochetted into the street. My father was on the way to the Hydrographic Museum when the pig hit him. Coming from that height and that angle it broke his neck.' This was really a masterly attempt to make an intrinsically interesting subject boring.

The other method Jerome rehearsed had the virtue of brevity.

'My father was killed by a pig.'

'Really? In India?'

'No, in Italy.'

'How interesting. I never realised there was pig-sticking in Italy. Was your father keen on polo?'

In course of time, neither too early nor too late, rather as though, in his capacity as a chartered accountant, Jerome had studied the statistics and taken the average, he became engaged to be married: to a pleasant fresh-faced girl of twenty-five whose father was a doctor in Pinner. Her name was Sally, her favourite author was still Hugh Walpole, and she had adored babies ever since she had been given a doll at the age of five which moved its eyes and made water. Their relationship was contented rather than exciting, as became the love-affair of a chartered accountant; it would never have done if it had inter-fered with the figures.

One thought worried Jerome, however. Now that within a year he might himself become a father, his love for the dead man increased; he realised what affection had gone into the picture-postcards. He felt a longing to protect his memory, and uncertain whether this quiet love of his would survive if Sally were so insensitive as to laugh when she heard the story of his father's death. Inevitably she would hear it when Jerome brought her to dinner with his aunt. Several times he tried to tell her himself, as she was naturally anxious to know all she could that concerned him.

'You were very small when your father died?'

'Just nine.'

'Poor little boy,' she said.

'I was at school. They broke the news to me.'

'Did you take it very hard?'

'I can't remember.'

'You never told me how it happened.'

'It was very sudden. A street accident.'

'You'll never drive fast, will you, Jemmy?' (She had begun to call him 'Jemmy'.) It was too late then to try the second method – the one he thought of as the pig-sticking one.

They were going to marry quietly in a registry office and have their honeymoon at Torquay. He avoided taking her to see his aunt until a week before the wedding, but then the night came, and he could not have told himself whether his apprehension was more for his father's memory or the security of his own love.

The moment came all too soon. 'Is that Jemmy's father?' Sally asked, picking up the portrait of the man with the umbrella.

'Yes, dear. How did you guess?'

'He has Jemmy's eyes and brow, hasn't he?'

'Has Jerome lent you his books?'

'No.'

'I will give you a set for your wedding. He wrote so tenderly about his travels. My own favourite is *Nooks and Crannies*. He would have had a great future. It made that shocking accident all the worse.'

'Yes?'

Jerome longed to leave the room and not see that loved face crinkle with irresistible amusement.

'I had so many letters from his readers after the pig fell on him.' She had never been so abrupt before.

And then the miracle happened. Sally did not laugh. Sally sat with open eyes of horror while his aunt told her the story, and at the end, 'How horrible,' Sally said. 'It makes you think, doesn't it? Happening like that. Out of a clear sky.'

Jerome's heart sang with joy. It was as though she had appeased his fear for ever. In the taxi going home he kissed her with more passion than he had ever shown and she returned it. There were babies in her pale blue pupils, babies that rolled their eyes and made water.

A week today,' Jerome said, and she squeezed his hand. 'Penny for your thoughts, my darling.'

'I was wondering,' Sally said, 'what happened to the poor pig?'

'They almost certainly had it for dinner,' Jerome said happily and kissed the dear child again.

The Invisible Japanese Gentlemen

There were eight Japanese gentlemen having a fish dinner at Bentley's. They spoke to each other rarely in their incomprehensible tongue, but always with a courteous smile and often with a small bow. All but one of them wore glasses. Sometimes the pretty girl who sat in the window beyond gave them a passing glance, but her own problem seemed too serious for her to pay real attention to anyone in the world except herself and her companion.

She had thin blonde hair and her face was pretty and *petite* in a Regency way, oval like a miniature, though she had a harsh way of speaking – perhaps the accent of the school, Roedean or Cheltenham Ladies' College, which she had not long ago left. She wore a man's signet-ring on her engagement finger, and as I sat down at my table, with the Japanese gentlemen between us, she said, 'So you see we could marry next week.'

'Yes?'

Her companion appeared a little distraught. He refilled their glasses with Chablis and said, 'Of course, but Mother . . . ' I missed some of the conversation then, because the eldest Japanese gentleman leant across the table, with a smile and a little bow, and uttered a whole paragraph like the mutter from an aviary, while everyone bent towards him and smiled and listened, and I couldn't help attending to him myself.

The girl's fiancé resembled her physically. I could
see them as two miniatures hanging side by side on
white wood panels. He should have been a young
officer in Nelson's navy in the days when a certain
weakness and sensitivity were no bar to promotion.

She said, 'They are giving me an advance of five
hundred pounds, and they've sold the paperback rights
already.' The hard commercial declaration came as a
shock to me; it was a shock too that she was one of my
own profession. She couldn't have been more than
twenty. She deserved better of life.

He said, 'But my uncle . . . '

'You know you don't get on with him. This way we
shall be quite independent.'

'*You* will be independent,' he said grudgingly.

'The wine-trade wouldn't really suit you, would it?
I spoke to my publisher about you and there's a very
good chance . . . if you began with some reading . . . '

'But I don't know a thing about books.'

'I would help you at the start.'

'My mother says that writing is a good crutch . . . '

'Five hundred pounds and half the paperback rights
is a pretty solid crutch,' she said.

'This Chablis is good, isn't it?'

'I dare say.'

I began to change my opinion of him – he had not
the Nelson touch. He was doomed to defeat. She
came alongside and raked him fore and aft. 'Do you
know what Mr Dwight said?'

'Who's Dwight?'

'Darling, you don't listen, do you? My publisher.
He said he hadn't read a first novel in the last ten
years which showed such powers of observation.'

'That's wonderful,' he said sadly, 'wonderful.'

'Only he wants me to change the title.'

'Yes?'

'He doesn't like *The Ever-Rolling Stream*. He wants to call it *The Chelsea Set*.'

'What did you say?'

'I agreed. I do think that with a first novel one should try to keep one's publisher happy. Especially when, really, he's going to pay for our marriage, isn't he?'

'I see what you mean.' Absent-mindedly he stirred his Chablis with a fork – perhaps before the engagement he had always bought champagne. The Japanese gentlemen had finished their fish and with very little English but with elaborate courtesy they were ordering from the middle-aged waitress a fresh fruit salad. The girl looked at them, and then she looked at me, but I think she saw only the future. I wanted very much to warn her against any future based on a first novel called *The Chelsea Set*. I was on the side of his mother. It was a humiliating thought, but I was probably about her mother's age.

I wanted to say to her, Are you certain your publisher is telling you the truth? Publishers are human. They may sometimes exaggerate the virtues of the young and the pretty. Will *The Chelsea Set* be read in five years? Are you prepared for the years of effort, 'the long defeat of doing nothing well'? As the years pass writing will not become any easier, the daily effort will grow harder to endure, those 'powers of observation' will become enfeebled; you will be judged, when you reach your forties, by performance and not by promise.

'My next novel is going to be about St Tropez.'

'I didn't know you'd ever been there.'

'I haven't. A fresh eye's terribly important. I thought

259

we might settle down there for six months.'

'There wouldn't be much left of the advance by that time.'

'The advance is only an advance. I get fifteen per cent after five thousand copies and twenty per cent after ten. And of course another advance will be due, darling, when the next book's finished. A bigger one if *The Chelsea Set* sells well.'

'Suppose it doesn't.'

'Mr Dwight says it will. He ought to know.'

'My uncle would start me at twelve hundred.'

'But, darling, how could you come then to St Tropez?'

'Perhaps we'd do better to marry when you come back.'

She said harshly, 'I mightn't come back if *The Chelsea Set* sells enough.'

'Oh.'

She looked at me and the party of Japanese gentlemen. She finished her wine. She said, 'Is this is a quarrel?'

'No.'

'I've got the title for the next book – *The Azure Blue*.'

'I thought azure *was* blue.'

She looked at him with disappointment. 'You don't really want to be married to a novelist, do you?'

'You aren't one yet.'

'I was born one – Mr Dwight says. My powers of observation . . . '

'Yes. You told me that, but, dear, couldn't you observe a bit nearer home? Here in London.'

'I've done that in *The Chelsea Set*. I don't want to repeat myself.'

The bill had been lying beside them for some time now. He took out his wallet to pay, but she snatched the paper out of his reach. She said, 'This is my celebration.'

'What of?'

'*The Chelsea Set*, of course. Darling, you're awfully decorative, but sometimes – well, you simply don't connect.'

'I'd rather . . . if you don't mind . . . '

'No, darling, this is on me. And Mr Dwight, of course.'

He submitted just as two of the Japanese gentlemen gave tongue simultaneously, then stopped abruptly and bowed to each other, as though they were blocked in a doorway.

I had thought the two young people matching miniatures, but what a contrast in fact there was. The same type of prettiness could contain weakness and strength. Her Regency counterpart, I suppose, would have borne a dozen children without the aid of anaesthetics, while he would have fallen an easy victim to the first dark eyes in Naples. Would there one day be a dozen books on her shelf? They have to be born without an anaesthetic too. I found myself hoping that *The Chelsea Set* would prove to be a disaster and that eventually she would take up photographic modelling while he established himself solidly in the wine trade in St James's. I didn't like to think of her as the Mrs Humphry Ward of her generation – not that I would live so long. Old age saves us from the realisation of a great many fears. I wondered to which publishing firm Dwight belonged. I could imagine the blurb he would have already written about her abrasive powers of observation. There would be a photo, if he was wise, on the back of the jacket, for reviewers, as well as publishers, are human, and she didn't look like Mrs Humphry Ward.

I could hear them talking while they found their coats at the back of the restaurant. He said, 'I wonder what all those Japanese are doing here?'

'Japanese?' she said. 'What Japanese, darling? Sometimes you are so evasive I think you don't want to marry me at all.'

Awful When You Think Of It

When the baby looked up at me from its wicker basket and winked – on the opposite seat somewhere between Reading and Slough – I became uneasy. It was as if he had discovered my secret interest.

It is awful how little we change. So often an old acquaintance, whom one has not seen for forty years when he occupied the neighbouring chopped and inky desk, detains one in the street with his unwelcome memory. Even as a baby we carry the future with us. Clothes cannot change us, the clothes are the uniform of our character, and our character changes as little as the shape of the nose and the expression of the eyes.

It has always been my hobby in railway trains to visualise in a baby's face the man he is to become – the bar-lounger, the gadabout, the frequenter of fashionable weddings; you need only supply the cloth cap, the grey topper, the uniform of the sad, smug or hilarious future. But I have always felt a certain contempt for the babies I have studied with such superior wisdom (they little know), and it was a shock last week when one of the brood not only detected me in the act of observation but returned that knowing signal, as if he shared my knowledge of what the years would make of him.

He had been momentarily left alone by his young mother on the seat opposite. She had smiled towards me with a tacit understanding that I would look after her baby for a few moments. What danger after all

263

could happen to *it*? (Perhaps she was less certain of his sex than I was. She knew the shape under the nappies, of course, but shapes can deceive: parts alter, operations are performed.) She could not see what I had seen – the tilted bowler and the umbrella over the arm. (No arm was yet apparent under the coverlet printed with pink rabbits.)

When she was safely out of the carriage I bent towards the basket and asked him a question. I had never before carried my researches quite so far.

'What's yours?' I said.

He blew a thick white bubble, brown at the edges. There could be no doubt at all that he was saying, 'A pint of the best bitter.'

'Haven't seen you lately – you know – in the old place,' I said.

He gave a quick smile, passing it off, then he winked again. You couldn't doubt that he was saying, 'The other half?'

I blew a bubble in my turn – we spoke the same language.

Very slightly he turned his head to one side. He didn't want anybody to hear what he was going to say now.

'You've got a tip?' I asked.

Don't mistake my meaning. It was not racing information I wanted. Of course I could not see his waist under all those pink-rabbit wrappings, but I knew perfectly well that he wore a double-breasted waistcoat and had nothing to do with the tracks. I said very rapidly because his mother might return at any moment, 'My brokers are Druce, Davis and Burrows.'

He looked up at me with bloodshot eyes and a little

line of spittle began to form at the corner of his mouth. I said, 'Oh, I know they're not all that good. But at the moment they are recommending Stores.'

He gave a high wail of pain – you could have mistaken the cause for wind, but I knew better. In his club they didn't have to serve dill water. I said, 'I don't agree, mind you,' and he stopped crying and blew a bubble – a little tough white one which lingered on his lip.

I caught his meaning at once. 'My round,' I said. 'Time for a short?'

He nodded.

'Scotch?' I know few people will believe me, but he raised his head an inch or two and gazed unmistakably at my watch.

'A bit early?' I said. 'Pink gin?'

I didn't have to wait for his reply. 'Make them large ones,' I said to the imaginary barman.

He spat at me, so I added, 'Throw away the pink.'

'Well,' I said, 'here's to you. Happy future,' and we smiled at each other, well content.

'I don't know what you would advise,' I said, 'but surely Tobaccos are about as low as they will go. When you think Imps were a cool eighty shillings in the early thirties and now you can pick them up for under sixty . . . This cancer scare can't go on. People have got to have their fun.'

At the word fun he winked again, looked secretively around, and I realised that perhaps I had been on the wrong track. It was not after all the state of the markets he had been so ready to talk about.

'I heard a damn good one yesterday,' I said. 'A man got into a tube train, and there was a pretty girl with one stocking coming down . . . '

He yawned and closed his eyes.

'Sorry,' I said, 'I thought it was new. You tell me one.'

And do you know that damned baby was quite ready to oblige? But he belonged to the school who find their own jokes funny and when he tried to speak, he could only laugh. He couldn't get his story out for laughter. He laughed and winked and laughed again – what a good story it must have been. I could have dined out for weeks on the strength of it. His limbs twitched in the basket; he even tried to get his hands free from the pink rabbits, and then the laughter died. I could almost hear him saying, 'Tell you later, old man.'

His mother opened the door of the compartment. She said, 'You've been amusing baby. How kind of you. Are you fond of babies?' And she gave me such a look – the love-wrinkles forming round the mouth and eyes – that I was tempted to reply with the warmth and hypocrisy required, but then I met the baby's hard relentless gaze.

'Well, as a matter of fact,' I said, 'I'm not. Not really,' I drooled on, losing all my chances before that blue and pebbly stare. 'You know how it is . . . never had one of my own . . . I'm fond of fishes though . . . '

I suppose in a way I got my reward. The baby blew a whole succession of bubbles. He was satisfied; after all a chap shouldn't make passes at another chap's mother, especially if he belongs to the same club – for suddenly I knew inevitably to what club he would belong in twenty-five years' time. 'On me,' he was obviously saying now. 'Doubles all round.' I could only hope that I would not live so long.

Dr Crombie

An unfortunate circumstance in my life has just recalled to mind a certain Dr Crombie and the conversations I used to hold with him when I was young. He was the school doctor until the eccentricity of his ideas became generally known. After he had ceased to attend the school the rest of his practice was soon reduced to a few old people, almost as eccentric as himself – there were, I remember, Colonel Parker, a British Israelite; Miss Warrender, who kept twenty-five cats; and a man called Horace Turner, who invented a system for turning the National Debt into a National Credit.

Dr Crombie lived all alone half a mile from the school in a red-brick villa in King's Road. Luckily he possessed a small private income, for at the end his work had come to be entirely paperwork – lengthy articles for the *Lancet* and the *British Medical Journal* which were never published. It was long before the days of television; otherwise a corner might have been found for him in some magazine programme, and his views would have reached a larger public than the random gossips of Bankstead – with who knows what result? – for he spoke with sincerity, and when I was young he certainly to me carried a measure of conviction.

Our school, which had begun as a grammar school during the reign of Henry VIII, had, by the twentieth century, just edged its way into the *Public Schools Year*

Book. There were many day-boys, of whom I was one, for Bankstead was only an hour from London by train, and in the days of the old London Midland and Scottish Railways there were frequent and rapid services for commuters. In a boarding-school where the boys are isolated for months at a time like prisoners on Dartmoor, Dr Crombie's views would have become known more slowly. By the time a boy went home for the holidays he would have forgotten any curious details, and the parents, dotted about England in equal isolation, would have been unable to get together and check up on any unusual stories. It was different at Bankstead, where parents lived a community life and attended sing-songs, but even here Dr Crombie's views had a long innings.

The headmaster was progressively minded and, when the boys emerged, at the age of thirteen, from the junior school, he arranged, with the consent of the parents, that Dr Crombie should address them in small groups on the problems of personal hygiene and the dangers which lay ahead. I have only faint memories of the occasion, of the boys who sniggered, of the boys who blushed, of the boys who stared at the ground as though they had dropped something, but I remember vividly the explicit and plain-speaking Dr Crombie, with his melancholy moustache, which remained blond from nicotine long after his head was grey, and his gold-rimmed spectacles – gold rims, like a pipe, always give me the impression of a rectitude I can never achieve. I understood very little of what he was saying, but I do remember later that I asked my parents what he meant by 'playing with oneself'. Being an only child I was accustomed to play with myself. For example, in the case of my model railway,

I was in turn driver, signalman and station-master, and I felt no need of an assistant.

My mother said she had forgotten to speak to the cook and left us alone.

'Dr Crombie,' I told my father, 'says that it causes cancer.'

'Cancer!' my father exclaimed. 'Are you sure he didn't say insanity?' (It was a great period for insanity: loss of vitality leading to nervous debility and nervous debility becoming melancholia and eventually melancholia becoming madness. For some reasons these effects were said to come before marriage and not after.)

'He said cancer. An incurable disease, he said.'

'Odd!' my father remarked. He reassured me about playing trains, and Dr Crombie's theory went out of my head for some years. I don't think my father can have mentioned it to anyone else except possibly my mother and that only as a joke. Cancer was as good a scare during puberty as madness – the standard of dishonesty among parents is a high one. They had themselves long ceased to believe in the threat of madness, but they used it as a convenience, and only after some years did they reach the conclusion that Dr Crombie was a strictly honest man.

I had just left school by that time and I had not yet gone up to the university; Dr Crombie's head was quite white by then, though his moustache stayed blond. We had become close friends, for we both liked observing trains, and sometimes on a summer's day we took a picnic-lunch and sat on the green mound of Bankstead Castle from which we could watch the line and see below it the canal with the bright-painted barges drawn by slow horses in the direction of Birmingham. We drank ginger-beer out of stone bottles and ate ham sandwiches while Dr Crombie studied *Bradshaw*. When I want an image for innocence I think of those afternoons.

But the peace of the afternoon I am remembering now was disturbed. An immense goods-train of coal-wagons went by us – I counted sixty-three, which approached our record, but when I asked for his confirmation, Dr Crombie had inexplicably forgotten to count.

'Is something the matter?' I asked.

'The school has asked me to resign,' he said, and he took off the gold-rimmed glasses and wiped them.

'Good heavens! Why?'

'The secrets of the consulting-room, my dear boy, are one-sided,' he said. 'The patient, but not the doctor, is at liberty to tell everything.'

A week later I learnt a little of what had happened. The story had spread rapidly from parent to parent, for this was not something which concerned small boys – this concerned all of them. Perhaps there was even an element of fear in the talk – fear that Dr Crombie might be right. Incredible thought!

A boy whom I knew, a little younger than myself, called Fred Wright, who was still in the sixth form, had visited Dr Crombie because of certain pains in the testicles. He had had his first woman in a street off Leicester Square on a half-day excursion – there were half-day excursions in those happy days of rival railway-companies – and he had taken his courage in his hands and visited Dr Crombie. He was afraid that he had caught what was then known as a social disease. Dr Crombie had reassured him – he was suffering from acidity, that was all, and he should be careful not to eat tomatoes, but Dr Crombie went on, rashly and unnecessarily, to warn him, as he had warned all of us at thirteen . . .

Fred Wright had no reason to feel ashamed. Acidity can happen to anyone, and he didn't hesitate to tell his parents of the further advice which Dr Crombie had given him. When I returned home that afternoon and questioned my parents, I found the story had already reached them as it had reached the school authorities. Parent after parent had checked with one another, and afterwards child after child was interrogated. Cancer as the result of masturbation was one thing – you had to discourage it somehow – but what right had Dr Crombie to say that cancer was the result of prolonged sexual relations, even in a proper marriage recognised by Church and State? (It was unfortunate that Fred Wright's very virile father, unknown to his son, had already fallen a victim to the dread disease.)

I was even a little shaken myself. I had great affection for Dr Crombie and great confidence in him. (I had never played trains all by myself after thirteen with the same pleasure as before his hygienic talk.) And the worst of it was that now I had fallen in love, hopelessly in love, with a girl in Castle Street with what we called then bobbed hair; she resembled in an innocent and provincial way two famous society sisters whose photographs appeared nearly every week in the *Daily Mail*. (The years seem to be returning on their tracks, and I see now everywhere the same face, the same hair, as I saw then, but alas, with little or no emotion.)

The next time I went out with Dr Crombie to watch the trains I tackled him – shyly; there were still words

I didn't like to use with my elders. 'Did you really tell Fred Wright that that – marriage – is a cause of cancer?'

'Not marriage in itself, my boy. Any form of sexual congress.'

'Congress?' It was the first time I had heard the word used in that way. I thought of the Congress of Vienna.

'Making love,' Dr Crombie said gruffly. 'I thought I had explained all that to you at the age of thirteen.'

'I just thought you were talking about playing trains alone,' I said.

'What do you mean, playing trains?' he asked with bewilderment as a fast passenger-train went by, in and out of Bankstead station, leaving a great ball of steam at either end of Platform 2. 'The 3.45 from Newcastle,' he said. 'I make it a minute and a quarter slow.'

'Three-quarters of a minute,' I said. We had no means of checking our watches. It was before the days of radio.

'I am ahead of the time,' Dr Crombie said, 'and I expect to suffer inconvenience. The strange thing is that people here have only just noticed. I have been speaking to you boys on the subject of cancer for years.'

'Nobody realised that you meant marriage,' I said.

'One begins with first things first. You were, none of you, in those symposiums which I held, of an age to marry.'

'But maiden ladies,' I objected, 'they die of cancer too.'

'The definition of maiden in common use,' Dr Crombie replied, looking at his watch as a goods-train went by towards Bletchley, 'is an unbroken hymen. A lady may have had prolonged sexual relations with herself or another without injuring the maidenhead.'

I became curious. A new world was opening to me.

'You mean girls play with themselves too?'

'Of course.'

'But the young don't often die of cancer, do they?'

'They can lay the foundations with their excesses. It was from that I wished to save you all.'

'And the saints,' I said, 'did none of them die of cancer?'

'I know very little about saints. I would hazard a guess that the percentage of such deaths in their case was a small one, but I have never taught that sexual congress is the sole cause of cancer: only that it is the most frequent.'

'But all married people don't die that way?'

'My boy, you would be surprised how seldom many married people make love. A burst of enthusiasm and then a long retreat. The danger is necessarily less in those cases.'

'The more you love the greater the danger?'

'I'm afraid that is a truth which applies to more than the danger of cancer.'

I was too much in love myself to be easily convinced, but his answers came, I had to admit, quickly and readily. When I made some remark about statistics he quickly closed that avenue of hope. 'If they demand statistics,' Dr Crombie said, 'statistics they shall have. They have suspected many causes in the past and based their suspicion on dubious and debatable statistics. White flour for example. It would not surprise me if one day they did not come to suspect even this little innocent comfort of mine' (he waved his cigarette in the direction of the Grand Junction Canal), 'but can they deny that statistically my solution outweighs all others? Almost one hundred per cent of those who die of cancer have practised sex.'

It was a statement impossible to deny, and for a little it silenced me. 'Aren't you afraid yourself?' I asked him at last.

'You know that I live alone. I am one of the few who have never been greatly tempted in that direction.'

'If all of us followed your advice,' I said gloomily, 'the world would cease to exist.'

'You mean the human race. The inter-pollination of flowers seems to have no ill side-effects.'

'And men were created only to die out?'

'I am no believer in the God of Genesis, young man. I think that the natural processes of evolution see to it that an animal becomes extinct when it makes a wrong accidental deviation. Man will perhaps follow the dinosaurs.' He looked at his watch. 'Now here is something wholly abnormal. The time is close on 4.10 and the four o'clock from Bletchley has not even been signalled. Yes, you may check the time, but this delay cannot be accounted for by a difference in watches.'

I have quite forgotten why the four o'clock was so delayed, and I had even forgotten Dr Crombie and our conversation until this afternoon. Dr Crombie survived his ruined practice for a few years and then died quietly one winter night of pneumonia following flu. I married four times, so little had I heeded Dr Crombie's advice, and I only remembered his theory today when my specialist broke to me with rather exaggerated prudence and gravity the fact that I am suffering from cancer of the lungs. My sexual desires, now that I am past sixty, are beginning to diminish, and I am quite content to follow the dinosaurs into obscurity. Of course the doctors attribute the disease to my heavy indulgence in cigarettes, but it amuses me all the same to believe with Dr Crombie that it has been caused by excesses of a more agreeable nature.

The Root of All Evil

This story was told me by my father who heard it directly from his father, the brother of one of the participants; otherwise I doubt whether I would have credited it. But my father was a man of absolute rectitude, and I have no reason to believe that this virtue did not then run in the family.

The events happened in 189—, as they say in old Russian novels, in the small market town of B—. My father was German, and when he settled in England he was the first of the family to go farther than a few kilometres from the home commune, province, canton or whatever it was called in those parts. He was a Protestant who believed in his faith, and no one has a greater ability to believe, without doubt or scruple, than a Protestant of that type. He would not even allow my mother to read us fairy-stories, and he walked three miles to church rather than go to one with pews. 'We've nothing to hide,' he said. 'If I sleep I sleep, and let the world know the weakness of my flesh. Why,' he added, and the thought touched my imagination strongly and perhaps had some influence on my future, 'they could play cards in those pews and no one the wiser.'

That phrase is linked in my mind with the fashion in which he would begin this story. 'Original sin gave man a tilt towards secrecy,' he would say. 'An open sin is only half a sin, and a secret innocence is only half innocent. When you have secrets, there, sooner or later, you'll have sin. I wouldn't let a Freemason cross my threshold. Where I come from secret societies were illegal, and the government had reason. Innocent though they might be at the start, like that club of Schmidt's.'

It appears that among the old people of the town where my father lived were a couple whom I shall continue to call Schmidt, being a little uncertain of the nature of the laws of libel and how limitations and the like affect the dead. Herr Schmidt was a big man and a heavy drinker, but most of his drinking he preferred to do at his own board to the discomfort of his wife, who never touched a drop of alcohol herself. Not that she wished to interfere with her husband's potations; she had a proper idea of a wife's duty, but she had reached an age (she was over sixty and he well past seventy) when she had a great yearning to sit quietly with another woman knitting something or other for her grandchildren and talking about their latest maladies. You can't do that at ease with a man continually on the go to the cellar for another litre. There is a man's atmosphere and a woman's atmosphere, and they don't mix except in the proper place, under the sheets. Many a time Frau Schmidt in her gentle way had tried to persuade him to go out of an evening to the inn. 'What and pay more for every glass?' he would say. Then she tried to persuade him that he had need of men's company and men's conversation. 'Not when I'm tasting a good wine,' he said.

So last of all she took her trouble to Frau Muller who suffered in just the same manner as herself. Frau Muller was a stronger type of woman and she set out to build an organisation. She found four other women starved of female company and female interests, and they arranged to foregather once a week with their sewing and take their evening coffee together. Between them they could summon up more than two dozen grandchildren, so you can imagine they were never short of subjects to talk about. When one child had finished with the chickenpox, at least two would have started the measles. There were all the varying treatments to compare, and there was one school of thought which took the motto 'starve a cold' to mean 'if you starve a cold you will feed a fever' and another school which took the more traditional view. But their debates were never heated like those they had with their husbands, and they took it in turn to act hostess and make the cakes.

But what was happening all this time to the husbands? You might think they would be content to go on drinking alone, but not a bit of it. Drinking's like reading a 'romance' (my father used the term with contempt, he had never turned the pages of a novel in his life): you don't need talk, but you need company, otherwise it begins to feel like work. Frau Muller had thought of that and she suggested to her husband – very gently, so that he hardly noticed – that, when the women were meeting elsewhere, he should ask the other husbands in with their own drinks (no need to spend extra money at the bar) and they could sit as silent as they wished with their glasses till bedtime. Not, of course, that they would be silent all the time. Now and then no doubt one of them would remark on the wet or the fine day, and another would mention the prospects for the harvest, and a third would say that they'd never had so warm a summer as the summer of 188—. Men's talk, which, in the absence of women, would never become heated.

But there was one snag in this arrangement and it was the one which caused the disaster. Frau Muller roped in a seventh woman, who had been widowed by something other than drink – by her husband's curiosity. Frau Puckler had a husband whom none of them could abide, and, before they could settle down to their friendly evenings, they had to decide what to do about him. He was a little vinegary man with a squint and a completely bald head who would empty any bar when he came into it. His eyes, coming together like that, had the effect of a gimlet, and he would stay in conversation with one man for ten minutes on end with his eyes fixed on the other's forehead until you expected sawdust to come out. Unfortunately Frau Puckler was highly respected. It was essential to keep from her any idea that her husband was unwelcome, so for some weeks they had to reject Frau Muller's proposal. They were quite happy, they said, sitting alone at home with a glass when what they really meant was that even loneliness was preferable to the company of Herr Puckler. But they got so miserable all this time that often, when their wives returned home, they would find their husbands tucked up in bed and asleep.

It was then Herr Schmidt broke his customary silence. He called round at Herr Muller's door, one evening when the wives were away, with a four-litre jug of wine, and he hadn't got through more than two litres when he broke silence. This lonely drinking, he said, must come to an end – he had had more sleep the last few weeks than he had had in six months and it was sapping his strength. 'The grave yawns for us,' he said, yawning himself from habit.

'But Puckler?' Herr Muller objected. 'He's worse than the grave.'

'We shall have to meet in secret,' Herr Schmidt said. 'Braun has a fine big cellar.' And that was how the secret began; and from secrecy, my father would moralise, you can grow every sin in the calendar. I pictured secrecy like the dark mould in the cellar where we cultivated our mushrooms, but the mushrooms were good to eat, so that their secret growth . . . I always found an ambivalence in my father's moral teaching.

It appears that for a time all went well. The men were happy drinking together – in the absence, of course, of Herr Puckler, and so were the women, even Frau Puckler, for she always found her husband in bed at night ready for domesticities. He was far too proud to tell her of his ramblings in search of company between the strokes of the town-clock. Every night he would try a different house and every night he found only the closed door and the darkened window. Once, in Herr Braun's cellar, the husbands heard the knocker hammering overhead. At the Gast-hof too he would look regularly in – and sometimes irregularly, as though he hoped that he might catch them off their guard. The street-lamp shone on his bald head, and often some late drinker going home would be confronted by those gimlet-eyes which believed nothing you said. 'Have you seen Herr Muller tonight?' or, 'Herr Schmidt, is he at home?' he would demand of another reveller. He sought them here, he sought them there – he had been content enough aforetime drinking in his own home and sending his wife down to the cellar for a refill, but he knew only too well, now he was alone, that there was no pleasure

possible for a solitary drinker. If Herr Schmidt and
Herr Muller were not at home, where were they? And
the other four with whom he had never been well
acquainted, where were they? Frau Puckler was the
very reverse of her husband, she had no curiosity, and
Frau Muller and Frau Schmidt had mouths which
clinked shut like the clasps of a well-made handbags.

Inevitably after a certain time Herr Puckler went to
the police. He refused to speak to anyone lower than
the Superintendent. His gimlet-eyes bored like a
migraine into the Superintendent's forehead. While
the eyes rested on the one spot, his words wandered
ambiguously. There had been an anarchist outrage at
Schloss – I can't remember the name; there were
rumours of an attempt on a Grand Duke. The Superintendent shifted a little this way and a little that way
on his seat, for these were big affairs which did not
concern him, while the squinting eyes bored con-
tinuously at the sensitive spot above his nose where
his migraine always began. Then the Superintendent
blew loudly and said, 'The times are evil,' a phrase
which he had remembered from the service on Sunday.

'You know the law about secret societies,' Herr
Puckler said.

'Naturally.'

'And yet here, under the nose of the police,' and
the squint-eyes bored deeper, 'there exists just such a
society.'

'If you would be a little more explicit . . . '

So Herr Puckler gave him the whole row of names,
beginning with Herr Schmidt. 'They meet in secret,'
he said. 'None of them stays at home.'

'They are not the kind of men I would suspect of
plotting.'

'All the more dangerous for that.'

'Perhaps they are just friends.'

'Then why don't they meet in public?'

'I'll put a policeman on the case,' the Super-intendent said half-heartedly, so now at night there were two men looking around to find where the six had their meeting-place. The policeman was a simple man who began by asking direct questions, but he had been seen several times in the company of Puckler, so the six assumed quickly enough that he was trying to track them down on Puckler's behalf and they became more careful than ever to avoid discovery. They stocked up Herr Braun's cellar with wine, and they took elaborate precautions not to be seen entering – each one sacrificed a night's drinking in order to lead Herr Puckler and the policeman astray. Nor could they confide in their wives for fear that it might come to the ears of Frau Puckler, so they pretended the scheme had not worked and it was every man for himself again now in drinking. That meant they had to tell a lot of lies if they failed to be the first home – and so, my father said, sin began to enter in.

One night too, Herr Schmidt, who happened to be the decoy, led Herr Puckler a long walk into the suburbs, and then seeing an open door and a light burning in the window with a comforting red glow and being by that time very dry in the mouth, he mistook the house in his distress for a quiet inn and walked inside. He was warmly welcomed by a stout lady and shown into a parlour, where he expected to be served with wine. Three young ladies sat on a sofa in various stages of undress and greeted Herr Schmidt with giggles and warm words. Herr Schmidt was afraid to leave the house at once, in case Puckler was lurking outside, and while he hesitated the stout lady entered with a bottle of champagne on ice and a number of glasses. So for the sake of the drink (though champagne was not his preference – he would have liked the local wine) he stayed, and thus out of secrecy, my father said, came the second sin. But it didn't end there with lies and fornication.

When the time came to go, if he were not to overstay his welcome, Herr Schmidt took a look out of the window, and there, in place of Puckler, was the policeman walking up and down the pavement. He must have followed Puckler at a distance, and then taken on his watch while Puckler went rabbiting after the others. What to do? It was growing late; soon the wives would be drinking their last cup and closing the file on the last grandchild. Herr Schmidt appealed to the kind stout lady; he asked her whether she hadn't a backdoor so that he might avoid the man he knew in the street outside. She had no backdoor, but she was a woman of great resource, and in no time she had decked Herr Schmidt out in a great cartwheel of a skirt, like peasant-women in those days wore at market, a pair of white stockings, a blouse ample enough and a floppy hat. The girls hadn't enjoyed themselves so much for a long time, and they amused themselves decking his face with rouge, eye-shadow and lipstick. When he came out of the door, the policeman was so astonished by the sight that he stood rooted to the spot long enough for Herr Schmidt to billow round the corner, take to his heels down a side street and arrive safely home in time to scour his face before his wife came in.

If it had stopped there all might have been well, but

the policeman had not been deceived, and now he reported to the Superintendent that members of the secret society dressed themselves as women and in that guise frequented the gay houses of the town. 'But why dress as women to do that?' the Superintendent asked, and Puckler hinted at orgies which went beyond the natural order of things. 'Anarchy,' he said, 'is out to upset everything, even the proper relationship of man and woman.'

'Can't you be more explicit?' the Superintendent asked him for the second time; it was a phrase of which he was pathetically fond, but Puckler left the details shrouded in mystery.

It was then that Puckler's fanaticism took a morbid turn; he suspected every large woman he saw in the street at night of being a man in disguise. Once he actually pulled off the wig of a certain Frau Hackenfurth (no one till that day, not even her husband, knew that she wore a wig), and presently he sallied out into the streets himself dressed as a woman with the belief that one transvestite would recognise another and that sooner or later he would find himself enlisted in the secret orgies. He was a small man and he played the part better than Herr Schmidt had done – only his gimlet-eyes would have betrayed him to an acquaintance in daylight.

The men had been meeting happily enough now for two weeks in Herr Braun's cellar, the policeman had tired of his search and the Superintendent was in hopes that all had blown over, when a disastrous decision was taken. Frau Schmidt and Frau Muller in the old days had the habit of cooking pasties for their husbands to go with the wine, and the two men began to miss this treat which they described to their fellow drinkers, their mouths wet with the relish of the memory. Herr Braun suggested that they should bring in a woman to cook for them – it would mean only a small contribution from each, for no one would charge very much for a few hours' work at the end of the evening. Her duty would be to bring in fresh warm pasties every half an hour or so as long as their wine-session lasted. He advertised the position openly enough in the local paper, and Puckler, taking a long chance – the advertisement had referred to a men's club – applied, dressed up in his wife's best Sunday blacks. He was accepted by Herr Braun, who was the only one who did not know Herr Puckler except by repute, and so Puckler found himself installed at the very heart of the mystery, with a grand opportunity to hear all their talk. The only trouble was that he had little skill at cooking and often with his ear to the cellar-door he allowed the pasties to burn. On the second evening Herr Braun told him that unless the pasties improved he would find another woman.

However Puckler was not worried by that because he had all the information he required for the Super-intendent, and it was a real pleasure to make his report in the presence of the policeman, who con-tributed nothing at all to the enquiry.

Puckler had written down the dialogue as he had heard it, leaving out only the long pauses, the gurgle of the wine-jugs and the occasional rude tribute that wind makes to the virtue of young wine. His report read as follows:

Inquiry into the Secret Meetings held in the Cellar of Herr Braun's House at 27 —strasse. The following dialogue was overheard by the investigator.

MULLER: If the rain keeps off another month, the wine harvest will be better than last year.

UNIDENTIFIED VOICE: Ugh.

UNIDENTIFIED VOICE: They say the postman nearly broke his ankle last week. Slipped on a step.

BRAUN: I remember sixty-one vintages.

DOBEL: Time for a pasty.

UNIDENTIFIED VOICE: Ugh.

MULLER: Call in that cow.

The investigator was summoned and left a tray of pasties.

BRAUN: Careful. They are hot.

SCHMIDT: This one's burnt to a cinder.

DOBEL: Uneatable.

KASTNER: Better sack her before worse happens.

BRAUN: She's paid till the end of the week. We'll give her till then.

MULLER: It was fourteen degrees at midday.

DOBEL: The town-hall clock's fast.

SCHMIDT: Do you remember that dog the mayor had with black spots?

UNIDENTIFIED VOICE: Ugh.

KASTNER: No, why?

SCHMIDT: I can't remember.

MULLER: When I was a boy we had plum-duff; they never make now.

DOBEL: It was the summer of '87.

UNIDENTIFIED VOICE: What was?

MULLER: The year Mayor Kalnitz died.

SCHMIDT: '88.

MULLER: There was a hard frost.

DOBEL: Not as hard as '86.

BRAUN: That was a shocking year for wine.

So it went on for twelve pages. 'What's it all about?' the Superintendent asked.

'If we knew that, we'd know all.'

'It sounds harmless.'

'Then why do they meet in secret?'

The policeman said, 'Ugh,' like the unidentified voice.

'My feeling is,' Puckler said, 'a pattern will emerge. Look at all those dates. They need to be checked.'

'There was a bomb thrown in '86,' the Superintendent said doubtfully. 'It killed the Grand Duke's best grey.'

'A shocking year for wine,' Puckler said. 'They missed. No wine. No royal blood.'

'The attempt was mistimed,' the Superintendent remembered.

'The town-hall clock's fast,' Puckler quoted.

'I can't believe it all the same.'

'A code. To break a code we have need of more material.'

The Superintendent agreed with some reluctance that the report should continue, but then there was the difficulty of the pasties. 'We need a good assistant-cook for the pasties,' Puckler said, 'and then I can listen without interruption. They won't object if I tell them that it will cost no more.'

The Superintendent said to the policeman, 'Those were good pasties I had in your house.'

'I cooked them myself,' the policeman said gloomily.

'Then that's no help.'

'Why no help?' Puckler demanded. 'If I can dress up as a woman, so can he.'

'His moustache?'

'A good blade and a good lather will see to that.'

'It's an unusual thing to demand of a man.'

'In the service of the law.'

So it was decided, though the policeman was not at all happy about the affair. Puckler, being a small man, was able to dress in his wife's clothes, but the policeman had no wife. In the end Puckler was forced to agree to buy the clothes himself; he did it late in the evening, when the assistants were in a hurry to leave and were unlikely to recognise his gimlet-eyes, as they judged the size of the skirt, blouse, knickers. There had been lies, fornication: I don't know in what further category my father placed the strange shopping expedition, which didn't, as it happened, go entirely unnoticed. Scandal – perhaps that was the third offence which secrecy produced, for a late customer coming into the shop did in fact recognise Puckler, just as he was holding up the bloomers to see if the seat seemed large enough. You can imagine how quickly that story got around, to every woman except Frau Puckler, and she felt at the next sewing-party an odd – well, it might have been deference or it might have been compassion. Everyone stopped to listen when she spoke; no one contradicted or argued with her, and she was not allowed to carry a tray or pour a cup. She began to feel so like an invalid that she developed a headache and decided to go home early. She could see them all nodding at each other as though they knew what was the matter better than she did, and Frau Muller volunteered to see her home.

Of course, she hurried straight back to tell them about it. 'When we arrived,' she said, 'Herr Puckler was not at home. Of course the poor woman pretended not to know where he could be. She got in quite a state about it. She said he was always there to welcome her when she came in. She had half a mind to go round to the police-station and report him missing, but I dissuaded her. I almost began to believe that she didn't know what he was up to. She muttered about the strange goings-on in town, anarchists and the like, and would you believe it, she said that Herr Puckler told her a policeman had seen Herr Schmidt dressed up in women's clothes.'

'The little swine,' Frau Schmidt said, naturally referring to Puckler, for Herr Schmidt had the figure of one of his own wine-barrels. 'Can you imagine such a thing?'

'Distracting attention,' Frau Muller said, 'from his own vices. For look what happened next. We come to the bedroom, and Frau Puckler finds her wardrobe door wide open, and she looks inside, and what does she find – her black Sunday dress missing. "There's truth in the story after all," she said, "and I'm going to look for Herr Schmidt," but I pointed out to her that it would have to be a very small man indeed to wear her dress.'

'Did she blush?'

'I really believe she knows nothing about it.'

'Poor, poor woman,' Frau Dobel said. 'And what do you think he does when he's all dressed up?' and they began to speculate. So thus it was, my father would say, that foul talk was added to the other sins of lies, fornication, scandal. Yet there still remained the most serious sin of all.

That night Puckler and the policeman turned up at Herr Braun's door, but little did they know that the story of Puckler had already reached the ears of the drinkers, for Frau Muller had reported the strange events to Herr Muller, and at once he remembered the gimlet-eyes of the cook Anna peering at him out of the shadows. When the men met, Herr Braun reported that the cook was to bring an assistant to help her with the pasties and as she had asked for no extra money he had consented. You can imagine the babble of voices that broke out from these silent men when Herr Muller told his story. What was Puckler's motive? It was a bad one or it would not have been Puckler. One theory was that he was planning with the help of an assistant to poison them with the pasties in revenge for being excluded. 'It's not beyond Puckler,' Herr Dobel said. They had good reason to be suspicious, so my father, who was a just man, did not include unworthy suspicion among the sins of which the secret society was the cause. They began to prepare a reception for Puckler.

Puckler knocked on the door and the policeman stood just behind him, enormous in his great black skirt with his white stockings crinkling over his boots because Puckler had forgotten to buy him suspenders. After the second knock the bombardment began from the upper windows. Puckler and the policeman were drenched with unmentionable liquids, they were struck with logs of wood. Their eyes were endangered by falling forks. The policeman was the first to take to his heels, and it was a strange sight to see so huge a woman go beating down the street. The blouse had come out of the waistband and flapped like a sail as its owner tacked to avoid the flying objects – which now included a toilet-roll, a broken teapot and a portrait of the Grand Duke.

Puckler, who had been hit on the shoulder by a rolling-pin, did not at first run away. He had his moment of courage or bewilderment. But when the frying-pan he had used for pasties struck him, he turned too late to follow the policeman. It was then that he was struck on the head with a chamber-pot and lay in the street with the pot fitting over his head like a vizor. They had to break it with a hammer to get it off, and by that time he was dead, whether from the blow on the head or the fall or from fear or from being stifled by the chamber-pot nobody knew, though suffocation was the general opinion. Of course there was an inquiry which went on for many months into the existence of an anarchist plot, and before the end of it the Superintendent had become secretly affianced to Frau Puckler, for which nobody blamed her, for she was a popular woman – except my father who resented the secrecy of it all. (He suspected that the Superintendent's love for Frau Puckler had extended the inquiry, since he pretended to believe her husband's accusations.)

Technically, of course, it was murder – death arising from an illegal assault – but the courts after about six months absolved the six men. 'But there's a greater court,' my father would always end his story, 'and in that court the sin of murder never goes unrequited. You begin with a secret,' and he would look at me as though he knew my pockets were stuffed with them, as indeed they were, including the note I intended to pass the next day at school to the yellow-haired girl in the second row, 'and you end with every sin in the calendar.' He began to recount them over again for my benefit. 'Lies, drunkenness, fornication, scandal-bearing, murder, the subornation of authority.'

'Subornation of authority?'

'Yes,' he said and fixed me with his glittering eye. I think he had Frau Puckler and the Superintendent in mind. He rose towards his climax. 'Men in women's clothes – the terrible sin of Sodom.'

'And what's that?' I asked with excited expectation.

'At your age,' my father said, 'some things must remain secret.'

Two Gentle People

They sat on a bench in the Parc Monceau for a long time without speaking to one another. It was a hopeful day of early summer with a spray of white clouds lapping across the sky in front of a small breeze: at any moment the wind might drop and the sky become empty and entirely blue, but it was too late now – the sun would have set first.

In younger people it might have been a day for a chance encounter – secret behind the long barrier of perambulators with only babies and nurses in sight. But they were both of them middle-aged, and neither was inclined to cherish an illusion of possessing a lost youth, though he was better looking than he believed, with his silky old-world moustache like a badge of good behaviour, and she was prettier than the looking-glass ever told her. Modesty and disillusion gave them something in common; though they were separated by five feet of green metal they could have been a married couple who had grown to resemble each other. Pigeons like old grey tennis balls rolled unnoticed around their feet. They each occasionally looked at a watch, though never at one another. For both of them this period of solitude and peace was limited.

The man was tall and thin. He had what are called sensitive features, and the cliché fitted him; his face was comfortably, though handsomely, banal – there would be no ugly surprises when he spoke, for a man may be sensitive without imagination. He had carried with him an umbrella which suggested caution. In her case one noticed first the long and lovely legs as unsensual as those in a society portrait. From her expression she found the summer day sad, yet she was reluctant to obey the command of her watch and go – somewhere – inside.

They would never have spoken to each other if two teenaged louts had not passed by, one with a blaring radio slung over his shoulder, the other kicking out at the preoccupied pigeons. One of his kicks found a random mark, and on they went in a din of pop, leaving the pigeon lurching on the path.

The man rose, grasping his umbrella like a riding-whip. 'Infernal young scoundrels,' he exclaimed, and the phrase sounded more Edwardian because of the faint American intonation – Henry James might surely have employed it.

'The poor bird,' the woman said. The bird struggled upon the gravel, scattering little stones. One wing hung slack and a leg must have been broken too, for the pigeon swivelled round in circles unable to rise. The other pigeons moved away, with disinterest, searching the gravel for crumbs.

'If you would look away for just a minute,' the man said. He laid his umbrella down again and walked rapidly to the bird where it thrashed around; then he picked it up, and quickly and expertly he wrung its neck – it was a kind of skill anyone of breeding ought to possess. He looked round for a refuse bin in which he tidily deposited the body.

'There was nothing else to do,' he remarked apologetically when he returned.

'I could not myself have done it,' the woman said, carefully grammatical in a foreign tongue.

'Taking life is *our* privilege,' he replied with irony rather than pride.

When he sat down the distance between them had narrowed; they were able to speak freely about the weather and the first real day of summer. The last week had been unseasonably cold, and even today . . . He admired the way in which she spoke English and apologised for his own lack of French, but she reassured him: it was no ingrained talent. She had been 'finished' at an English school at Margate.

'That's a seaside resort, isn't it?'

'The sea always seemed very grey,' she told him, and for a while they lapsed into separate silences. Then perhaps thinking of the dead pigeon she asked him if he had been in the army. 'No, I was over forty when the war came,' he said. 'I served on a government mission, in India. I became very fond of India.' He began to describe to her Agra, Lucknow, the old city of Delhi, his eyes alight with memories. The new Delhi he did not like, built by a Britisher – Lut-Lut-Lut- ? No matter. It reminded him of Washington.

'Then you do not like Washington?'

'To tell you the truth,' he said, 'I am not very happy in my own country. You see, I like old things. I found myself more at home – can you believe it? – in India, even with the British. And now in France, I find it's the same. My grandfather was British Consul in Nice.'

'The Promenade des Anglais was very new then,' she said.

'Yes, but it aged. What we Americans build never ages beautifully. The Chrysler Building, Hilton hotels . . . '

'Are you married?' she asked. He hesitated a moment before replying, 'Yes,' as though he wished to be quite, quite accurate. He put out his hand and felt for his umbrella – it gave him confidence in this surprising situation of talking so openly to a stranger.

'I ought not to have asked you,' she said, still careful with her grammar.

'Why not?' He excused her awkwardly.

'I was interested in what you said.' She gave him a little smile. 'The question came. It was *imprévu*.'

'Are *you* married?' he asked, but only to put her at her ease, for he could see her ring.

'Yes.'

By this time they seemed to know a great deal about each other, and he felt it was churlish not to surrender his identity. He said, 'My name is Greaves, Henry C. Greaves.'

'Mine is Marie-Claire. Marie-Claire Duval.'

'What a lovely afternoon it has been,' the man called Greaves said.

'But it gets a little cold when the sun sinks.' They escaped from each other again with regret.

'A beautiful umbrella you have,' she said, and it was quite true – the gold band was distinguished, and even from a few feet away one could see there was a monogram engraved there – an H certainly, entwined perhaps with a C or a G.

'A present,' he said without pleasure.

'I admired so much the way you acted with the pigeon. As for me I am *lâche*.'

'That I am quite sure is not true,' he said kindly.

'Oh, it is. It is.'

'Only in the sense that we are all cowards about something.'

'You are not,' she said, remembering the pigeon with gratitude.

'Oh yes, I am,' he replied, 'in one whole area of life.' He seemed on the brink of a personal revelation, and she clung to his coat-tail to pull him back; she literally clung to it, for lifting the edge of his jacket she exclaimed, 'You have been touching some wet paint.' The ruse succeeded; he became solicitous about her dress, but examining the bench they both agreed the source was not there. 'They have been painting on my staircase,' he said.

'You have a house here?'

'No, an apartment on the fourth floor.'

'With an *ascenseur*?'

'Unfortunately not,' he said sadly. 'It's a very old house in the dix-septième.'

The door of his unknown life had opened a crack, and she wanted to give something of her own life in return, but not too much. A 'brink' would give her vertigo. She said, 'My apartment is only too depressingly new. In the huitième. The door opens electrically without being touched. Like in an airport.'

A strong current of revelation carried them along. He learned how she always bought her cheeses in the Place de la Madeleine – it was quite an expedition from her side of the huitième, near the Avenue George V, and once she had been rewarded by finding Tante Yvonne, the General's wife, at her elbow choosing a Brie. He on the other hand bought his cheeses in the Rue de Tocqueville, only round the corner from his apartment.

'You yourself?'

'Yes, I do the marketing,' he said in a voice suddenly abrupt.

She said, 'It is a little cold now. I think we should go.'

'Do you come to the Parc often?'

'It is the first time.'

'What a strange coincidence,' he said. 'It's the first time for me too. Even though I live close by.'

'And I live quite far away.'

They looked at one another with a certain awe, aware of the mysteries of providence. He said, 'I don't suppose you would be free to have a little dinner with me.'

Excitement made her lapse into French. 'Je suis libre, mais vous . . . votre femme . . . ?'

'She is dining elsewhere,' he said. 'And your husband?'

'He will not be back before eleven.'

He suggested the Brasserie Lorraine, which was only a few minutes' walk away, and she was glad that he had not chosen something more chic or more flamboyant. The heavy bourgeois atmosphere of the brasserie gave her confidence, and, though she had small appetite herself, she was glad to watch the comfortable military progress down the ranks of the sauerkraut trolley. The menu too was long enough to give them time to readjust to the startling intimacy of dining together. When the order had been given, they both began to speak at once. 'I never expected . . .'

'It's funny the way things happen,' he added, laying unintentionally a heavy inscribed monument over that conversation.

'Tell me about your grandfather, the consul.'

'I never knew him,' he said. It was much more difficult to talk on a restaurant sofa than on a park bench.

'Why did your father go to America?'

'The spirit of adventure perhaps,' he said. 'And I suppose it was the spirit of adventure which brought me back to live in Europe. America didn't mean Coca-Cola and *Time-Life* when my father was young.'

'And have you found adventure? How stupid of me to ask. Of course you married here?'

'I brought my wife with me,' he said. 'Poor Patience.'

'Poor?'

'She is fond of Coca-Cola.'

'You can get it here,' she said, this time with intentional stupidity.

'Yes.'

The wine-waiter came and he ordered a Sancerre. 'If that will suit you?'

'I know so little about wine,' she said.

'I thought all French people . . .'

'We leave it to our husbands,' she said, and in his turn he felt an obscure hurt. The sofa was shared by a husband now as well as a wife, and for a while the sole meunière gave them an excuse not to talk. And yet silence was not a genuine escape. In the silence the two ghosts would have become more firmly planted, if the woman had not found the courage to speak.

'Have you any children?' she asked.

'No. Have you?'

'No.'

'Are you sorry?'

She said, 'I suppose one is always sorry to have missed something.'

'I'm glad at least I did not miss the Parc Monceau today.'

'Yes, I am glad too.'

The silence after that was a comfortable silence: the two ghosts went away and left them alone. Once their fingers touched over the sugar-castor (they had chosen strawberries). Neither of them had any desire for further questions; they seemed to know each other more completely than they knew anyone else. It was like a happy marriage; the stage of discovery was over – they had passed the test of jealousy, and now they were tranquil in their middle age. Time and death remained the only enemies, and coffee was like the warning of old age. After that it was necessary to hold sadness at bay with a brandy, though not successfully. It was as though they had experienced a lifetime, which was measured as with butterflies in hours.

He remarked of the passing head waiter, 'He looks like an undertaker.'

'Yes,' she said. So he paid the bill and they went outside. It was a death-agony they were too gentle to resist for long. He asked, 'Can I see you home?'

'I would rather not. Really not. You live so close.'

'We could have another drink on the *terrasse*?' he suggested with half a sad heart.

'It would do nothing more for us,' she said. 'The evening was perfect. *Tu es vraiment gentil.*' She noticed too late that she had used 'tu' and she hoped his French was bad enough for him not to have noticed. They did not exchange addresses or telephone numbers, for neither of them dared to suggest it: the hour had come too late in both their lives. He found her a taxi and she drove away towards the great illuminated Arc, and he walked home by the Rue Jouffroy, slowly. What is cowardice in the young is wisdom in the old, but all the same one can be ashamed of wisdom.

Marie-Claire walked through the self-opening doors and thought, as she always did, of airports and escapes. On the sixth floor she let herself into the flat. An abstract painting in cruel tones of scarlet and yellow faced the door and treated her like a stranger.

She went straight to her room, as softly as possible, locked the door and sat down on her single bed. Through the wall she could hear her husband's voice and laugh. She wondered who was with him tonight – Toni or François. François had painted the abstract picture, and Toni, who danced in ballet, always claimed, especially before strangers, to have modelled for the little stone phallus with painted eyes that had a place of honour in the living-room. She began to undress. While the voice next door spun its web, images of the bench in the Parc Monceau returned and of the sauerkraut trolley in the Brasserie Lorraine. If he had heard her come in, her husband would soon proceed to action: it excited him to know that she was a witness. The voice said, 'Pierre, Pierre,' reproachfully. Pierre was a new name to her. She spread her fingers on the dressing-table to take off her rings and she thought of the sugar-castor for the strawberries, but at the sound of the little yelps and giggles from next door the sugar-castor turned into the phallus with painted eyes. She lay down and screwed beads of wax into her ears, and she shut her eyes and thought how different things might have been if fifteen years ago she had sat on a bench in the Parc Monceau, watching a man with pity killing a pigeon.

'I can smell a woman on you,' Patience Greaves said with pleasure, sitting up against two pillows. The top pillow was punctured with brown cigarette burns.

'Oh no, you can't. It's your imagination, dear.'

'You said you would be home by ten.'

'It's only twenty past now.'

'You've been up in the Rue de Douai, haven't you, in one of those bars, looking for a *fille*.'

'I sat in the Parc Monceau and then I had dinner at the Brasserie Lorraine. Can I give you your drops?'

'You want me to sleep so that I won't expect anything. That's it, isn't it, you're too old now to do it twice.'

He mixed the drops with water from the carafe on the table between the twin beds. Anything he might say would be wrong when Patience was in a mood like this. Poor Patience, he thought, holding out the drops towards the face crowned with red curls, how she misses America – she will never believe that the Coca-Cola tastes the same here. Luckily this would not be one of their worst nights, for she drank from the glass without further argument, while he sat beside her and remembered the street outside the brasserie and how – by accident he was sure – he had been called 'tu'.

'What are you thinking?' Patience asked. 'Are you still in the Rue de Douai?'

'I was thinking that things might have been different,' he said.

It was the biggest protest he had ever allowed himself to make against the condition of life.

THE FALLEN IDOL

Preface

The Fallen Idol unlike *The Third Man* was not written for the films. That is only one of many reasons why I prefer it. The story, published as 'The Basement Room' in 1935, was conceived on the cargo steamer on the way home from Liberia to relieve the tedium of the voyage. *The Fallen Idol* is, of course, a meaningless title for the original story printed here, and even for the film it always reminded me of the problem paintings of John Collier. It was chosen by the distributors.

I was surprised when Carol Reed suggested that I should collaborate with him on a film of 'The Basement Room' because it seemed to me that the subject was unfilmable – a murder committed by the most sympathetic character and an unhappy ending which would certainly have imperilled the £250,000 that films nowadays cost.

However we went ahead, and in the conferences that ensued the story was quietly changed, so that the subject no longer concerned a small boy who unwittingly betrayed his best friend to the police, but dealt instead with a small boy who believed that his friend was a murderer and nearly procured his arrest by telling lies in his defence. I think this, especially with Reed's handling, was a good subject, but the reader must not be surprised by not finding it the subject of the original story.

Why was the scene changed to an Embassy? This

was Reed's idea since we both felt that the large Belgravia house was already in these post-war years a period piece, and we did not want to make an historical film. I fought the solution for a while and then wholeheartedly concurred.

It is always difficult to remember which of us made which change in the original story except in certain details. For example the cross-examination of the girl beside the bed that she had used with Baines was mine; the witty interruption of the man who came to wind the clock was Reed's. The snake was mine (I have always liked snakes), and for a short while it met with Reed's sympathetic opposition.

Of one thing about both these films I have complete certainty, that their success is due to Carol Reed, the only director I know with that particular warmth of human sympathy, the extraordinary feeling for the right face for the right part, the exactitude of cutting, and not least important the power of sympathising with an author's worries and an ability to guide him.

When the front door had shut them out and the butler
Baines had turned back into the dark heavy hall,
Philip began to live. He stood in front of the nursery
door, listening until he heard the engine of the taxi
die out along the street. His parents were gone for a
fortnight's holiday; he was 'between nurses', one dis-
missed and the other not arrived; he was alone in the
great Belgravia house with Baines and Mrs Baines.

He could go anywhere, even through the green
baize door to the pantry or down the stairs to the
basement living-room. He felt a stranger in his home
because he could go into any room and all the rooms
were empty.

You could only guess who had once occupied
them: the rack of pipes in the smoking-room beside
the elephant tusks, the carved wood tobacco jar; in
the bedroom the pink hangings and pale perfumes
and the three-quarter-finished jars of cream which
Mrs Baines had not yet cleared away; the high glaze
on the never-opened piano in the drawing-room, the
china clock, the silly little tables and the silver: but
here Mrs Baines was already busy, pulling down the
curtains, covering the chairs in dust-sheets.

'Be off out of here, Master Philip,' and she looked
at him with her hateful peevish eyes, while she moved
round, getting everything in order, meticulous and
loveless and doing her duty.

Philip Lane went downstairs and pushed at the
baize door; he looked into the pantry, but Baines was

not there; then he set foot for the first time on the stairs to the basement. Again he had the sense: this is life. All his seven nursery years vibrated with the strange, the new experience. His crowded busy brain was like a city which feels the earth tremble at a distant earthquake shock. He was apprehensive, but he was happier than he had ever been. Everything was more important than before.

Baines was reading a newspaper in his shirtsleeves. He said, 'Come in, Phil, and make yourself at home. Wait a moment and I'll do the honours,' and going to a white cleaned cupboard he brought out a bottle of ginger beer and half a Dundee cake. 'Half-past eleven in the morning,' Baines said. 'It's opening time, my boy,' and he cut the cake and poured out the ginger-beer. He was more genial than Philip had ever known him, more at his ease, a man in his own home.

'Shall I call Mrs Baines?' Philip asked, and he was glad when Baines said no. She was busy. She liked to be busy, so why interfere with her pleasure?

'A spot of drink at half-past eleven,' Baines said, pouring himself out a glass of ginger-beer, 'gives an appetite for chop and does no man any harm.'

'A chop?' Philip asked.

'Old Coasters,' Baines said, 'call all food chop.'

'But it's not a chop?'

'Well, it might be, you know, cooked with palm oil. And then some paw-paw to follow.'

Philip looked out of the basement window at the dry stone yard, the ash-can and the legs going up and down beyond the railings.

'Was it hot there?'

'Ah, you never felt such heat. Not a nice heat, mind, like you get in the park on a day like this. Wet,'

Baines said, 'corruption.' He cut himself a slice of cake. 'Smelling of rot,' Baines said, rolling his eyes round the small basement room, from clean cupboard to clean cupboard, the sense of bareness, of nowhere to hide a man's secrets. With an air of regret for something lost he took a long draught of ginger-beer.

'Why did father live out there?'

'It was his job,' Baines said, 'same as this is mine now. And it was mine then too. It was a man's job. You wouldn't believe it now, but I've had forty niggers under me, doing what I told them to.'

'Why did you leave?'

'I married Mrs Baines.'

Philip took the slice of Dundee cake in his hand and munched it round the room. He felt very old, independent and judicial; he was aware that Baines was talking to him as man to man. He never called him Master Philip as Mrs Baines did, who was servile when she was not authoritative.

Baines had seen the world; he had seen beyond the railings, beyond the tired legs of typists, the Pimlico parade to and from Victoria. He sat there over his ginger pop with the resigned dignity of an exile; Baines didn't complain; he had chosen his fate: and if his fate was Mrs Baines he had only himself to blame.

But today, because the house was almost empty and Mrs Baines was upstairs and there was nothing to do, he allowed himself a little acidity.

'I'd go back tomorrow if I had the chance.'

'Did you ever shoot a nigger?'

'I never had any call to shoot,' Baines said. 'Of course, I carried a gun. But you didn't need to treat them bad. That just made them stupid. Why,' Baines said, bowing his thin grey hair with embarrassment over the ginger pop, 'I loved some of those damned niggers. I couldn't help loving them. There they'd be laughing, holding hands; they liked to touch each other; it made them feel fine to know the other fellow was round. It didn't mean anything we could understand; two of them would go about all day without losing hold, grown men; but it wasn't love; it didn't mean anything we could understand.'

'Eating between meals,' Mrs Baines said. 'What would your mother say, Master Philip?'

She came down the steep stairs to the basement, her hands full of pots of cream and salve, tubes of grease and paste. 'You oughtn't to encourage him, Baines,' she said, sitting down in a wicker armchair and screwing up her small ill-humoured eyes at the Coty lipstick, Pond's cream, the Leichner rouge and Cyclax powder and Elizabeth Arden astringent.

She threw them one by one into the wastepaper basket. She saved only the cold cream. 'Telling the boy stories,' she said. 'Go along to the nursery, Master Philip, while I get lunch.'

Philip climbed the stairs to the baize door. He heard Mrs Baines's voice like the voice in a nightmare when the small Price light has guttered in the saucer and the curtains move; it was sharp and shrill and full of malice, louder than people ought to speak, exposed.

'Sick to death of your ways, Baines, spoiling the boy. Time you did some work about the house,' but he couldn't hear what Baines said in reply. He pushed open the baize door, came up like a small earth animal in his grey flannel shorts into a wash of sunlight on a parquet floor, the gleam of mirrors dusted and polished and beautified by Mrs Baines.

Something broke downstairs, and Philip sadly mounted the stairs to the nursery. He pitied Baines; it occurred to him how happily they could live together in the empty house if Mrs Baines were called away. He didn't want to play with his Meccano set; he wouldn't take out his train or his soldiers; he sat at the table with his chin on his hands: this is life; and suddenly he felt responsible for Baines, as if he were the master of the house and Baines an ageing servant who deserved to be cared for. There was not much one could do; he decided at least to be good.

He was not surprised when Mrs Baines was agreeable at lunch; he was used to her changes. Now it was 'another helping of meat, Master Philip', or 'Master Philip, a little more of this nice pudding'. It was a pudding he liked, queen's pudding with a perfect meringue, but he wouldn't eat a second helping lest she might count that a victory. She was the kind of woman who thought that any injustice could be counterbalanced by something good to eat.

She was sour, but she liked making sweet things; one never had to complain of a lack of jam or plums; she ate well herself and added soft sugar to the meringue and the strawberry jam. The half light through the basement window set the motes moving above her pale hair like dust as she sifted the sugar, and Baines crouched over his plate saying nothing.

Again Philip felt responsibility. Baines had looked forward to this, and Baines was disappointed: everything was being spoilt. The sensation of disappointment was one which Philip could share; knowing nothing of love or jealousy or passion he could understand better than anyone this grief, something hoped for not happening, something promised not fulfilled, something exciting turning dull. 'Baines,' he said, 'will you take me for a walk this afternoon?'

'No,' Mrs Baines said, 'no. That he won't. Not with all the silver to clean.'

'There's a fortnight to do it in,' Baines said.

'Work first, pleasure afterwards.' Mrs Baines helped herself to some more meringue.

Baines suddenly put down his spoon and fork and pushed his plate away. 'Blast,' he said.

'Temper,' Mrs Baines said softly, 'temper. Don't you go breaking any more things, Baines, and I won't have you swearing in front of the boy. Master Philip, if you've finished you can get down.' She skinned the rest of the meringue off the pudding.

'I want to go for a walk,' Philip said.

'You'll go and have a rest.'

'I will go for a walk.'

'Master Philip,' Mrs Baines said. She got up from the table leaving her meringue unfinished, and came towards him, thin, menacing, dusty in the basement room. 'Master Philip, you do as you're told.' She took him by the arm and squeezed it gently; she watched him with a joyless passionate glitter and above her head the feet of the typists trudged back to the Victorian offices after the lunch interval.

'Why shouldn't I go for a walk?' But he weakened; he was scared and ashamed of being scared. This was life; a strange passion he couldn't understand moving in the basement room. He saw a small pile of broken glass swept into a corner by a wastepaper basket. He looked to Baines for help and only intercepted hate; the sad hopeless hate of something behind bars.

'Why shouldn't I?' he repeated.

'Master Philip,' Mrs Baines said, 'you've got to do

as you're told. You mustn't think just because your father's away, there's nobody here to – '

'You wouldn't dare,' Philip cried, and was startled by Baines's low interjection: 'There's nothing she wouldn't dare.'

'I hate you,' Philip said to Mrs Baines. He pulled away from her and ran to the door, but she was there before him; she was old, but she was quick.

'Master Philip,' she said, 'you'll say you're sorry.' She stood in front of the door quivering with excitement. 'What would your father do if he heard you say that?'

She put a hand out to seize him, dry and white with constant soda, the nails cut to the quick, but he backed away and put the table between them, and suddenly to his surprise she smiled; she became again as servile as she had been arrogant. 'Get along with you, Master Philip,' she said with glee, 'I see I'm going to have my hands full till your father and mother come back.'

She left the door unguarded and when he passed her she slapped him playfully. 'I've got too much to do today to trouble about you. I haven't covered half the chairs,' and suddenly even the upper part of the house became unbearable to him as he thought of Mrs Baines moving about shrouding the sofas, laying out the dust-sheets.

So he wouldn't go upstairs to get his cap but walked straight out across the shining hall into the street, and again, as he looked this way and that way, it was life he was in the middle of.

It was the pink sugar cakes in the window on a paper doily, the ham, the slab of mauve sausage, the wasps driving like small torpedoes across the pane that caught Philip's attention. His feet were tired by pavements; he had been afraid to cross the road, had simply walked first in one direction, then in the other. He was nearly home now; the square was at the end of the street; this was a shabby outpost of Pimlico, and he smudged the pane with his nose looking for sweets, and saw between the cakes and ham a different Baines. He hardly recognised the bulbous eyes, the bald forehead. It was a happy, bold and buccaneering Baines, even though it was, when you looked closer, a desperate Baines.

Philip had never seen the girl. He remembered Baines had a niece and he thought that this might be her. She was thin and drawn, and she wore a white mackintosh; she meant nothing to Philip; she belonged to a world about which he knew nothing at all. He couldn't make up stories about her, as he could make them up about withered Sir Hubert Reed, the Permanent Secretary, about Mrs Wince-Dudley, who came up once a year from Penstanley in Suffolk with a green umbrella and an enormous black handbag, as he could make them up about the upper servants in all the houses where he went to tea and games. She just didn't belong; he thought of mermaids and Undine, but she didn't belong there either, nor to the adventures of Emil, nor the Bastables. She sat there looking at an iced pink cake in the detachment and mystery of the completely disinherited, looking at the half-used pots of powder which Baines had set out on the marble-topped table between them.

Baines was urging, hoping, entreating, commanding, and the girl looked at the tea and the china pots and cried. Baines passed his handkerchief across the table, but she wouldn't wipe her eyes; she screwed it in her palm and let the tears run down, wouldn't do anything, wouldn't speak, would only put up a silent despairing resistance to what she dreaded and wanted and refused to listen to at any price. The two brains battled over the teacups loving each other, and there came to Philip outside, beyond the ham and wasps and dusty Pimlico pane, a confused indication of the struggle.

He was inquisitive and he did not understand and he wanted to know. He went and stood in the door-way to see better; he was less sheltered than he had ever been; other people's lives for the first time touched and pressed and moulded. He would never escape that scene. In a week he had forgotten it; but it conditioned his career, the long austerity of his life; when he was dying he said: 'Who is she?'

Baines had won; he was cocky and the girl was happy. She wiped her face, she opened a pot of powder, and their fingers touched across the table. It occurred to Philip that it would be amusing to imitate Mrs Baines's voice and call 'Baines' to him from the door. It shrivelled them; you couldn't describe it in any other way, it made them smaller, they weren't happy any more and they weren't bold. Baines was the first to recover and trace the voice, but that didn't make things as they were.

The sawdust was spilled out of the afternoon; nothing you did could mend it, and Philip was scared. 'I didn't mean . . . ' He wanted to say that he loved

Baines, that he had only wanted to laugh at Mrs
Baines. But he had discovered that you couldn't
laugh at Mrs Baines. She wasn't Sir Hubert Reed,
who used steel nibs and carried a pen-wiper in his
pocket; she wasn't Mrs Wince-Dudley; she was
darkness when the night-light went out in a draught;
she was the frozen blocks of earth he had seen one
winter in a graveyard when someone said, 'They
need an electric drill'; she was the flowers gone bad
and smelling in the little closet room at Penstanley.
There was nothing to laugh about. You had to
endure her when she was there and forget about her
quickly when she was away, suppress the thought of
her, ram it down deep.

Baines said, 'It's only Phil,' beckoned him in and
gave him the pink iced cake the girl hadn't eaten, but
the afternoon was broken, the cake was like dry bread
in the throat. The girl left them at once; she even
forgot to take the powder; like a small blunt icicle in
her white mackintosh she stood in the doorway with
her back to them, then melted into the afternoon.

'Who is she?' Philip asked. 'Is she your niece?'

'Oh, yes,' Baines said, 'that's who she is; she's my
niece,' and poured the last drops of water on to the
coarse black leaves in the teapot.

'May as well have another cup,' Baines said.

'The cup that cheers,' he said hopelessly, watching
the bitter black fluid drain out of the spout.

'Have a glass of ginger pop, Phil?'

'I'm sorry. I'm sorry, Baines.'

'It's not your fault, Phil. Why, I could believe it
wasn't you at all, but her. She creeps in everywhere.'
He fished two leaves out of his cup and laid them
on the back of his hand, a thin soft flake, and a

hard stalk. He beat them with his hand: 'Today,' and the stalk detached itself, 'tomorrow, Wednesday, Thursday, Friday, Saturday, Sunday,' but the flake wouldn't come off, stayed where it was, drying under his blows, with a resistance you wouldn't believe it to possess. 'The tough one wins,' Baines said.

He got up and paid the bill and out they went into the street. Baines said, 'I don't ask you to say what isn't true, but you needn't mention to Mrs Baines you met us here.'

'Of course not,' Philip said, catching something of Sir Hubert Reed's manner, 'I understand, Baines.' But he didn't understand a thing; he was caught up in other people's darkness.

'It was stupid,' Baines said. 'So near home, but I hadn't got time to think, you see. I'd got to see her.'

'Of course, Baines.'

'I haven't time to spare,' Baines said. 'I'm not young. I've got to see that she's all right.'

'Of course you have, Baines.'

'Mrs Baines will get it out of you if she can.'

'You can trust me, Baines,' Philip said in a dry important Reed voice; and then, 'Look out. She's at the window watching.' And there indeed she was, looking up at them, between the lace curtains, from the basement room, speculating. 'Need we go in, Baines?' Philip asked, cold lying heavy on his stomach like too much pudding; he clutched Baines's arm.

'Careful,' Baines said softly, 'careful.'

'But need we go in, Baines? It's early. Take me for a walk in the park.'

'Better not.'

'But I'm frightened, Baines.'

'You haven't any cause,' Baines said. 'Nothing's

319

going to hurt you. You just run along upstairs to the nursery. I'll go down by the area and talk to Mrs Baines.' But even he stood hesitating at the top of the stone steps pretending not to see her, where she watched between the curtains. 'In at the front door, Phil, and up the stairs.'

Philip didn't linger in the hall; he ran, slithering on the parquet Mrs Baines had polished, to the stairs. Through the drawing-room doorway on the first floor he saw the draped chairs; even the china clock on the mantel was covered like a canary's cage; as he passed it, it chimed the hour, muffled and secret under the duster. On the nursery table he found his supper laid out: a glass of milk and a piece of bread and butter, a sweet biscuit, and a little cold queen's pudding without the meringue. He had no appetite; he strained his ears for Mrs Baines's coming, for the sound of voices, but the basement held its secrets; the green baize door shut off that world. He drank the milk and ate the biscuit, but he didn't touch the rest, and presently he could hear the soft precise footfalls of Mrs Baines on the stairs: she was a good servant, she walked softly; she was a determined woman, she walked precisely.

But she wasn't angry when she came in; she was ingratiating as she opened the night-nursery door – 'Did you have a good walk, Master Philip?' – pulled down the blinds, laid out his pyjamas, came back to clear his supper. 'I'm glad Baines found you. Your mother wouldn't like you being out alone.' She examined the tray. 'Not much appetite, have you, Master Philip? Why don't you try a little of this nice pudding? I'll bring you up some more jam for it.'

'No, no, thank you, Mrs Baines,' Philip said.

'You ought to eat more,' Mrs Baines said. She sniffed round the room like a dog. 'You didn't take any pots out of the wastepaper basket in the kitchen, did you, Master Philip?'

'No,' Philip said.

'Of course you wouldn't. I just wanted to make sure.' She patted his shoulder and her fingers flashed to his lapel; she picked off a tiny crumb of pink sugar. 'Oh, Master Philip,' she said, 'that's why you haven't any appetite. You've been buying sweet cakes. That's not what your pocket money's for.'

'But I didn't,' Philip said. 'I didn't.'

She tasted the sugar with the tip of her tongue.

'Don't tell lies to me, Master Philip. I won't stand for it any more than your father would.'

'I didn't, I didn't,' Philip said. 'They gave it me. I mean Baines,' but she had pounced on the word 'they'. She had got what she wanted; there was no doubt about that, even when you didn't know what it was she wanted. Philip was angry and miserable and disappointed because he hadn't kept Baines's secret. Baines oughtn't to have trusted him; grown-up people should keep their own secrets, and yet here was Mrs Baines immediately entrusting him with another.

'Let me tickle your palm and see if you can keep a secret.' But he put his hand behind him; he wouldn't be touched. 'It's a secret between us, Master Philip, that I know all about them. I suppose she was having tea with him,' she speculated.

'Why shouldn't she?' he said, the responsibility for Baines weighing on his spirit, the idea that he had got to keep her secret when he hadn't kept Baines's making him miserable with the unfairness of life. 'She was nice.'

321

'She was nice, was she?' Mrs Baines said in a bitter voice he wasn't used to.

'And she's his niece.'

'So that's what he said,' Mrs Baines struck softly back at him like the clock under the duster. She tried to be jocular. 'The old scoundrel. Don't tell him I know, Master Philip.' She stood very still between the table and the door, thinking very hard, planning something. 'Promise you won't tell. I'll give you that Meccano set, Master Philip . . . '

He turned his back on her; he wouldn't promise, but he wouldn't tell. He would have nothing to do with their secrets, the responsibilities they were determined to lay on him. He was only anxious to forget. He had received already a larger dose of life than he had bargained for, and he was scared. 'A 2A Meccano set, Master Philip.' He never opened his Meccano set again, never built anything, never created anything, died, the old dilettante, sixty years later with nothing to show rather than preserve the memory of Mrs Baines's malicious voice saying good-night, her soft determined footfalls on the stairs to the basement, going down, going down.

3

The sun poured in between the curtains and Baines was beating a tattoo on the water-can. 'Glory, glory,' Baines said. He sat down on the end of the bed and said, 'I beg to announce that Mrs Baines has been called away. Her mother's dying. She won't be back till tomorrow.'

'Why did you wake me up so early?' Philip said.

He watched Baines with uneasiness; he wasn't going to be drawn in; he'd learnt his lesson. It wasn't right for a man of Baines's age to be so merry. It made a grown person human in the same way that you were human. For if a grown-up could behave so childishly, you were liable too to find yourself in their world. It was enough that it came at you in dreams: the witch at the corner, the man with a knife. So, 'It's very early,' he complained, even though he loved Baines, even though he couldn't help being glad that Baines was happy. He was divided by the fear and the attraction of life.

'I want to make this a long day,' Baines said. 'This is the best time.' He pulled the curtains back. 'It's a bit misty. The cat's been out all night. There she is, sniffing round the area. They haven't taken in any milk at 59. Emma's shaking out the mats at 63.' He said, 'This was what I used to think about on the Coast: somebody shaking mats and the cat coming home. I can see it today,' Baines said, 'just as if I was still in Africa. Most days you don't notice what you've got. It's a good life if you don't weaken.' He put a penny on the washstand. 'When you've dressed, Phil, run and get a *Mail* from the barrow at the corner. I'll be cooking the sausages.'

'Sausages?'

'Sausages,' Baines said. 'We're going to celebrate today. A fair bust.' He celebrated at breakfast, restless, cracking jokes, unaccountably merry and nervous. It was going to be a long long day, he kept on coming back to that: for years he had waited for a long day, he had sweated in the damp Coast heat, changed shirts, gone down with fever, lain between the blankets and sweated, all in the hope of this long day, that cat sniffing round the area, a bit of mist, the mats beaten at 63. He propped the *Mail* in front of the coffee-pot and read pieces aloud. He said, 'Cora Down's been married for the fourth time.' He was amused, but it wasn't his idea of a long day. His long day was the Park, watching the riders in the Row, seeing Sir Arthur Stillwater pass beyond the rails ('He dined with us once in Bo; up from Freetown; he was governor there'), lunch at the Corner House for Philip's sake (he'd have preferred himself a glass of stout and some oysters at the York bar), the Zoo, the long bus ride home in the last summer light: the leaves in the Green Park were beginning to turn and the motors nuzzled out of Berkeley Street with the low sun gently glowing on their windscreens. Baines envied no one, not Cora Down, or Sir Arthur Stillwater, or Lord Sandale, who came out on to the steps of the Naval and Military and then went back again because he hadn't got anything to do and might as well look at another paper. 'I said don't let me see you touch that black again.' Baines had led a man's life; everyone on top of the bus pricked their ears when he told Philip all about it.

'Would you have shot him?' Philip asked, and Baines put his head back and tilted his dark respectable man-servant's hat to a better angle as the bus swerved round the Artillery Memorial.

'I wouldn't have thought twice about it. I'd have shot to kill,' he boasted, and the bowed figure went by, steel helmet, the heavy cloak, the down-turned rifle and the folded hands.

'Have you got the revolver?'

'Of course I've got it,' Baines said. 'Don't I need it with all the burglaries there've been?' This was the

Baines whom Philip loved: not Baines singing and carefree, but Baines responsible, Baines behind barriers, living this man's life.

All the buses streamed out from Victoria like a convoy of aeroplanes to bring Baines home with honour. 'Forty blacks under me,' and there waiting near the area steps was the proper conventional reward, love at lighting-up time.

'It's your niece,' Philip said, recognising the white mackintosh, but not the happy sleepy face. She frightened him like an unlucky number; he nearly told Baines what Mrs Baines had said; but he didn't want to bother, he wanted to leave things alone.

'Why, so it is,' Baines said, 'I shouldn't wonder if she was going to have a bite of supper with us.' But he said they'd play a game, pretend they didn't know her, slip down the area steps, 'and here,' Baines said, 'we are,' lay the table, put out the cold sausages, a bottle of beer, a bottle of ginger pop, a flagon of harvest burgundy. 'Everyone his own drink,' Baines said. 'Run upstairs, Phil, and see if there's been a post.'

Philip didn't like the empty house at dusk before the lights went on. He hurried. He wanted to be back with Baines. The hall lay there in quiet and shadow prepared to show him something he didn't want to see. Some letters rustled down, and someone knocked. 'Open in the name of the Republic.' The tumbrils rolled, the head bobbed in the bloody basket. Knock, knock, and the postman's footsteps going away. Philip gathered the letters. The slit in the door was like the grating in a jeweller's window. He remembered the policeman he had seen peer through. He had said to his nurse, 'What's he doing?'

and when she said, 'He's seeing if everything's all right,' his brain immediately filled with images of all that might be wrong. He ran to the baize door and the stairs. The girl was already there and Baines was kissing her. She leant breathless against the dresser. 'This is Emmy, Phil.'

'There's a letter for you, Baines.'

'Emmy,' Baines said, 'it's from her.' But he wouldn't open it. 'You bet she's coming back.'

'We'll have supper, anyway,' Emmy said. 'She can't harm that.'

'You don't know her,' Baines said. 'Nothing's safe. Damn it,' he said, 'I was a man once,' and he opened the letter.

'Can I start?' Philip asked, but Baines didn't hear; he presented in his stillness and attention an example of the importance grown-up people attached to the written word: you had to write your thanks, not wait and speak them, as if letters couldn't lie. But Philip knew better than that, sprawling his thanks across a page to Aunt Alice who had given him a doll he was too old for. Letters could lie all right, but they made the lie permanent: they lay as evidence against you; they made you meaner than the spoken word.

'She's not coming back till tomorrow night,' Baines said. He opened the bottles, he pulled up the chairs, he kissed Emmy again against the dresser.

'You oughtn't to,' Emmy said, 'with the boy here.'

'He's got to learn,' Baines said, 'like the rest of us,' and he helped Philip to three sausages. He only took one for himself; he said he wasn't hungry; but when Emmy said she wasn't hungry either he stood over her and made her eat. He was timid and rough with her; he made her drink the harvest burgundy because he said she needed building up; he wouldn't take no for an answer, but when he touched her his hands were light and clumsy too, as if he were afraid to damage something delicate and didn't know how to handle anything so light.

'This is better than milk and biscuits, eh?'

'Yes,' Philip said, but he was scared, scared for Baines as much as for himself. He couldn't help wondering at every bite, at every draught of the ginger pop, what Mrs Baines would say if she ever learnt of this meal; he couldn't imagine it, there was a depth of bitterness and rage in Mrs Baines you couldn't sound. He said, 'She won't be coming back tonight?' but you could tell by the way they immediately understood him that she wasn't really away at all; she was there in the basement with them, driving them to longer drinks and louder talk, biding her time for the right cutting word. Baines wasn't really happy; he was only watching happiness from close to instead of from far away.

'No,' he said, 'she'll not be back till late tomorrow.' He couldn't keep his eyes off happiness; he'd played around as much as other men, he kept on reverting to the Coast as if to excuse himself for his innocence; he wouldn't have been so innocent if he'd lived his life in London, so innocent when it came to tenderness. 'If it was you, Emmy,' he said, looking at the white dresser, the scrubbed chairs, 'this'd be like a home.' Already the room was not quite so harsh; there was a little dust in corners, the silver needed a final polish, the morning's paper lay untidily on a chair. 'You'd better go to bed, Phil; it's been a long day.'

They didn't leave him to find his own way up through the dark shrouded house; they went with him, turning on lights, touching each other's fingers on the switches; floor after floor they drove the night back; they spoke softly among the covered chairs; they watched him undress, they didn't make him wash or clean his teeth, they saw him into bed and lit the night-light and left his door ajar. He could hear their voices on the stairs, friendly like the guests he heard at dinner-parties when they moved down to the hall, saying good-night. They belonged; wherever they were they made a home. He heard a door open and a clock strike, he heard their voices for a long while, so that he felt they were not far away and he was safe. The voices didn't dwindle, they simply went out, and he could be sure that they were still somewhere not far from him, silent together in one of the many empty rooms, growing sleepy together as he grew sleepy after the long day.

He just had time to sigh faintly with satisfaction, because this too perhaps had been life, before he slept and the inevitable terrors of sleep came round him: a man with a tricolour hat beat at the door on His Majesty's service, a bleeding head lay on the kitchen table in a basket, and the Siberian wolves crept closer. He was bound hand and foot and couldn't move; they leapt around him breathing heavily; he opened his eyes and saw Mrs Baines was there, her grey untidy hair in threads over his face, her black hat askew. A loose hairpin fell on the pillow and one musty thread brushed his mouth. 'Where are they?' she whispered. 'Where are they?'

4

Philip watched her in terror. Mrs Baines was out of breath as if she had been searching all the empty rooms, looking under loose covers.

With her untidy grey hair and her black dress buttoned to her throat, her gloves of black cotton, she was so like the witches of his dreams that he didn't dare to speak. There was a stale smell in her breath.

'She's here,' Mrs Baines said, 'you can't deny she's here.' Her face was simultaneously marked with cruelty and misery; she wanted to 'do things' to people, but she suffered all the time. It would have done her good to scream, but she daren't do that: it would warn them. She came ingratiatingly back to the bed where Philip lay rigid on his back and whispered, 'I haven't forgotten the Meccano set. You shall have it tomorrow, Master Philip. We've got secrets together, haven't we? Just tell me where they are.'

He couldn't speak. Fear held him as firmly as any nightmare. She said, 'Tell Mrs Baines, Master Philip. You love your Mrs Baines, don't you?' That was too much; he couldn't speak, but he could move his mouth in terrified denial, wince away from her dusty image.

She whispered, coming closer to him. 'Such deceit. I'll tell your father. I'll settle with you myself when I've found them. You'll smart; I'll see you smart.' Then immediately she was still, listening. A board had creaked on the floor below, and a moment later, while she stooped listening above his bed, there came the whispers of two people who were happy and sleepy together after a long day. The night-light stood beside the mirror and Mrs Baines could see bitterly there her own reflection, misery and cruelty wavering in the glass, age and dust and nothing to hope for. She sobbed without tears, a dry, breathless sound; but her cruelty was a kind of pride which kept her going; it was her best quality, she would have been merely pitiable without it. She went out of the door on tiptoe, feeling her way across the landing, going so softly down the stairs that no one behind a shut door could hear her. Then there was complete silence again; Philip could move; he raised his knees; he sat up in bed; he wanted to die. It wasn't fair, the walls were down again between his world and theirs; but this time it was something worse than merriment that the grown people made him share; a passion moved in the house he recognised but could not understand.

It wasn't fair, but he owed Baines everything: the Zoo, the ginger pop, the bus ride home. Even the supper called on his loyalty. But he was frightened; he was touching something he touched in dreams: the bleeding head, the wolves, the knock, knock, knock. Life fell on him with savagery: you couldn't blame him if he never faced it again in sixty years. He got out of bed, carefully from habit put on his bedroom slippers, and tiptoed to the door: it wasn't quite dark on the landing below because the curtains had been taken down for the cleaners and the light from the street came in through the tall windows. Mrs Baines had her hand on the glass doorknob; she was carefully turning it; he screamed, 'Baines, Baines.'

Mrs Baines turned and saw him cowering in his

pyjamas by the banisters; he was helpless, more helpless even than Baines, and cruelty grew at the sight of him and drove her up the stairs. The nightmare was on him again and he couldn't move; he hadn't any more courage left for ever; he'd spent it all, had been allowed no time to let it grow, no years of gradual hardening; he couldn't even scream.

But the first cry had brought Baines out of the best spare bedroom and he moved quicker than Mrs Baines. She hadn't reached the top of the stairs before he'd caught her round the waist. She drove her black cotton gloves at his face and he bit her hand. He hadn't time to think, he fought her savagely like a stranger, but she fought back with knowledgeable hate. She was going to teach them all and it didn't really matter whom she began with; they had all deceived her; but the old image in the glass was by her side, telling her she must be dignified, she wasn't young enough to yield her dignity; she could beat his face, but she mustn't bite; she could push, but she mustn't kick.

Age and dust and nothing to hope for were her handicaps. She went over the banisters in a flurry of black clothes and fell into the hall; she lay before the front door like a sack of coals which should have gone down the area into the basement. Philip saw; Emmy saw; she sat down suddenly in the doorway of the best spare bedroom with her eyes open as if she were too tired to stand any longer. Baines went slowly down into the hall.

It wasn't hard for Philip to escape; they'd forgotten him completely; he went down the back, the servants' stairs, because Mrs Baines was in the hall; he didn't understand what she was doing lying there; like the startling pictures in a book no one had read to him, the things he didn't understand terrified him. The whole house had been turned over to the grown-up world; he wasn't safe in the night-nursery; their passions had flooded it. The only thing he could do was to get away, by the back stairs, and up through the area, and never come back. You didn't think of the cold, of the need for food and sleep; for an hour it would seem quite possible to escape from people for ever.

He was wearing pyjamas and bedroom slippers when he came up into the square, but there was no one to see him. It was that hour of the evening in a residential district when everyone is at the theatre or at home. He climbed over the iron railings into the little garden: the plane trees spread their large pale palms between him and the sky. It might have been an illimitable forest into which he had escaped. He crouched behind a trunk and the wolves retreated; it seemed to him between the little iron seat and the tree trunk that no one would ever find him again. A kind of embittered happiness and self-pity made him cry; he was lost; there wouldn't be any more secrets to keep; he surrendered responsibility once and for all. Let grown-up people keep to their world and he would keep to his, safe in the small garden between the plane trees. 'In the lost childhood of Judas, Christ was betrayed'; you could almost see the small unformed face hardening into the deep dilettante selfishness of age.

Presently the door of 48 opened and Baines looked this way and that; then he signalled with his hand and Emmy came; it was as if they were only just in time for a train, they hadn't a chance of saying goodbye;

she went quickly by like a face at a window swept past the platform, pale and unhappy and not wanting to go. Baines went in again and shut the door; the light was lit in the basement, and a policeman walked round the square, looking into the areas. You could tell how many families were at home by the lights behind the first-floor curtains.

Philip explored the garden: it didn't take long: a twenty-yard square of bushes and plane trees, two iron seats and a gravel path, a padlocked gate at either end, a scuffle of old leaves. But he couldn't stay: something stirred in the bushes and two illuminated eyes peered out at him like a Siberian wolf, and he thought how terrible it would be if Mrs Baines found him there. He'd have no time to climb the railings; she'd seize him from behind.

He left the square at the unfashionable end and was immediately among the fish-and-chip shops, the little stationers selling bagatelle, among the accommodation addresses and the dingy hotels with open doors. There were few people about because the pubs were open, but a blowsy woman carrying a parcel called out to him across the street and the commissionaire outside a cinema would have stopped him if he hadn't crossed the road. He went deeper: you could go farther and lose yourself more completely here than among the plane trees. On the fringe of the square he was in danger of being stopped and taken back: it was obvious where he belonged; but as he went deeper he lost the marks of his origin. It was a warm night: any child in those free-living parts might be expected to play truant from bed. He found a kind of camaraderie even among grown-up people; he might have been a neighbour's child as he went quickly by, but they weren't going to tell on him, they'd been young once themselves. He picked up a protective coating of dust from the pavements, of smuts from the trains which passed along the backs in a spray of fire. Once he was caught in a knot of children running away from something or somebody, laughing as they ran; he was whirled with them round a turning and abandoned, with a sticky fruit-drop in his hand.

He couldn't have been more lost; but he hadn't the stamina to keep on. At first he feared that someone would stop him; after an hour he hoped that someone would. He couldn't find his way back, and in any case he was afraid of arriving home alone; he was afraid of Mrs Baines, more afraid than he had ever been. Baines was his friend, but something had happened which gave Mrs Baines all the power. He began to loiter on purpose to be noticed, but no one noticed him. Families were having a last breather on the doorsteps, the refuse bins had been put out and bits of cabbage stalks soiled his slippers. The air was full of voices, but he was cut off; these people were strangers and would always now be strangers; they were marked by Mrs Baines and he shied away from them into a deep class-consciousness. He had been afraid of policemen, but now he wanted one to take him home; even Mrs Baines could do nothing against a policeman. He sidled past a constable who was directing traffic, but he was too busy to pay him any attention. Philip sat down against a wall and cried.

It hadn't occurred to him that that was the easiest way, that all you had to do was to surrender, to show you were beaten and accept kindness. . . . It was lavished on him at once by two women and a pawnbroker. Another policeman appeared, a young man with a sharp incredulous face. He looked as if he noted everything he saw in pocketbooks and drew conclusions. A woman offered to see Philip home, but he didn't trust her: she wasn't a match for Mrs Baines immobile in the hall. He wouldn't give his address: he said he was afraid to go home. He had his way; he got his protection. 'I'll take him to the station,' the policeman said, and holding him awkwardly by the hand (he wasn't married; he had his career to make), he led him round the corner and up the stone stairs into the little bare over-heated room where Justice waited.

5

Justice waited behind a wooden counter on a high stool; it wore a heavy moustache; it was kindly and had six children ('three of them nippers like yourself'); it wasn't really interested in Philip, but it pretended to be; it wrote the address down and sent a constable to fetch a glass of milk. But the young constable was interested; he had a nose for things.

'Your home's on the telephone, I suppose,' Justice said. 'We'll ring them up and say you are safe. They'll fetch you very soon. What's your name, sonny?'

'Philip.'

'Your other name.'

'I haven't got another name.' He didn't want to be fetched; he wanted to be taken home by someone who would impress even Mrs Baines. The constable watched him, watched the way he drank the milk, watched him when he winced away from questions.

335

'What made you run away? Playing truant, eh?'

'I don't know.'

'You oughtn't to do it, young fellow. Think how anxious your father and mother will be.'

'They are away.'

'Well, your nurse.'

'I haven't got one.'

'Who looks after you, then?' That question went home. Philip saw Mrs Baines coming up the stairs at him, the heap of black cotton in the hall. He began to cry.

'Now, now, now,' the sergeant said. He didn't know what to do; he wished his wife were with him; even a policewoman might have been useful.

'Don't you think it's funny,' the constable said, 'that there hasn't been an enquiry?'

'They think he's tucked up in bed.'

'You are scared, aren't you?' the constable said. 'What scared you?'

'I don't know.'

'Somebody hurt you?'

'No.'

'He's had bad dreams,' the sergeant said. 'Thought the house was on fire, I expect. I've brought up six of them. Rose is due back. She'll take him home.'

'I want to go home with you,' Philip said; he tried to smile at the constable, but the deceit was immature and unsuccessful.

'I'd better go,' the constable said. 'There may be something wrong.'

'Nonsense,' the sergeant said. 'It's a woman's job. Tact is what you need. Here's Rose. Pull up your stockings, Rose. You're a disgrace to the Force. I've got a job of work for you.' Rose shambled in: black

cotton stockings drooping over her boots, a gawky
Girl Guide manner, a hoarse hostile voice. 'More
tarts, I suppose.'

'No, you've got to see this young man home.' She
looked at him owlishly.

'I won't go with her,' Philip said. He began to cry
again. 'I don't like her.'

'More of that womanly charm, Rose,' the sergeant
said. The telephone rang on his desk. He lifted the
receiver. 'What? What's that?' he said. 'Number 48?
You've got a doctor?' He put his hand over the
telephone mouth. 'No wonder this nipper wasn't
reported,' he said. 'They've been too busy. An
accident. Woman slipped on the area stairs.'

'Serious?' the constable asked. The sergeant
mouthed at him; you didn't mention the word death
before a child (didn't he know? he had six of them),
you made noises in the throat, you grimaced, a complicated shorthand for a word of only five letters
anyway.

'You'd better go, after all,' he said, 'and make a
report. The doctor's there.'

Rose shambled from the stove; pink apply-dapply
cheeks, loose stockings. She stuck her hands behind
her. Her large morgue-like mouth was full of blackened
teeth. 'You told me to take him and now just because
something interesting . . . I don't expect justice from a
man . . . '

'Who's at the house?' the constable asked.

'The butler.'

'You don't think,' the constable said, 'he saw . . . '

'Trust me,' the sergeant said. 'I've brought up six. I
know 'em through and through. You can't teach me
anything about children.'

'He seemed scared about something.'

'Dreams,' the sergeant said.

'What name?'

'Baines.'

'This Mr Baines,' the constable said to Philip, 'you like him, eh? He's good to you?' They were trying to get something out of him; he was suspicious of the whole roomful of them; he said yes without conviction because he was afraid at any moment of more responsibilities, more secrets.

'And Mrs Baines?'

'Yes.'

They consulted together by the desk. Rose was hoarsely aggrieved; she was like a female impersonator, she bore her womanhood with an unnatural emphasis even while she scorned it in her creased stockings and her weather-exposed face. The charcoal shifted in the stove; the room was over-heated in the mild late summer evening. A notice on the wall described a body found in the Thames, or rather the body's clothes: wool vest, wool pants, wool shirt with blue stripes, size ten boots, blue serge suit worn at the elbows, fifteen-and-a-half celluloid collar. They couldn't find anything to say about the body, except its measurements, it was just an ordinary body.

'Come along,' the constable said. He was interested, he was glad to be going, but he couldn't help being embarrassed by his company, a small boy in pyjamas. His nose smelt something, he didn't know what, but he smarted at the sight of the amusement they caused: the pubs had closed and the streets were full again of men making as long a day of it as they could. He hurried through the less frequented streets, chose the darker pavements, wouldn't loiter, and

Philip wanted more and more to loiter, pulling at his hand, dragging with his feet. He dreaded the sight of Mrs Baines waiting in the hall: he knew now that she was dead. The sergeant's mouthings had conveyed that; but she wasn't buried; she wasn't out of sight; he was going to see a dead person in the hall when the door opened.

The light was on in the basement, and to his relief the constable made for the area steps. Perhaps he wouldn't have to see Mrs Baines at all. The constable knocked on the door because it was too dark to see the bell, and Baines answered. He stood there in the doorway of the neat bright basement room and you could see the sad complacent plausible sentence he had prepared wither at the sight of Philip; he hadn't expected Philip to return like that in the policeman's company. He had to begin thinking all over again; he wasn't a deceptive man; if it hadn't been for Emmy he would have been quite ready to let the truth lead him where it would.

'Mr Baines?' the constable asked.

He nodded; he hadn't found the right words; he was daunted by the shrewd knowing face, the sudden appearance of Philip there.

'This little boy from here?'

'Yes,' Baines said. Philip could tell that there was a message he was trying to convey, but he shut his mind to it. He loved Baines, but Baines had involved him in secrets, in fears he didn't understand. The glowing morning thought 'This is life' had become under Baines's tuition the repugnant memory 'That was life': the musty hair across the mouth, the breathless cruel tortured enquiry, 'Where are they?', the heap of black cotton tipped into the hall. That was

what happened when you loved: you got involved;
and Philip extricated himself from life, from love,
from Baines with a merciless egotism.

There had been things between them, but he laid
them low, as a retreating army cuts the wires, destroys
the bridges. In the abandoned country you may leave
much that is dear – a morning in the park, an ice at a
Corner House, sausages for supper – but more is
concerned in the retreat than temporary losses. There
are old people who, as the tractors wheel away,
implore to be taken, but you can't risk the rearguard
for their sake: a whole prolonged retreat from life,
from care, from human relationship is involved.

'The doctor's here,' Baines said. He nodded at the
door, moistened his mouth, kept his eyes on Philip,
begging for something like a dog you can't understand. 'There's nothing to be done. She slipped on
those stone basement stairs. I was in here. I heard
her fall.' He wouldn't look at the constable's spidery
writing which got a terrible lot on one page.

'Did the boy see anything?'

'He can't have done. I thought he was in bed.
Hadn't we better go up? It's a shocking thing. Oh,'
Baines said, losing control, 'it's a shocking thing for a
child.'

'She's through here?' the constable asked.

'I haven't moved her an inch,' Baines said.

'He'd better then – '

'Go up the area and through the hall,' Baines said
and again he begged dumbly like a dog: one more
secret, keep this secret, do this for old Baines, he
won't ask another.

'Come along,' the constable said. 'I'll see you up
to bed. You're a gentleman; you must come in the

proper way through the front door like the master should. Or will you go along with him, Mr Baines, while I see the doctor?'

'Yes,' Baines said, 'I'll go.' He came across the room to Philip, begging, begging, all the way with his soft old stupid expression: this is Baines, the old Coaster; what about a palm-oil chop, eh? a man's life; forty niggers; never used a gun; I tell you I couldn't help loving them: it wasn't what we call love, nothing we could understand. The messages flickered out from the last posts at the border, imploring, beseeching, reminding: this is your old friend Baines; what about an elevens; a glass of ginger-pop won't do you any harm; sausages; a long day. But the wires were cut, the messages just faded out into the enormous vacancy of the neat scrubbed room in which there had never been a place where a man could hide his secrets.

'Come along, Phil, it's bedtime. We'll just go up the steps . . . ' tap, tap, tap, at the telegraph; you may get through, you can't tell, somebody may mend the right wire . . . 'and in at the front door.'

'No,' Philip said, 'no. I won't go. You can't make me go. I'll fight. I won't see her.'

The constable turned on them quickly. 'What's that? Why won't you go?'

'She's in the hall,' Philip said. 'I know she's in the hall. And she's dead. I won't see her.'

'You moved her then?' the constable said to Baines. 'All the way down here? You've been lying, eh? That means you had to tidy up. . . . Were you alone?'

'Emmy,' Philip said, 'Emmy.' He wasn't going to keep any more secrets: he was going to finish once and for all with everything, with Baines and Mrs

Baines and the grown-up life beyond him; it wasn't his business and never, never again, he decided, would he share their confidences and companionship. 'It was all Emmy's fault,' he protested with a quaver which reminded Baines that after all he was only a child; it had been hopeless to expect help there; he was a child; he didn't understand what it all meant; he couldn't read this shorthand of terror; he'd had a long day and he was tired out. You could see him dropping asleep where he stood against the dresser, dropping back into the comfortable nursery peace. You couldn't blame him. When he woke in the morning, he'd hardly remember a thing.

'Out with it,' the constable said, addressing Baines with professional ferocity, 'who is she?' just as the old man sixty years later startled his secretary, his only watcher, asking, 'Who is she? Who is she?' dropping lower and lower into death, passing on the way perhaps the image of Baines: Baines hopeless, Baines letting his head drop, Baines 'coming clean'.

MACMILLAN COLLECTOR'S LIBRARY

Own the world's great works of literature in one beautiful collectible library

Designed and curated to appeal to book lovers everywhere, Macmillan Collector's Library editions are small enough to travel with you and striking enough to take pride of place on your bookshelf. These much-loved literary classics also make the perfect gift.

Beautifully produced with gilt edges, a ribbon marker, bespoke illustrated cover and real cloth binding, every Macmillan Collector's Library hardback adheres to the same high production values.

Discover something new or cherish your favourite stories with this elegant collection.

Macmillan Collector's Library: own, collect, and treasure

Discover the full range at
macmillancollectorslibrary.com